AF005231

NAUTANKI DIARIES

Dominic Franks graduated from Bangalore Medical College. His passion for sports led him to give up his career in medicine and join a premier sports channel. In September 2010, he decided to go on a cross-country bicycle journey from Bengaluru to New Delhi to witness the Commonwealth Games. *It's Not About the Cycle*—winner of Best Adventure Film at the 2017 Toronto Beaches Film Festival—stars Nautanki, his bicycle, the central character of *Nautanki Diaries*.

Currently, he is working on producing his first documentary feature about human-animal relationships.

When not working to travel, or travelling on work, Franks holes up in Bengaluru where he lives, laughs and loves.

NAUTANKI DIARIES

DOMINIC FRANKS

RUPA

Published by
Rupa Publications India Pvt. Ltd 2018
7/16, Ansari Road, Daryaganj
New Delhi 110002

Sales Centres:
Allahabad Bengaluru Chennai
Hyderabad Jaipur Kathmandu
Kolkata Mumbai

ISBN: 978-81-291-5074-5

First impression 2018

10 9 8 7 6 5 4 3 2 1

Printed in India by Thomson Press India Ltd., Faridabad

To Mr H. Shivaprakash, and
Ma & Pops,
for teaching me to dream incessantly.

Contents

Prologue

29 August 2010

First 100-km Cycle Ride

I woke up around five. I no longer needed an alarm clock, but I still needed a kick in the backside to get out of bed. Ordinarily, an hour (or three) lapsed before I roused myself from the sheets. That morning was different. All the preparations had been made the night before—rope to lash my bag to the carrier, weighty medical textbooks occupying the bag, apples and bananas on the table, knife to chop the fruits, tiffin box to carry them, a sweatshirt in case it rained. The morning was silent save for the first few feet trudging the dark streets of dawn. Even the wind slept on.

The previous night, while watching the pipettes of rain, I sent Sibi a message:

Even if it rains, we cycle tomorrow.

In a minor indictment of our times, the Nokia T9 dictionary interpreted the text as: *Even if it pains, we cycle tomorrow.*

Sibi replied: *Pains or rains?*

Both, I texted back. It was a measure of how eager I was the night before my first 100-km cycle ride.

We headed out to Savandurga, a large monolith on the outskirts of Bengaluru. Sibi always planned the long weekend rides; one of the cycling blogs had labelled this one 'Killer Ride'.

We cruised down several slopes. I told Sibi we were having fun freewheeling down, but it would be hard work cycling back, that too in the afternoon when the sun would be out. Sibi was unconcerned. We could return by Magadi Road if we wanted, although it meant six extra kilometres, he warned. We went back to our cycles and our silences, revelling in the crisp clean air that deepened in tone the further we slipped from the city.

We stopped for breakfast at Big Banyan Tree; the sun began to lose her shyness. A small tough incline had us panting. It dipped without warning and unexpectedly—the incredible vista of Manchanabele Reservoir! A large grey swathe of water lazed to our right; before we had time to admire it, we clattered down a steep slope. As was usual, my cycle gathered speed quicker than Sibi's Trek. I stole a glimpse as I hurtled by. Eyes locked on the road, his face was alive with the exhilaration of shooting down a slope with only his brakes and good luck for recourse. 'How quick are we going?' I yelled. He glanced at the iPhone strapped to his handlebar. '55!' I focused as the earth rushed by, a mere leg-length from my eyes, and though Sibi was in the present, he was already in my past.

I crouched as the wind rushed me in a head-on tackle. We splashed through a cradle of water puddled at the end of the slope. The road went to pieces. I thought about the steep descent we had come down. It meant a steep ascent too—an ascent so steep I had already decided I would push my cycle through it. I didn't have the stamina or the strength to take a slope that gaunt. The road narrowed. A few steady rises later we were cycling through forest—thick trees on both sides, few motorcycles, fewer pedestrians. There was just the wind singing, the trees sighing, the insects ringing, the birds chirping, the cycle churning as the wheels went turning, and only us and our laboured breathing for company.

The road began a deceitful rise where the harshness of the climb hid behind the make-up of gentle inclines. We didn't know how difficult it was until we began to gasp for breath. We lost our rhythms on those gradual forested slopes. Our cycles lost the straight lines they were always intended to have; they lolled like drunks, we swayed with them. Initially, I had stood on the pedals. Now I was stamping down on them, willing my body weight to drive me forward. Every downstroke ended in a virtual genuflection. Finally, my cycle stopped dead. With a resolve marked by immobility, it refused to move an inch further. I shook my head and muttered to Sibi through gulps of inrushing air, 'I can't cycle anymore.'

He had stopped too. We pushed our cycles and laughed—at least there were declines to look forward to. After recovering a semblance of steady breath, we proceeded to ride more slowly, more gently, without hurling ourselves at the road. Occasionally, someone went by on a motorcycle. Savandurga was a popular weekend cycle ride and Sibi half-expected a group of cyclists to descend on us at any moment. It wasn't our lucky day. After one more unavoidable stop for similar reasons, we reached Savandurga.

We did some cursory stretches as we waited for our tender coconuts. Sibi ran through an app on his iPhone. It chronicled the ride with statistical unnecessaries—bar charts, diagrams, heat maps—an endless orgy of details. In between heavy breaths, he read it out to me.

Maximum speed: 58 km/hr

Total descent: 50 m

Total ascent: 35 m

I was surprised. The slow climbs hadn't seemed as dramatic as the steep fall at the reservoir. We surveyed the large monolith that looked like it had been dropped in place overnight. It was an hour's trek to the top. We gulped and left it for another day.

We retired to a few rocks abutting the government guest house. A curious dog was our companion; he gambolled, we stretched. After about an hour of lounging on the rocks, I told Sibi about the *keeda* that Shree had planted. To my mind, Shree was the God of cross-country cycling. He had cycled over 12,500 km of India's vast sweeps in five trips. He had also responded to my first email with incredible speed—11 minutes. The previous day, I had met him to tap into the bank of his experience. I was surprised at his girth, but remembered he was recovering from a back injury. Shree suggested I put in three back-to-back 100-km days before I took off. His reasoning was simple: I had never attempted a long cycle ride before, and was better off finding out my limitations before I set out. Besides, he argued, 'It will be a solid confidence booster before the trip'.

Sibi thought it was a good idea and said I should do it the following week. I wasn't so sure. I already had my training schedule down, and it was the same as it had been for the previous three weeks, except that all the running and jumping I did, I would do faster and longer than I had before. Besides, I didn't want to mix up training plans so close to the head-out. But the *keeda* about confidence had been sown and it wormed round ceaselessly in my head.

Truthfully, I was concerned because I didn't think I was cycling enough. Even Ponappa (my trainer) was bemused when I showed him Shikaari's training schedule that had me running five days a week and cycling for just one. Eyebrows raised, he questioned, 'Are you sure this is right? It must be wrong! Shouldn't it be five days of cycling?' I had my doubts too about a training schedule that seemingly worked in an upside-down manner, and for the past three weeks, I had doggedly lapped the 400-m cinder track in 3rd Block, Jayanagar, and run circles around the lake in Lalbagh, wondering why I was running more than I was cycling. But it was Shikaari's blueprint and I was following it blindly. He knew better, he'd done it before.

We decided to head back. The last few kilometres into Savandurga, the roads were shot-up, all uphill too. We wanted to enjoy the descents before the killer climb began. In seconds, the ride was on. I whizzed past Sibi, gripping the handlebar as the jolts from the ragged road gently hammered my body. I hadn't yet learnt the technique of staying slack-limbed and loose-jointed when the roads ran to rot. I imagined I was the star in a mountain-biking video. At a turn in the road, I heard Sibi shout my name. Not wanting to stop at a speed too delicious for slow, I barrelled along. I heard my name again—this time further away, more insistent. I braked. The forest we were in housed sloth bears and leopards. I retraced my cycle-treads, hoping Sibi had spotted a leopard. He had dismounted and was gazing forlornly at the Trek's rear wheel. Its ego had been deflated by the excessive demands of the road.

I ribbed Sibi about his 'useless 35,000-rupee cycle', telling him how 'fancy foreign cycles' weren't invented for Indian roads. 'One year on Indian roads without a problem *marm*, it must be a good cycle,' he countered. We were so far out neither of us had reception on our mobile phones. I told him his cycle was called Trek because if someone was stupid enough to buy it, it was exactly what they would end up doing—trekking more than they cycled. Sibi laughed. After a lazy cup of chai and the return of the reception, he called a close friend Nishant who gallantly accepted to ship Trek home.

We walked our cycles to stay limber and kill time. Our legs got tight, we sat on a culvert. 'You know when I was in school,' Sibi searched for the right words, 'I knew older people were doing something wrong with their lives. And I was always confused *marm*...about how I wanted to live when I grew up. All I knew was I didn't want to live like them. And I was convinced that when I did grow up...I wouldn't be confused because I'd finally be living life the way I wanted to. Now I've grown up *marm*...and I'm doing whatever shit I want to do, and I'm even more confused than before. But you know what *marm*?' he said conspiratorially, 'I don't mind being confused anymore.'

We laughed convulsively. Water gushed over stones through a breach in a flimsy rusted pipe. I envied Sibi his evolved equanimity. I knew exactly what he was talking about—one of the reasons I so desperately wanted to get on the road was to have time and solitude enough to think things over at my own pace, take stock of all the years I had spent experimenting with love and careers and try and make some sense of the tangled mass of confusion my life had become.

I told Sibi Achyu would be coming to Bengaluru to shoot the documentary. Achyu was an ex-television colleague of mine who had recently quit his job. When he heard about the trip, he called to ask if he could document it. I agreed on the condition that I wouldn't have to playact for the camera. I had worked in the television industry for the past five years, and I knew how much of it was a sham—even the bits that masqueraded as reality. Besides, all my energy would be consumed in cycling. Sibi was pleased with the idea. 'I'm worried the purity of the trip will be ruined,' I whined. Sibi stopped wheeling his cycle and burst out laughing, 'What is this "purity of the trip" bullshit?' He said it with such incredulous vehemence I had to laugh too. He carried on, 'How do you measure this "purity"? The next time I go travelling, even I would like to tell people, "I had so much purity on my trip". Purity of the trip it seems!

Where do people come up with this nonsense? You want to travel, just travel man, don't expect anything from it.'

We walked some more. The unexpected trek had made for good conversation; it was good practice for the journey ahead. Now when something similar happened, I wouldn't grunt and curse. I'd just wheel my cycle and think about Sibi and our unseen leopards. Nishant arrived with another mutual friend Uzef. Everyone was in splits about calling a car to tow a cycle. Uzef wondered at my Hercules. Sibi told him it was my ride for the journey ahead. Uzef turned to me and asked, 'You've finally gone crazy?'

My mind cycled back to the day I had first told Shikaari I wanted to emulate his 1982 expedition. He had smiled softly and advised, 'Many people will laugh at you. They will call you mad, *huchchaa*. Then you can do one of two things—ignore them, or laugh with them...but make sure you listen to them. It will only help to motivate yourself further.'

Nishant got busy inspecting my cycle. 'No ass-fucking *marm*!' Sibi gushed as Nishant slapped the seat to confirm the padding beneath. I stood there proudly. It was the first time Sibi had referred to my cycle in complimentary terms. Nishant asked if I wanted a ride back. I considered, and declined. There was no way a big sturdy Hercules would fit in the back of Nishant's Innova. Sibi disengaged the punctured wheel from his cycle in less than ten seconds. I was fascinated. The only other time I had seen this done was on TV, during the Tour de France. A minute later, the flat tyre and a disembodied Trek were packed into the car. Sibi gave me the last of his chocolate and I headed out.

Now that I was alone, I set my own pace. All through the walk with the flat tyre, I had wondered—should I climb back to Manchanabele Reservoir or return via Magadi Road?

Sibi suggested I take Magadi Road. He said the trek with the cycles (we must have walked 10 km) would make the climbs tougher than they seemed. But I didn't want to turn away from the slopes. I decided to give it a shot. If I couldn't scale it, I'd get off and walk.

Rather than tiring me out, the trek had galvanized me. I found a good rhythm along the gradual dips in the road. At some places, I shook my head in happy disbelief at the speed I was generating. I knew it would stop soon. In the distance, past a curve, I saw the reservoir. I gathered speed. As I turned into the mammoth climb, from out of nowhere, I felt a second wind. Instinctively, I started pedalling faster—easier, lighter, smoother.

Ascending steadily when I least expected to, at the place I was convinced I would falter and flail, I was surprised at how easily I managed the first climb. Once it was done, the road ran flat before rising like the hypotenuse of a right-angled triangle. I recovered my breath on the flat stretch. As I built a new head of speed into the second slope, the expert machinery of Shikaari's training regime revealed itself like a weird flower which blossoms once every 28 years. The flat before a slope was suicide; but strength let me hit the slope without diminishing speed; and when strength failed and I had to climb on the pedals to inch upwards—that was endurance. For three weeks without knowing the science behind it all, I had doggedly run myself silly wondering why I wasn't cycling enough. Now the unassuming architect's master plans were beginning to bear fruit.

Climbing with a good cadence, my breath not breaking rhythm, a mischievous glint crowded my face. A few minutes earlier, I'd been bracing myself for a long hike uphill, dragging my cycle and its attendant 15-kg weight of textbooks. And here I was now, cycling with an ease that surprised and filled me to bursting, an ease that made my heart wheelie excitedly, because for the first time since I had decided to cycle to New Delhi, I felt a step closer to my destination. As I crested the final slope of the Manchanabele Reservoir, I leaned over the handlebar and christened my cycle, whispering in her ear, 'From now on Nautanki, it's you and me against the weather and the roads.'

6 September 2010

Shikaari

We cycled down to my old school to shoot with Shikaari. It was a name Mr H. P. Shivaprakash had already been given when I joined in 1988. Growing up, I thought the moniker was a reference to Shikari Shambu because of the wide brimmed hat he wore to ward off the tropical heat while performing his duties as PT instructor. Over the years, the name had come to mean different things to me. He told us the antecedents of his nickname: he was from a place called Shikaaripura. I had been relieved—it seemed legitimate to call him Shikaari after that.

I asked to visit the Sports Room. He threw open its warped wooden doors. We walked into the musty darkness; I sniffed the air. I couldn't smell it instantly but gradually the old scent of stale sweat, damp socks, sodden underwear and shared camaraderie came filtering in. I couldn't tell if it was what the Sports Room in St. Joseph's Boys' High School actually smelled like, or if it was another memory distorting reality into the makings of my imagination. I examined the room for the artifacts of my childhood. Hockey sticks—so old their elongated blades curved with the languor of highways—still lined the rack. The first time

I had seen them, I had thought they were for playing ice hockey.

I asked Shikaari if kids still used them; they did, he said. Even the posters adorning the paint-peeling walls were the same: Steffi Graf and her dreamy legs, Stefan Edberg's blue eyes and blonde hair damp with sweat, Boris Becker's back arched like a bow before it went boom, Gary Kirsten in whites and he was bald then too, Hansie Cronje with his riveting gaze—they were still stuck on the wall, all the retired giants and dead kings.

This was the room where the dream of a cross-country cycle ride had been spawned 15 years ago. It was the finals of the Centenary Shield—at the time, the only hockey tournament for high school boys in (then) Bangalore. Shikaari sent word calling the senior team out of class two hours before the usual time. It had never happened in six years. We didn't care—we were happy to bunk three extra periods despite wondering why. Brojo, Joseph, Viren and I walked into the Sports Room. It was empty. A wooden easel balancing a blackboard stood ominously in a corner—there had never been a blackboard in the Sports Room. On the blackboard was written in bold scrawl with coloured chalk, 'WE PLAY TO WIN'. Viren, who was possibly the only person in our team who didn't think much of Shikaari, said scornfully, 'What! That bald bastard thinks we're playing to lose?' We all laughed. Suddenly, Shikaari popped up from the dark shadows behind the blackboard. We hushed, we swallowed, we acted guilty, we waited to be rebuked. Shikaari pointed to Viren and said emphatically, 'That's a good attitude son,' and carried on with whatever he was doing, crouched behind the easel. We began to change into our school colours but Shikaari stopped us. We waited for the rest of the team to filter in.

When we were settled down, Shikaari told us the story of

him cycling from (then) Bangalore to Delhi to watch the 1982 Asian Games. He spoke for almost an hour, saying how most of us in the hockey team had played for years and never won a hockey tournament together—it was our final year in school too. He spoke of the joys of accomplishment, what it meant to feel things you knew you would remember forever. He talked about things that were meant to be simply because one had worked hard for it. He passed around newspaper articles of his cycle ride and photographs of incredibly talented hockey teams that didn't win finals because they were too cocky. He drew parallels between his cycle ride and us practising stodgily for six years, but I couldn't pay attention to the switch in the stories. I was taken with the idea of a man on a cycle, discovering his country. I was so impressed I filed the story away for future use. I sat down when I heard Shikaari give that speech. I felt calm and resolved, in equal measure—like I always used to before a hockey game. After 15 years, I was finally following through.

We set up an interview. Shikaari now had an office to himself. He was no longer the PT instructor, he was the Sports Director of the only school he had ever taught in—a school that has consistently produced international athletes. A vivid cross section of sporting luminaries had passed through Shikaari's tutelage. The names ran like an honour roll of Indian sports: Anil Aldrin, Sandeep Somesh, Rahul Dravid, Hakimuddin Habibullah, Anup Sridhar, Rehan Poncha, Robin Uthappa. Add to that the not so inconsiderable number of schoolboy-sportspeople like me.

So when Shikaari put down an accurate appraisal of my sporting ability 15 years after I had passed under the banner of his understanding, I was stunned. In the interview, Achyu asked Shikaari what I was like in school, and when he said I had enthusiasm but needed to be trained, it was a milder way of saying I had no talent and needed to be polished over the years until I was an imperfect jewel in a tournament-winning team. From the fifth standard, I would show up for practice religiously. I had neither skill nor sporting ability and had tried my clumsy hand at every position except goalkeeper, that too only because I was too scared to constantly face the music of hockey balls thudding into limbs scarcely protected by cane-and-coir pads. When I was selected to represent school (less often than I desired), I spent most of the time 'preventing the bench from flying off' as was said jocularly of us substitutes. In my final year in St. Joseph's, I was one of the senior players by default of longevity. I was convinced I would get the game-time and big-match atmosphere I craved. Because I had played in so many different positions, that year Shikaari shunted me around during practice sessions to even out the number of attackers and defenders. It was the last chance I would have to play the sport I loved for the school I was obsessed with, and I was sorely frustrated at not knowing my position or place in the team.

One morning after practice, I took the extreme step of confronting Shikaari to ask what my specific role was. I had to wrestle with my courage to do it because he was always so big on respect. Shikaari looked at me quietly for a while and said, 'Son, you are my utility player. I know you can fit into any position. Within a few days, I'll tell you where you will be playing.' That evening he slotted me in as a left-back, a position I've never strayed from since.

Listening to Shikaari answer Achyu's questions in his quiet measured way now, I was taken with his humility. A few weeks earlier, Shikaari and I had unfurled a huge 'Survey of India' roadmap across the long table in the library to chart a course for the trip. The new coach who had been assigned to ease

Shikaari's workload was stunned to learn that a young Shikaari had fearlessly cycled across the country to watch the '82 Asiad. When we went to film the principal of the school, he was unaware of the feat too. Sitting opposite Shikaari, I heard for the first time how he had 'broken his head' knocking on the stately pillars of Vidhana Soudha looking for a generous hand or a kind ear to lend him some assistance. Finally, he had given up, borrowed a cycle from a friend and ventured forth with money showered on him from all quarters. 'The donations were of all denominations,' he said, '1 rupee, 2 rupees, 3 rupees, 20 rupees, and what people couldn't donate in cash they made up for with encouragement, prayers and well wishes.'

The interview being concluded I asked Shikaari what my training plan for the next four days should be. Ponappa had suggested I ease up and cool down, get a nice long massage; focus, meditate, calm the body, still the mind. Shikaari shot the idea down. 'Carry on training the way you have been. Training isn't done as yet. You want to peak on the trip. Not now.'

8 September 2010

Ponappa

We went to the gym where Ponappa worked. I had gotten in touch with him on Shikaari's advice. The first time I had met Ponappa, he had looked at me and said, 'Your shoulders are weak.' I had liked him instantly; he was no-nonsense man. He knew why I had come and wasted no time sharing his wisdom. When Ponappa, Shikaari and I met to chalk up a training schedule (after Ponappa was confused by how little I was cycling), Ponappa and I stood beneath the stone arches looking onto the field where he and I had spent a large part of our childhoods and Shikaari, most of his adult life.

'Sometimes all you want to do is run again,' Ponappa said. 'Just be out in the open and run, like when we were kids—feel the breeze, watch the clouds. I wish more of my clients would ask me to train them outdoors. But everyone wants to train in a gym. The funny thing is I don't need a gym to kill them. I can kill them much more in a field. I only need 20 metres, but no one wants to train in the open. I guess it's easier in a gym, you're less self-conscious that way.' It was Ponappa who introduced me to dynamic workouts, stressing the necessity to move away from warming up with static stretches because it was more detrimental than good. His mantra was simple: eat clever, hydrate well, stretch long, sleep enough. Ponappa also suggested I designate Monday as my 'Rest Day'—while everyone else suffered with a new week's work, I could sleep off the effort of the previous week's training and let my body recover and rest. But Monday was 'Rest Day' by default because Sibi and I had appointed Sundays for the long weekend cycle rides. We wanted to have the run of the roads to ourselves while the city rested from the drudge of the previous week's labour or slept off Saturday night's excesses.

The shoot being done, I joked with Ponappa about all the palpable changes that had taken place in my body since I had started training. A month ago, I spat too often because I smoked too much; I knew which food items set off a bout of gastritis and avoided them religiously (or if I liked them too much I popped a Rantac to ward off the heartburn); I couldn't eat food from outside without wanting to crap within half an hour of finishing the meal; every day some new niggle in my neck sniggered or some back muscle complained; I carried a strip of Viagra in my bag because I couldn't gather an erection worthy of the name. 'This is no way for a 30-year-old body to be!' I would think. Now I rarely crapped more than once a day, I had stopped spitting, I hadn't taken a Rantac since the day I started training, and sex was ecstasy and fun once more.

The Crew

By the time we returned home, the rest of the crew had arrived. Arjun Negi, a good-looking boy from Uttarakhand, was the assistant director; Prashanth would be the sound recordist. The crew was complete save one. Prashanth didn't wait to get shown around, he simply asked Achyu what time he would be required and set out to explore the city on foot.

We shot with a bunch of my friends that evening. Nayantara ran PlayWrite—a Public Relations firm in the sports vertical. I told her I wanted to meet Saina Nehwal in Hyderabad and shake her hand—it would be the highlight of the trip. She said it would be done. I told her I wasn't joking, she said she wasn't either. How she was going to accomplish it I didn't know, but I trusted her implicitly. I sat there like I had done during all the interviews, listening to everything that people said, paying heed to only what I wanted and discarding the rest, thinking how strange it was to hear myself being discussed so earnestly by the ones who thought they knew me best. I heard so many say they were convinced I would complete the trip—for them it was a given.

In a subdued nervous silence I wondered where all this ill-placed confidence came from, until one of my oldest friends spoke of the days when I would spend all my time in class, surreptitiously mapping plans for the daily lunch-break football matches. I was transported back 20 years when in the double sheet of a notebook, I'd sit and strategize for games that involved 22-member-a-side teams; games that took place simultaneously with other similar ones on the same field, where for a frenzied 30-minute duration, a thousand schoolboys would roam the field, aimlessly kicking any football that happened to cross their path. The few hundred 'football players' scampered after the balls, trying to pass it to the next teammate from among the many they had tried to memorize before the match started. If you kicked the ball four times during the lunch break, you went back to class thinking you had a great game. And every day I had tried to plot those games!

Hadn't I employed the same belligerent planning over the last one month, poring over maps and exploring alternate routes? Hadn't I abandoned plotting and planning (forget writing) *Light Black*—my 99-chapter novel that was going nowhere? Hadn't I spent hours on the Internet hunting for videos to train from, trawling through pages of information for cyclists, by cyclists and about cycling, scouring for one small tip that might be of possible use on the trip? Hadn't I already broken up the journey into five legs—from Bengaluru to Hyderabad to Nagpur to Jhansi or Gwalior before finally and triumphantly rolling into Delhi? Hadn't I already calculated the individual distances for each leg and the best time frames in which I could hope to make them? Hadn't I only recently, when someone asked me the route I was taking, reeled off the names of every single possible stop that I could make from Bengaluru to Hyderabad—there were more than 13 names in between—as if it were a litany? And didn't I also know that I hadn't bothered to memorize the rest of the route because I was only concerned with reaching Hyderabad—it was the only place I was convinced I could cycle to, and also because I got bored so quickly I could never see anything through to its logical tiresome conclusion. It was true! For the last one month I had done nothing but dream—not of reaching Delhi because it was too far away, but of enjoying cycling across the country.

Remembering the days I had tried to be the 'special one' for many, I recognized the same foolish zeal with which I had trained for the last one month, neglecting everything and everyone to focus on one single question: what was the easiest way I could drag Nautanki and myself across the length of India?

I spun home slowly that night, thinking how some friends had insisted the trip be longer. Vinay—a doctor friend who had travelled more in India than anyone else I knew too had said the same thing. In response to my email, he had written back saying, 'Take as long as you must to complete the trip *Dom*, and make a photo essay out of it'. But the date of the Opening Ceremony of the 2010 Commonwealth Games was set in stone and although I had abandoned the idea of a rudderless trip, I still dreamt about it incessantly.

9 September 2010

Final Practice Session

Achyu wanted to shoot me while I was training. I wanted to look good on camera and had lengthened my strides considerably to demonstrate the elegance of athleticism when I felt a sharp searing streak down my right thigh. It wasn't a pain as much as a sensation of something hot and sharp shearing through, like a pair of scissors cutting through paper. I eased up.

I had felt the same flash the previous day and had curtailed my workout. I kept up the running because the filming needed to get done. When I felt I had given it enough time, I tested my leg out again. I felt the same strange slashing sensation. This time I didn't bother trying to run it off. I wasn't an advocate of pushing through the pain barrier, nor did I want to know how fragile I might be. I didn't want to be saddled with any more self-doubt. I'd just wait for the breakdown on the road. I was eager to finish quickly so I could attend to Nautanki's accoutrements for the trip, but Achyu wanted to do a long interview, because as he said, 'We'll never get this moment back, the day before the trip, and how you feel'. I struggled to articulate strongly felt emotions that ended up sounding vague in translation.

When we returned, my small home had been overtaken. For a month, I had done nothing but train and dream. Now I no longer had a place to laze, and it was supposed to be the last day before the head-out. I had planned on finishing all preparations the previous night, so I could get a massage to cool the body down and calm the mind like Ponappa had advised. With all the shooting, there hadn't been time for such luxuries. All of a sudden, there was too much to do—Nautanki needed one last 'overall', I wanted to customize a padded seat, I still had to buy a waterproof bag, and I was caught in the middle of documentary production chaos.

I was so sick of having left everything for the last minute, I lost interest in following through on my carefully laid out plans. Instead of scouting for the perfect waterproof travelling bag, I stopped at the first shop Nautanki passed and bought the biggest brightest bag they had. I also dropped the idea of a padded seat. Nautanki would have to make do with one last 'overall'. I asked Rajanna, the cycle-mechanic, if she would reach Delhi without a hitch; '*USA tanka hogathe,*' (It will reach USA) he prophesied.

Pride

In the evening, the family gathered to celebrate my parents' 39th wedding anniversary. The customary cake was cut. My father believed no celebration was complete without a cake; my mother thought cakes were a wasteful indulgence unless you were a child. I couldn't imagine how two people so disparate had managed to stay together for so long. The round of interviews with the family began. Apparently, the *keeda* about confidence didn't extend to kin; no one doubted I would reach Delhi. The weight of expectation was too much to bear. I had a sudden urge to be away from it all.

After a quick dinner, I cycled down to my old medical college, thinking how my father had told me how proud he was of me when I had wished him goodnight. It was the first time I had heard him speak about being proud of me since I graduated as a doctor. My poor father—a pure princeling of the lower middle class! Somehow he had risen above the cudgels of poverty to educate his children, had even contrived to make one of them a doctor. And I had gone and chucked it all up so I could become a writer. And for five years I hadn't even gotten close to finishing something, let alone sending it out into the publishing world. I had stolen all the pride my father had dreamt of for years.

The medicos whom I knew from the Reading Room came out to wish me. It had been 12 years since I had passed out of Bangalore Medical College and Research Institute, and I still went back there—to read, to write, to play badminton, to drink, to stretch. I was like one of those guys in the movies who never left college because they were too afraid of the realities of the working world, too happy with playing make-believe kings in their little sandbox castles. When the well-wishers emptied, I thought about the friends whom I had studied medicine with. For seven years, we had lived together in laboratories and classrooms, hospital wards and libraries, educating ourselves and learning about one another. I wished there was at least one with whom I could speak that night. But they were all pursuing their medical careers, travelling where their desires took them. Where were they, and what were they doing? Shilpa was in Louisville studying to be a neonatologist; Chitra in Chennai, Renu in Florida and Prasun in Michigan were all preparing to become internal medicine specialists; Goutham was in Pittsburgh training to be a liver surgeon; and Beesh was in the Caribbean, not studying medicine but working as a research student. All the birds except one had flown the nest, and for the last 12 years, I had taken the same blessed 3½-km route—from my home in Siddapura to my college in Kalasipalyam and back. And I had no idea why. No matter! On the morrow I would be starting my first big jaunt as a traveller; I promised myself I'd make up for all the ground lost over the years. It was time to head back.

If during the day the cyclists are solitary and unique, at night, they band together in packs. They cycle together, alongside one another, talking and laughing while musing over their thoughts. They hog the roads and don't bother about straight lines, veering instead from side to side—especially the young ones—singing and whistling in the alternating darkness of street lights after another day of work. I watched them all that night as I passed them or they passed me, thinking I was lesser than every one of those midnight cyclists simply because I didn't have a regular job.

EASE IN

Bengaluru to Hyderabad

10 September 2010

Naveen arrived at six. He was going to drive the documentary crew to Delhi. He was fair and clean-shaven except for a neatly manicured moustache. His hair fell in waves; he dressed casually. He was unlike any driver I had ever seen. He came upstairs to take my luggage, and as he said, to tell me how proud he was of me for undertaking such a journey. I wheeled Nautanki out. He took one look at her and said in Kannada, 'What Sir! Is this the cycle you are riding?' I nodded. 'This is an agricultural cycle, Sir!' he suppressed a laugh. He wanted me to place a red-and-yellow Karnataka flag on Nautanki. I told him I was interested in my countrymen, not in my countrymen getting to know my roots. He suggested the Indian national flag instead. He even knew a flag-selling shop which would be open at that time of the day. I refused. I had wanted to travel incognito and I already had a camera crew heralding me along the way; now Naveen wanted to add the tricolour to the ensemble.

It is customary to say a prayer in my family before anyone goes on a long journey. My father made all manner of requests to Jesus. Just to be on the safe side, he invoked Jesus' heavenly Father, Mother Mary, and many other religious dignitaries. All the while I was thinking it was to be the longest journey I had ever undertaken; I was delirious with anticipation. My father fashioned a cross on my forehead with a dab of holy oil. He handed me a plastic packet containing two xeroxed copies of my election ID card and a certificate from my college stating I had graduated as a doctor; a laminated prayer to St. Jude—the Patron Saint of Hopeless Cases—was also in the packet for good measure. My sister had bought a garland; she wanted me to wear it around my neck. I ignored the suggestion; the garland was twisted around Nautanki's stock instead. It would become a ritual. After a quick round of kisses, hugs, promises, suggestions and aborted tears, it was goodbye and good luck.

The early morning emptiness of roads was a revelation and I set a quick pace. On my first day, I didn't intend to lean into the ride. I was going to cycle hard until I met Shikaari at Hebbal Lake (around 15 km from home), after which I'd ease up and enjoy the ride with him. Once he turned back, I would take the roads as they unfolded. Shikaari was waiting at the side of the road looking dapper in his sunglasses. He looked at me and smiled, 'Sweating already.' I stiffened, but he was only remarking.

My bag had come loose. He suggested I pick up some cloth rope on the way; cloth wouldn't slip as much as nylon, he counselled. It was the same advice my father had administered the first day I had strapped a bag to Nautanki. Shikaari had also suggested a padded seat, easily fashioned at any shop that made seat covers for motorcycles, where I could choose the foam of a desired thickness to cushion the bumps of the variegated road surfaces ahead. He had suggested a waterproof bag with plastic hooks on the sides, so that it could be strapped tightly by simply slipping the rope through the hooks. I had passed up all his hard-earned advice. I was embarrassed and waited for a reproach. He let it pass smiling, telling me to enjoy the trip and everything it wrought. He cautioned against not having water close at hand. I told him I planned to get a netted appendage stitched to the sides of my bag so that I could replenish on the go. Shikaari helped me tie the bag firmly, and though I listened carefully to what he said, I was on pins to start cycling again.

We set out almost immediately, Shikaari tailing Nautanki

on his white Kinetic Honda in the thickening traffic of Friday morning. I had intended to ride slowly, but I had worked up such a steady head of pace, I didn't want to ease up. I was so nervous, I wanted to put as much distance as possible between myself and Bengaluru. Shikaari was almost disappointed there was no one accompanying me. When he had set out, there'd been nearly 25 people tailing him on cycles, scooters and motorcycles.

I told Shikaari my general plans of breaking up the cycling into three-hour segments—6–9 where I hoped to cover 40 km, 10–1 where I would finish another 35 km, and 3–6 where I would wind down the last 25 km for the day. I assumed that by the time night fell, I would want to know where I'd be sleeping. Shikaari remarked how nice the roads were now and I was transported to 1982. I was filled with the sheer enormity of what this man had accomplished; my affair looked like a piddling joyride in comparison. He told me to reflect on the things I would see, the people I'd meet, the real meaning of the cycling trip. I listened carefully to all Shikaari said, hoping to ferret out one last tip.

About 10 km later, we were at the Yelahanka Air Force station. We dismounted to say goodbye, but the armed guards outside the station didn't want us flashing cameras. A documentary shot was lost; Achyu fumed.

I tried to keep the same solid rhythm; the idea was to get to Chikballapur (56 km from Bengaluru) by noon. I slipped under a signboard that proclaimed, 'Nagpur: 976 km'—I winced, it was too far to think about. I looked left; Hyderabad: 536 km—manageable. Anantapur: 179 km—I was thrilled. A couple of hours earlier, Anantapur had been 200 km away. 'Twenty-one kilometre down—1/100th of the journey complete!' I thought happily and pushed on. We went past the up-ramp of the traffic trumpet leading into Bengaluru International Airport; Nautanki was breaking in a new stretch of road. I had never cycled this far. I told myself gleefully, 'From now on, every experience is original, every feeling is new.'

Nandi Hills loomed in the distance; even from afar she looked huge. I had read so many names for her in the previous one month—the bull, the beast, the elephant. She was Bengaluru's most written about weekend cycle ride location. When I had asked Shree whether it was tough, he had shrugged it off saying, 'Some people like to think it's a great thing to cycle up Nandi Hills.' For me, Nandi had acquired mythic proportions. On the Internet, everyone wrote of Curve Number 32. It was where everyone stopped, whether they wanted to or not. One cyclist wrote, 'I was telling myself "don't stop, don't stop, don't stop", but when I came to Curve Number 32, I stopped. I had to.' Another cyclist had uploaded a 3D-map that showed Nandi Hills in all her twisting, swooping, winding, arching, hairpin-turning glory. I looked at the hulking mass of rock that rose to an elevation of 550 m in 8 km; I was glad I hadn't attempted to tame 'The Bull'. Her sheer size was overwhelming. I leaned over the handlebar and whispered, 'We'll tame Nandi when we come back, Nautanki. For now, let's focus on the hills of Madhya Pradesh.'

The road slipped by as I pedalled. I was surprised at how quickly the highway emptied out. There was nothing to watch out for in front or behind. According to the *Eicher India Road Atlas*, Palasamudram was 124 km away from Bengaluru. All of a sudden, the prospect of clocking 124 km in a day (something I had never done before) was beguiling. It would do my confidence a world of good. 'The more the merrier!' I thought and turned the pedals, trying not to step too hard as I pushed on. We went by fields of orange flowers; we passed stacks of corncobs glowing orange in the September breeze. Achyu wanted to stop because they looked so picturesque, I cycled on.

I devised a plan to count down the days. I'd pretend I was Jesus getting tempted in the desert. He'd done it for 40 days. Every day I cycled would amount to two days of me roaming in the wilderness resisting the temptation to give up. By around two in the afternoon, I began to tire. We stopped for lunch. Naveen was garrulous. Straightaway he confessed: he didn't smoke, he didn't drink—his only demand was to eat chicken every day. We ordered eggs; already Telugu had become the lingua franca. After stretching, eating lunch and lying down for half an hour, I ploughed on. It was only four and I had finished my appointed 100 km. Achyu wanted me to call it a day. He was nervous about me overdoing it, but I carried on in the hope of breaching Palasamudram. The moment I began to tire, I gave up.

A few abandoned bum shacks abutted NH7's edge. They were uninhabited and untooled except for an assortment of large wooden benches and wood blocks. I thought they were the remnants of roadside workshops and businesses gone bust in the developing economic recession. I asked the fruit-sellers at the highway's edge if I could sleep there that night. They stared at me curiously, horror mixed with disgust, until an old man pointed out the errors of my perception—the empty shacks were fully functional meat stalls on Wednesdays and Sundays! Another villager pointed out a spanking new temple opposite the road. We turned around; there it stood, upright and pretty against a cotton-fluff sky—a pristine white temple that the villagers promised was safe. It had a caretaker too, and could be used by anyone who needed a place to sleep at night. We hadn't even noticed the temple because it was on the opposite side of the road. We were learning quickly.

Bad Luck and Barbwire

After a quick conversation with the caretaker (he lived with his wife who was as old as him), it was decided it would be our sanctuary for the night. Achyu was overjoyed. The temple had innumerable plug points, both two-pinned and three-pinned. The crew could transfer all the footage, make backup copies, empty the memory cards, vet the footage, check the audio, and charge the batteries and their phones. Without unpacking my bag or parking Nautanki, I lay down, face flat on the temple floor. The clean marble brought cool relief and I fell into a deep sleep. When I woke up, it was early evening and I wanted chai. The untended grassy lawns of the temple were fenced by barbwire that sagged in a few places. Spotting a low patch of fence, I tried to climb it. Groggy with hypnopompia, I tripped clumsily on the barbwire, slipped down the fence and tore my skin from knee to ankle. *That* woke me up. I ran water on the wound; it wasn't as deep as I had imagined. I was relieved. Achyu, ordinarily squeamish at the sight of blood, was aghast. When he saw the white flesh shining through, he got nervous. I dried out the groove the barbwire had inscribed. He lectured me, I tried to make jokes about it. He kept muttering to himself, 'It's only the first day and this happens'.

Visions of Shikaari in the stuffy Sports Room telling a set of rapt hockey players the story of his incredible journey came back. On the first day of his trip, he had developed a puncture and thought to himself, 'My first day and I already have a puncture. How will I ever cycle all the way to Delhi?' He had been so disappointed and constrained by doubt, he had contemplated chucking it and turning back. Then he had decided to carry on and leave everything to the Gods who were scattered across the land. 'And would you believe it? I didn't have another puncture until I reached Delhi!' he had told the story with a flourish. What was even more incredible about the solitary puncture story was that the resultant search for a cycle-repair shop led Shikaari to discover what he called 'the guardian angels of the road'.

At Gauribidanur, 76 km out of Bengaluru, Shikaari had told a few farmers at a chai stall about his trip. The farmers had pointed him in Basavva's direction. Basavva was a young man from Gauribidanur who had undertaken a similar cross-country ride a year ago. Shikaari asked the way to Basavva's house; he had to wait until nightfall for Basavva to show up. After sharing route-maps and stories, Basavva had decided to accompany Shikaari to Delhi on a whim. A day had been lost as Basavva roamed Gauribidanur gathering funds for his impromptu expedition, but Shikaari had gained a cycling companion for the entire trip. 'And what a companion Basavva was!' Shikaari had remarked—a companion well-suited to him, a companion who didn't drink every night and leave in the middle of the afternoon, but one who woke at the break of dawn and cycled with vigour every day.

11 September 2010

When I woke up, the caretaker and his wife were gone. No traces of their beds remained. Apprehensive about the constant ache and itch of a bruise, I set out for Anantapur. The flat lands and fields of the previous evening gave way to rocky rugged landscape as the road swooped and grew serpentine. I knew my body well enough to realize it would take the better part of 30 minutes to get into the ride—it was when all the muscles would begin to work in concert. Till that happened, different parts of my body would make me suspicious. But I had learnt to not listen to the false alarms. The first half an hour was when I tuned my instrument.

It was breezy without being windy: a good day to cycle briskly. I figured I was making good time. I stopped for tea at a stick-and-plastic chai shop and listened to the sounds of the morning. I stayed longer than intended because one of the men running the chai shop spoke Kannada. I was already agonizing about not knowing Telugu now that we were in Andhra Pradesh. I learnt to recognize the groundnut plant and uprooted a few. They hadn't ripened to succulent pleasures, but they were fresh from the earth. Two days into the trip and I was already sampling raw groundnuts. These were my simple pleasures early on.

About 40 km into the day I saw a sign that read 'Timbaktu: 3 km'. I continued cycling thinking how as a child, Timbaktu had been a euphemism for any place that was far away. I still didn't know where Timbaktu was, or whether it was even a place. I made jokes to myself about telling my friends I had been to Hyderabad, and Nagpur, and Timbaktu. And when they'd say in surprise, 'Timbaktu? No chance, where is that?' I'd shoot back, '100 km from Bengaluru.' I turned around towards the sign—it wasn't good form to have nothing to say to the follow-up questions.

Timbaktu

The detour from the tarmac gave way to a mud track; a few minutes later we were awash in swathes of green vegetation. It began to drizzle. The sounds of birds, the slightest hint of rain, the green leaves waving to the breezes speaking in Chinese whispers—it seemed I was cycling through utopia. The *kachcha* road began to heave and dip and while this made the cycling more difficult, the surroundings were beautiful enough to be immersed in. When you're cycling, 3 km on a mud track is longer than 3 km on a highway—or so it seemed. I began to tire.

We came across five large huts grouped inside latticed bamboo fences. Assuming it was the fringe of the village I carried on, no more huts came. In a space of open clearing, I surveyed the landscape. Surrounded by green hills, each one of us was surprised by splotches of black rock that stood out like ugly scars amidst the dense foliage. Why hadn't they been greened over? Prashanth wondered if it was volcanic rock. I cycled Nautanki back to the village. As I approached the door of one of the large huts, a bespectacled man walked out. I asked if water was available; he said food was available too. I jumped at the offer.

The man was Babloo Ganguly, Benagli by birth, social worker by vocation, and resident of Andhra Pradesh for the last 30 years by choice. He was in a hurry to go somewhere, but threw open his grounds to us. I took a walk. The place was faultlessly clean. There was hardly any iron and steel. It was all stone, trees, thatch and wood. I bit into some raw tamarind drying on stone benches in an open clearing. We were called for breakfast. After washing off the sand from the groundnut-pulling in a spotlessly clean stone washbasin, I sat down on the cloth mats rimming the cool black-slabbed floor under the tiled roof topped with thatch. Light crept into the large commodious space. *Chitranna* and *puliyogare* was the menu. I had met my guardian angels of the road. Where in a city could you stop at someone's house to ask coyly for a glass of water and have six people invited in to gorge on a fresh meal, besides the run of the land to roam and inspect? The food was delicious and less oily. I was convinced the groundnuts in the *puliyogare* grew in the backyard, possibly every ingredient grew in the bosom of that bamboo-picketed village. Only the rice was bought in a store probably. I was famished from the cycling and helped myself generously.

After breakfast, I got talking to Vinod, the contractor for the village. He was from Madhya Pradesh, a witness and victim of the Latur earthquake of 1993. Forty members of his family died in that earthquake, he was merely struck on the head by falling debris. His work with the United Nations Development Programme led to him witnessing the aftermath of the Bhuj earthquake in 2001 and the tsunami in 2004. After working for a while with Babloo Ganguly, he gave up the travel of UNDP to settle down in Timbaktu. Vinod was searing in his honesty; since he had arrived in Timbaktu he had never felt like leaving, he said. He thought he might live there forever. It was many an itinerant workers' dream—a place to take root. Babloo Ganguly had recently given him a house in the village; he had married four months ago, aided by a loan he was paying off easily because his wife too had become a salaried employee of the Timbaktu collective, the NGO that Babloo ran.

Vinod said the village lived collectively, partaking in each others' lives—there was not one above the other. That struck a chord. All through my short working life, I hated the sham of offering respect where none was due—it was one of the many reasons I wanted to live without a regular job. Now I had met a man who had found his ideal place and position in society. Vinod liked to work hard, as was evidenced by the pride with which he pointed out the pathways he had paved and the guest rooms he had built. He had wanted a job that promised advancement and just rewards as fruit for his toil, and he had not wanted to pay obeisance: he had found it all in Timbaktu. The way he spoke, I imagined Timbaktu had softened him considerably. He seemed at ease, content, more than happy, like he was on a drug, and everyone we met in Timbaktu seemed to be spun from that same fibre. They were all genial and warm, welcoming without being effusive, with receptive smiles leaping to their faces. I was embarrassed at being unable to keep up with the conviviality; even worse, I didn't know Telugu.

We walked through the village to the school that was run by the collective and came across a bunch of girls studying under trees. I thought of the days when I would study anatomy in Lalbagh, twirling bones and fondling them to study their ridges and grooves, and the people who walked by walked a little faster when I looked up and examined them.

Chelluvaraj (one of the school teachers) spoke in clear, halting, ungrammatical English. He said the school had 50 students—30 girls and 20 boys. It was a school dedicated to dropouts and children too poor to afford an education. They lived in dormitories and studied in the corridors. Everyone looked eager and bright. In the afternoon, Chelluvaraj told me, the children were taught crafts. The heart leapt!

Shailesh (a classmate from school) and I, both of us ill-equipped to deal with life, would often sit in his apartment in Delhi and bemoan the fact that our education never involved the necessities of life—how to bargain, how to operate a bank account, how to haggle over a bribe while smiling and not talking about it, how to woo a woman. Here, children spent the afternoon learning 'crafts'—bamboo work and origami, things they could teach their hands to master. I imagined one of those children becoming an ardent worker like Vinod, fashioning simple, elegant and effective fences out of strips of bamboo.

We met another teacher called Gangamma. Vinod introduced her as the 'mother' of all the children in Timbaktu. She was responsible for the 50 children being spotlessly clean. I didn't get to see her mothering skills, but I watched her wield her pedagogical finesse. Gangamma didn't understand Kannada and

I was mute in Telugu; more was to be gained by watching Gangamma than speaking to her. I joined the class in progress. Around 20 students were ranged around Gangamma on the floor of the shaded open classroom. Fruits and flowers hung from the wooden beams of the roof, one corner was deified with a Ganesha icon. Breezes blew untrammelled through the class, birds could be heard, insects sang outside. Here education was conducted in close confluence with nature; in this school the classrooms gave free vent to the numerous outlets of imagination. It was true about the school in Timbaktu being different from the schools Vinod had seen in Madhya Pradesh and Gujarat. 'There, beatings were the preferred way of disciplining children,' he said.

I watched some of the children straying, their eyes wandering, their minds dreaming; Gangamma saw this too and didn't say a word—she carried on her narrative uninterrupted. No one was admonished for staring out of the window—in fact half the wall was the window—no child was belittled for yawning, no child berated for not paying attention. Gangamma merely kept an eye on them while continuing to teach the ones who listened to the ebb and flow of her voice. Occasionally, she would bring back the mind of a child who strayed, but mostly she concentrated on taking the children through a fascinating story that they responded to with a never-ending series of 'oohs' and 'aahs'. Here was a teacher who taught her students using the blackboard of imagination. Listening to Gangamma's voice intone and modulate, watching the children's faces change with the drift of her story, everything seemed so perfect I could have been forgiven for imagining I was witnessing a well-directed play. Timbaktu was remarkable because not one of its inhabitants seemed bored.

Vinod took us for a walk in the hillocks that ringed Timbaktu;

he showed us the solar plant that took care of the village's electricity needs. He pointed out places where the children had recently planted trees. The only two trees whose names I was convinced of were the rain tree and the silver oak; that too only because on some sunny afternoon when I was six years old, our EVS teacher walked us through the playground in St. Anthony's, telling us the names of trees after we were instructed to look long and hard at them. It was the only field trip of my entire school life. I envied these children who grew up so close to the land. I was amazed at the intelligent planning, the neat huts, the underlying presence of a certain warmth that seemed to pervade everything that made up this little oasis of happiness, best exemplified by a mentally challenged child who had the biggest smile in the world, and eyes for nothing but the uppermost thought in his mind.

Even he was effusive and unrestrained; he clung to me, I couldn't understand why I felt so happy when he did. He was my favourite child of all the kids I met in Timbaktu. I tried to memorize the names of everyone I spoke to; I wanted to lengthen the 'Litany for the Hills'. I wished the entire expedition wasn't a time-bound trip after all. I wanted to settle down in Timbaktu to watch and learn the secrets that Babloo Ganguly had woven into the seams of the village. Vinod had already showed me the guest rooms. I could surely find some work I was capable of doing here, and I could write in my spare time; I was convinced I would find plenty of it in Timbaktu. We walked past an empty rooster coop which a peacock used when he visited occasionally, uncalled for and alone; he ate and lived there when he wanted, free to roam when he pleased—a peaceful perch always awaited him.

I was constantly consulting my watch hoping Babloo would return. I didn't want to leave without picking his brain. It was already noon. Anantapur was 60 km away. Eventually Babloo came back. When Arjun trained the cameras on him, he tiredly asked, 'You guys still haven't finished?' We packed up and went inside his house, the five of us ranged around him like disciples before a teaching monk. I explained my journey to him; he told a few stories about his own road trips in the heady swirl of the '70s. Inspired by Jayaprakash Narayan's clarion call to university students 'to go back to the villages' and armed with only a Yezdi and three mechanic's tools, Babloo had travelled the country. He didn't think the youngsters of today had as much fun as the youth of his times, but looking at us, he thought we 'were managing all right'. It was true—we were managing all right. Hearing Babloo commend us so, it only corroborated my suspicion that every generation, no matter where they are in the timeline of mankind, pities the generation that comes after because they aren't privy to the particular spirit of their times.

Babloo told us how he, 'an upper middle-class child of privilege', had come into a little money and started the Timbaktu collective. He cleared up the mystery of the black rocks—when he had arrived, the large range behind the little hills had been all black and mostly rock. They had started replanting and 'nature having an extraordinary capacity to regenerate responded to the little push'. In 1992 when they conducted a species count, they had about 17 species of fauna, Babloo said; ten years later, another survey had thrown up close to a 100 different species of animal life. The Timbaktu collective was involved in all the right things in India, the essential things—women's emancipation, the upliftment of lower castes, upholding minority rights, microfinance, ecological restoration. Funding was always a source of concern, but the collective subsisted on what was offered and generated what was unavailable.

Babloo invited us to lunch, but breakfast was still heavy upon me. 'One more meal at Timbaktu and I will become a convert,'

I thought. It was time to head out. Babloo wished me luck and cautioned me about my bandaged leg. We all left Timbaktu in a stupor, dazed at how one man had created his own little island of perfected zeal, imbued it with the warmth of his personality and was doling out hope and opportunities to the ones who needed it most. Here was a man, and a village, worthy of emulation. Timbaktu would be the last untroubled village we would see on the entire trip. Going back on the mud track, hauling my 72-kg body of unemployed flesh over the trail that rose and fell like a wave, I thought about Vinod who had said that in three years in Timbaktu he had gained eight kilograms. He tipped the scales at 43 kilograms and he was 26 years old.

12 September 2010

Like Inzamam, But on a Cycle

The previous night's bath and early sleep left me fresh as a daisy. It was the first time I was going to attempt three consecutive 100-km days and I was apprehensive. Depending on how the day's ride went, hinged the decision whether to make Hyderabad in five days or six. Bent on eating up the road in the waft of the cool morning breezes, I tried to work up a good rhythm. Achyu exulted when we came across a railway crossing with the bars turned down. I didn't understand why. He and Arjun quickly jumped the railings to get to the opposite side. They set up the camera and sat cross-legged on the road, waiting for the train.

Within an hour, the wind had drawn apart the curtain of clouds; the sun stretched slowly, indulgently, like she had woken from a deep sleep. I had a vague premonition it was going to be a tough day in the saddle. Not wanting to blow myself, I stopped for breakfast at a dhaba. It was my first real breakfast on the road and being a city boy, my expectations were those one had from the city. But prompt service is not an urgent necessity at a highway dhaba—it was something I would learn throughout the trip.

The dhaba was still rising; a majority of its inhabitants lay curled under blankets on charpoys deep within—it was both a home and business establishment. The *saagoo* was being prepared; finally the puris came. I shelved all dietary concerns about deep-fried food. I had shunned it since I had started training. I threw out all embargos concerning smoking too. It was wise to give up all resolutions on the road—it was the only decent way to travel. It was too hot to cycle. I wondered if it was wiser to recalibrate my sights to a more conservative 90 km. I wanted to pace myself, and it was as good a time as any to read Vivekananda. After an hour of the Swami's ramblings that I was carrying, I headed to Gooty. Unaccustomed to cycling in the heat, I made slow progress, as slow as the buffaloes who impressed me with their intelligence while ambling across the road.

As I neared scores of them on the highway, I watched carefully to see if they did something daft like make sudden darts or break into quick trots like the countless carcases of roadkill on the highway no doubt must have. I wound up admiring how they slowed their crawl as we approached, watching from the corner of their eyes as big as eggs, waiting motionlessly, almost with polite indifference, until we had overreached them—not once taking their eyes off Nautanki's nose. The sun beat shamelessly on everything in sight. I made my peace with taking a little help by borrowing fruit and water from the car. I imagined I was cycling a Tour de India in slow motion. I began to yawn. Shikaari had told me the closer I got to Hyderabad, the hotter and more humid it would get. I didn't feel like cycling but had no intention of taking a break; it would set a terrible precedent for the rest of the journey.

Unknowingly, I began to nod off on Nautanki. Twice, I jerked myself awake as she swayed uncertainly. It was ridiculous—I couldn't believe I was falling asleep on a cycle. I was like Inzamam in the slip cordon. I couldn't understand the phenomenon. Shree had documented such an occurrence on his blog, but that was at the end of a crazed attempt to cycle 500 km in 24 hrs. I wasn't through 50 km as yet. I ploughed through each revolution in a stupefied daze. I stopped and tanked up on Electral. The problem of water not being readily available was solved—any one-litre packaged drinking water bottle could be cradled in the circular shock absorbers beneath Nautanki's seat.

Cautious by nature, I decided that Shikaari's suggestion of getting blow-refilled every 350 to 400 km was best left for the faithful. I stopped at a cycle shop and got Nautanki filled with air. Wrestling with her had torn the crotch of the seat cover. I asked for a new seat. Padded seats were unavailable, but when the cycle-shop man heard I was cycling to Delhi, he threaded a couple of particoloured brushes through the spokes. Nautanki was getting pimped.

Gooty was the first major town since Bengaluru; after the lush solitude of the highway, I wanted to get away from the swarms choking the town's thin roads like a tight collar. The road got choppy and crowded, it began to hump and haw; Nautanki rolled with it. I was determined to finish 100 km. The rises started. By two in the afternoon, Achyu asked if I wanted to stop for lunch. I wasn't hungry and wanted to plough a little longer—better to leave as little as possible for the third leg. Ten kilometres later, I wanted a break. I had assumed the dhabas would be littered like dead dogs across the highway. We stopped and asked for places to eat. No one mentioned the same dhaba twice. Opinions varied when asked about the distance of the nearest dhaba; some said 3 km, others assured us it was 10. We were pointed in both directions. The crew car went ahead to see what lay in store food-wise. I ran out of drinking water, my body complained as much as my parched throat. I got peevish; there wasn't a place to stop and drink chai either. The crew car returned without any luck.

Achyu wanted me to wrangle lunch in a village home; I didn't want to turn on the charm to forage for food. I wanted to stretch when I stopped, the politeness required while eating strangers' food I didn't have the energies for. I plodded along. I pretended I was Mr Plod and Noddy rolled into one. I passed a board pointing the way to Peapulli. I loved the name. 'They must pull peas in Peapulli!' I thought. Achyu asked if I wanted to venture inside. I looked at the steep decline that swooped away from the NH7. Even if I got lucky with a free meal, I'd still have to cycle up the imposing slope—it would be an impossible feat post prandial indulgence. I shook my head. I was irritated for not stopping when I could have. It was the third day of shooting and Achyu was getting nervous about the documentary going to pot. He was insistent about eating at a village; I was fagged out and tetchy.

Late afternoon, we found a spacious clean dhaba. It was worth the wait. While we waited for our stock meal of egg curry, rice, chapattis, dal and sabzi, I stretched on the lawns adjoining the dhaba, wondering how many drunk people had peed in the grass over the nights. When we were done, I set out early. If I loitered, I would sleep. The crew stayed behind. When they caught up with me, they had a horrific story to tell.

Not soon after I had left, they had been roused from their post-lunch dreams by squealing brakes. I had heard it too. Just 50 m from the dhaba, a motorcyclist had fallen from his bike after colliding with a truck. Blood ran from his head, an ambulance had whistled him away. Naveen was convinced the motorcyclist had died on the spot; Arjun thought so too; Prashanth didn't put forth such a dire opinion, but said it looked really bad. Achyu hadn't bothered to decide. He had taken one look at the fallen motorcyclist, his stomach had churned and he had turned away. I was relieved I hadn't witnessed the accident. Each time I saw a smashed vehicle on the highway my stomach acquired the depth of a coal mine.

A Place to Sleep?

I carried on the laborious cycling. It was enough that I pedalled, form wasn't important. The sun cast broadside glances; thankfully, the sides of the road had grown leafy with trees. The crew car couldn't be bothered with my pace, they drove up ahead and waited. It was the first time I was cycling alone. I was floating on a cushion of air on a national highway so empty it could have been built just for me. A few homes hung carelessly at the edge of the highway, a woman stood outside. I was cycling so slowly, I watched everything at the side of the road. The woman raised her eyebrows at me, I raised mine back at her. She said something in Telugu, I slowed Nautanki to a crawl. I asked if I could refill water. She wore make-up in the middle of the afternoon, an uneven spread of powder with a blotch of lipstick; jasmine fell from her hair. She asked where I was headed, I told her. She threw more questions at me in Telugu. It was more than I could understand. We communicated in sign language. She motioned me inside. I was surprised at how informal and friendly she was, but I jumped at the offer. When I meet women who shun the unwritten laws society expects them to abide by, I always enjoy their company. I parked Nautanki and locked her up. I strode into the little house and looked around while I waited.

Despite the dark environs, I could tell the house was kept fastidiously clean. I drank water slowly; she tried to ask me more questions but I shook my head and hands. 'Hindi? Hindi?' she asked helpfully, I nodded. She returned with a matronly woman who plugged me with questions in Hindi. She was made up garishly too, and she was brusque. I asked if she knew places I could sleep at night. I wondered how these women spoke to me so freely. I wished there were some men around. She said I could sleep but I would have to pay. I told her I had four companions and they needed rooms too. Her eyes widened in surprise. She asked where they were, I said they were coming in a car. She ran onto the highway and scanned the horizon. She saw Nautanki and asked whose cycle it was. I told her I was travelling to Delhi on it. Then she saw the train of shit I had inadvertently designed from the highway to her doorstep by stepping on it. She shouted at me, the way she talked veered on abuse. She stormed back into the house and shouted something in Telugu. Another young girl appeared scurrying; this one looked timid and scared.

A volley of instructions were barked, the girl disappeared and returned with a coconut broom and a bucket of water. I watched as she started cleaning. The matron turned to me and asked what I had come for. I said water. She said we couldn't sleep the night but we could stay for a while and enjoy ourselves—we would have to pay though. And it would have to be one at a time, she added firmly. It slowly dawned upon me that unknowingly, I was bargaining the terms of sexual union. I mulled the offer, she waited impatiently. I remembered Achyu's crestfallen face from the previous day every time a prospective story had bombed. I told the madam we were travelling around the country trying to discover what people were doing with their lives. I asked if she would allow us to film her and her establishment, it would only take 15 minutes. The matron's face grew expressive by degrees. When I stopped speaking, she physically hustled me out, shoving my shoulders, slapping my back, shouting insults and curses. I hurried outside, I didn't need much encouragement. The doorway was shining wet from being scrubbed clean. I was impressed at the efficiency of the housekeeping. My mother would have been too. I picked up my shoes and walked away chastened; the madam harangued behind my back. I got on Nautanki and waved goodbye. The madam snarled and shook her head in disgust. When she disappeared inside her office, I allowed myself to smile.

I cycled meditatively, musing at my naiveté. The experience of the brothel had run counter to everything I'd imagined about a hooker's home. I'd always wanted to sleep with a prostitute to enjoy the notion that sex was a commodity, and feel the convenience of a communion ceasing the moment congress was complete. But I'd never had the courage to rid myself of the errors of my conditioning. I was also faintly encumbered by the night I saw my mother break down. It was easy to remember vividly the times I'd seen her cry because they were so rare.

In the days when street lamps were a luxury—I must have been eight—we used to wait for my mother to return from her evening shift as a midwife to have dinner. It was a must that the family ate together with the TV supervising the proceedings. When my mother walked in that day, my father glanced at her usually unyielding impassive face trembling in shock. He jumped as quickly as his arthritic joints allowed him to, and made the distance to put a comforting arm around her. My sisters crowded around her, everyone raining questions at her while helping her sit and unburden herself of her purse. She settled into the chair, my father leaned towards her and asked, 'What happened, La? Tell us what happened?' My mother broke down. She covered her face with her hands and sobbed. It startled me. I had seen her cry—never weep—and she always cried inconspicuously. She didn't believe grief was worthy of public spectacle. Even in the depths of her sorrows (it had to be when she turned lachrymose), she had always attempted to be dignified. That day was different. She seemed to have shrunk, shoulders convulsing, making loud sounds as she tried to swallow and still her tears. Her breath came in jerks, her torso spasmed constantly. I was frightened to see her behave that way.

The story was this—while waiting for a bus, she eschewed the dark vestibule of the bus stop for the openness of the footpath because there were no other women. She stood apart from the few fellow passengers waiting with her. A bright red car with music blaring slowed to a stop. The windows rolled down and a young boy looked up at my stunned motionless mother to ask how much she would cost. She was so shocked at the suggestion she couldn't muster the courage to react—verbally, or physically. She merely walked back to the bus stop, struggling with the dichotomy of seeking the security of the same men who had watched her being shamed into silence for being mistaken a sex worker.

My poor proud mother who held herself to the highest moral standards and hence was always appalled and dissatisfied at the naked turpitude of India bawled, 'How could he even think of me like that? He was so young, he must have been a teenager. Can't he see how old I am? How could he, Duncan? I'm so ashamed of myself,' and the tears wouldn't stop falling.

What if I did something similar? What sort of writer was I if I didn't have the temerity to sleep with a prostitute? Thinking this, I wrapped up for the day.

It was a dead day as far as footage was concerned—just like the previous one. Achyu wanted me to sleep in someone's house, I agreed. It was decided Naveen would interpret considering I was mute in Telugu. We detoured at the next village crossroads; we knocked on the first house we saw. A woman emerged. We asked for water. I watched Naveen as he initiated conversation. I wanted to pay attention to the words he used, how he asked for a place to sleep. Naveen told the woman who we were, our destination, our aims for the documentary. Water being consumed, we waited for Naveen to ask if beds were available (preferably free of charge and without sexual favour). He didn't really ask as much as he reeled her in. Naveen wasn't ghoulishly straightforward like me. He didn't walk into a house and ask if five people could sleep there. He didn't even make eye contact. He scuffed the floor with a downward gaze, smiled at her bashfully, ran his hand through his hair, smoothed his moustache gently, and with an air bordering on embarrassment, asked softly if there wasn't a spare terrace 'they' could use to sleep, indicating us with a paternal helplessness. 'I'll sleep in the car,' he said gallantly, 'it's only them who need a place.' The woman had softened considerably as Naveen led up to his request. She said we could come upstairs and ask her husband. We went and waited. The woman's two kids were doing homework on the terrace. I sat next to them and conversed in English. They replied shyly, the mother beamed proudly. The husband came out towelling himself after a bath, he had just returned from work. Naveen went through the same drill with him but without any of the bashfulness. He spoke to the apparent head of the house differently. The man consented grudgingly; he was too polite to refuse. He mentioned a restaurant we could eat at and asked what time we would be back so he could make arrangements. We left for dinner. Achyu too had noticed the man's discomfiture when Naveen asked for boarding. It was best not to impose.

13 September 2010

Time to Farm

Tired from the heat and winds, I was looking for a place to rest. I took a break to eat some bananas and apples. It was a gorgeous morning—the cycling had been rigorous though the pace was slow, and there I was, after partaking in it all, lounging like a king in his gardens of blossoming pink flowers on the NH7's median, listening to the music of the wheels as his faithful steed lay motionless in the mid-morning sun with flies flitting around her. I was assailed by a tremendous desire to sleep, but the bushes on the median offered scant protection from the sun's rays. I pedalled on.

Further ahead, I came up against a Tata Ace; a young boy directed the unloading of sacks. I stopped to find out what was happening. Seenu studied in a college in Kurnool—as it turned out, he also played volleyball for Andhra Pradesh. My instinctive admiration for athletes taking over, I began to examine Seenu's impressive anatomy as we spoke. Thick-wristed and strong-necked, well-muscled forearms tattooed with veins, Seenu's torso rippled beneath his tight T-shirt; he was farming the cotton fields his family owned. The rains had come and ripened the fields. Seenu had no time for idle talk (thankfully, he knew Hindi) and quickly terminated the conversation with a polite handshake. I was eager to see what it was like to farm and fertilize. After watching his crew of four men unloading 50-kg sacks of urea, I pitched in. Walking down the banked slopes of the highway to the cotton fields with the sack balanced on my shoulder, I was careful with my footing. I felt my legs quiver under the weight as my feet sank in the black clayey soil. Naveen succeeded in wrangling a ploughing session by telling Seenu we were 'from the Press'.

After a quick tutorial and a warning to watch the sharp iron blades of the plough so they didn't cut my feet, I was given the reins of the cows whose mouths were muzzled with cloth rope. I thought of all the mornings I had cycled on the outskirts of Bengaluru watching farmers walk their cows, admiring their work ethic for being up so early on a Sunday—now I was the one standing on a plough. It was difficult to balance while holding the reins lightly, so I wound the reins around my wrist to get a better grip; it resulted in a mild throttling of one of the cows. I was duly corrected. Trying to stay steady, I subconsciously pulled the left rein a little more than the right. The cow on the left veered off the neat straight furrows and tore up a few plants. I gave up farming and spoke to an old man who belonged to the crew. He knew the answer to every question I threw at him and answered with such quiet authority, one could tell he took immense pride in his work. Meanwhile, Seenu was directing the other three men to transfer the fertilizer from the sacks to the bags tied around their waist. That is when I saw how farming was actually done. It wasn't enough to merely stand on the plough and guide the cows in a straight line. With one hand holding the reins, the other hand was dipped into the waist bags of the fertilizer, and handfuls were poured into a long bamboo pole at regular intervals.

The cows' hooves sank deep in the soil; it gave me a sense of how heavy they were. I must have worked for 10 minutes but I was sweating as if I'd been cycling for an hour at full tilt. I had had enough; besides Seenu seemed too busy to attend to trifles. In two days, he and his crew would rake and fertilize six acres of cotton field. And what an efficient crew they were! All reed-thin (except for Seenu) and strong.

The Lake Shining with White Birds

I came to a bridge under which River Krishna swirled in countless eddies. Without dismounting Nautanki, I watched the river snaking and sallying in either direction. A little further on, we stopped for lunch where I indulged myself in some freshly slaughtered *nati koli*. With a little help from Arjun, Naveen and I polished off the entire chicken. After a brief yet deep sleep on a charpoy, we were off for the evening leg. I couldn't get rid of the notion that I wanted to take an urgent dump. I tried to put it out of my head and cycled on. But having trained myself since medical college to always give in to the fickle demands of any physiological emission, I was soon on the lookout for a place to stop. I didn't have great rhythm and looked forward to combining the crap with a smoke break, when out of the blue skies at the edge of the highway, we chanced upon a large lake. We took the break in the highway; tyre tracks led the way to the lake's sandy banks strewn with beer bottles. Achyu complained about the bottles. I pointed out the fact that I would be dirtying up the shores soon. 'Crap is organic man, beer bottles are not,' Achyu responded.

I took off my shoes and socks, drank the water in the bottle and substituted it with water from the lake. At the far end of the lake where the reeds grew tall amidst the marshes, countless birds lay perched atop slender grass stalks. I wanted a secluded spot and walked some distance. I sat on my haunches for one of the most beautiful craps I've ever taken. The sun glossed the water creating a column of light so bright and liquid, it changed with every ripple. The birds were mostly white, large, slim and elegant; they swallow-swooped and shallow-dived, emerging with silvery fish, struggling and gleaming fractionally between their talons. Some skimmed the lake in long glides. There were hundreds of them. We were all in thrall of the beauty that seemed carelessly scattered across the land. We watched the sun dance sensually atop the delicate waves, each one of us musing privately.

Even Nautanki watched closely with all the meditative concentration of a tonga-cart horse eating hay at the end of a working day. The cameras had stopped rolling. A Tata Ace landed, two men got out. They hung around, not doing anything except act fidgety. I couldn't imagine what they waited for. I told Achyu they were most likely the source of the beer bottles since they had a couple in their hands. As it turned out, the bottles were empty and all the men wanted was to take a shit too. We were in no mood to forsake our beautiful little lake. We continued watching the captivating antics of the quivering light on the flickering water; the men settled down. I wanted to see the sun sink, watch the column of gold change colour, and witness the canvas of water turn red as the stage in the sky changed sets. But Hyderabad was still 140 km away and I wanted to roll in early, settle down, shoot the breeze with Aarthi—a close medical college friend I hadn't seen in years—and make it seem like I had two days of rest instead of one before I began for Nagpur.

Reluctantly, I wheeled Nautanki away from the lake shining with white birds. Despite the testing times on the road that day, on account of the trance-like state the lake had induced, I had a vague inkling I was in for a good ride. I got on NH7 hoping for a slow truck or tractor to get me started. On a loping incline, a lumbering tractor carrying old rusted farm equipment rolled. My guardian angel of the road! After the necessary acceleration, I latched on. The iron chain I held on to as the truck led me up the slope was coated with rust, dust and dirt. It mixed with the sweat of my palms to form a fine paste. At the top of the slope, I bade goodbye and assumed my hunched back position. It was a small decline, but coming out of it, I built a steady cadence—and I held it for the next hour, letting myself go once in a while to see how much the body could take, and how far it had come. The sky was an orgy of colours, nocturnal breezes stirred, the highway was empty and I could blow as hard as I wanted to. I pretended it was another practice session except now I forgot about time and kilometres. I simply cycled, watching the sky, feeling the breeze, pounding the legs, marshalling the breathing, trying to make everything last forever. It was an exhilarating effort as a fiery red horizon glowed like thousand orange lampshades in an indigo-drenched sky—it was the most perfect cycling session since I had started from Bengaluru.

Achyu asked if I wanted to stop. The sun had set but the colours hadn't run dry. It would soon be night and we needed a place to sleep. Achyu wanted to shoot a piece before the fading light made it impossible. We stopped, but the light was already useless. I cycled on until we came to the beginning of a small village with its shops and houses strung like beads along the edge of the highway. I stopped at a *kaaka kade* on the chance of chai and a possible bed. After watching Naveen the previous night, I wanted to give it a shot. Men sat around. It wasn't difficult striking up a conversation, dressed as I was in shorts and sweat with a big bag strapped to Nautanki. Fortunately, one of the men knew Hindi. I abandoned my useless Telugu; I gave up that night. I couldn't wrap my tongue around the words. How can a language whose script bears such a remarkable similarity to Kannada sound so dissimilar?

The man I spoke to ran the *kaaka kade*; he permitted me to sleep in his house behind the shop. When I said I had four companions, he came up with a better idea. He owned the rice mill next door and we could all sleep there, he would tell the watchman. We could take our pick—verandah or the terrace. The guardian angels were scattered like birds on the highway that day. We were overjoyed. The cycle yatra was turning out to be a whole lot easier than expected.

I had a quick wash at the mill's borewell surrounded by dense foliage. I treaded my way to and fro nervously; I was terrified of frogs and snakes. Dinner was at a dhaba close to the rice mill. I pulled out my phone for the first time since I had left. There was a call from my parents, and Shikaari too. He had called on the first night of the trip. I called Nayantara who gave me the number of Nidhi (one of her colleagues) who was scheduled to meet Pullela Gopichand the following day. I called Nidhi and told her that all I wanted to do was conduct a small interview with Gopichand and shake Saina Nehwal's hand. Nidhi said she couldn't promise anything but would ask. She said it might be difficult because Saina had just gotten into a spot with her comments about facilities in foreign stadiums being better than Siri Fort Stadium. I tried to convince Nidhi that I wasn't a journalist looking for the next earth-shattering news.

It was a toss-up between the verandah and the terrace. Sleeping under the stars held tremendous attraction, but the owner had informed us that the tube light on the verandah doubled up as effective mosquito repellent. After spending extra time on my progressive relaxation exercises, I went to sleep dreaming. On the morrow, I would roll into Hyderabad.

14 September 2010

The Joy of Cycling Alone

I had been lucky with the weather but after a deep and restful sleep, we woke up to a slight drizzle. I donned my tracks and windcheater for the first time hoping the drizzle wouldn't turn into a downpour. In the city, rain inevitably banked the sides of the road with mud and slowed me down. But the empty highway didn't pose the same problem. Shikaari had advised me to remove the mudguards and chainguard to lessen Nautanki's weight. When Ponappa had seen her for the first time, he had pointed to the mudguards and roared, 'Strip it!'

The week before I had started, the TV and newspapers had been overflowing with stories of incessant rains across India, and I had left the rainguards on. I was glad for the protection they now provided—to me and Nautanki. The spray from the wheels of vehicles hit us like a spout from a water gun.

It was a fascinating weather to cycle in—neither cold nor hot or humid, just a film of breeze, a dash of rain, a light wind and the smooth empty highway. The rain cloaked the road in a silken sweat. It had come to wash away the strain of the past two days. I sweated inside. There was no traffic that morning and for 30 km I didn't flick the brakes once. Not wanting to stop too long for breakfast, I overdid the chai and cigarettes while gazing at a low hill crested with grey clouds. I didn't attempt to make any conversation. There was no need for talk, there was beauty all around and heat within. The crew headed out to Hyderabad to sort out a camera-charger problem.

I was on my own. The drizzle stopped and the sun began a game of hide-and-seek that lasted all day. The idea of being Jesus spending 40 days in the wilderness had turned distinctly unappealing. I had resisted for eight days, by the time Hyderabad was breached, it would only be ten. It was taking too long. I abandoned the ruse and adopted a new one instead. When I had started training, I had told myself—5 weeks to get fit. Then, I had assigned a training goal to each of the weeks.

Week 1: *Ease in:* This was when I got my body used to the idea of training for an hour every morning. Apparently the body is not as supple as the mind, and cannot be called upon to suddenly punch above its weight.

Week 2: *Train the mind to not listen to the body:* I knew my body was the dumb oaf. If I could convince my mind to not listen to its pleadings, I would be able to run a little longer, sprint a little quicker, skip a little slicker, pump a little heavier.

Week 3: *To Failure:* Whatever training I did, I did until I could do it no more.

Week 4: *Suffer:* Since I already knew failure, I would suffer beyond (even if it was only one step further).

Week 5: *Fly:* After three days of relaxing, cooling down, and getting a nice therapeutic massage, I would fly on Nautanki all the way to Delhi.

I drafted a simpler plan this time. I wasn't cycling to Delhi—I had merely started my second stint of training. I designated each leg of the journey as another week of training.

Leg 1: *Bengaluru–Hyderabad:* Ease in.

Leg 2: *Hyderabad–Nagpur:* Train the mind to not listen to the body (or Nautanki).

Leg 3: *Nagpur–Jhansi (or Gwalior):* Cycle to failure and suffer beyond.

Leg 4: *Jhansi (or Gwalior)–Delhi:* Fly.

Content with this new scheme, I led into Hyderabad from its southern side as NH7 displayed a never-ending series of small heaves and slow dips to bypass the innumerable villages it cut through. The hills of Madhya Pradesh loomed. I used the vertical undulations as practice. I alternated 25 revolutions seated with 25 revolutions standing on the pedals, trying not to vary the speed too much. I gradually upped it to 40 revolutions apiece, adding 20 revolutions of cycling tiptoed. It was disciplined cycling—an hour of cycling broken by a 15-minute break where I stretched on stopping and before starting too. I was so focused, I even stretched while smoking, sipping on my chai intermittently.

Bhootnagar, Mahbubnagar, Jadcherla, Rajahpur—they dropped like flies in Nautanki's wake. I exulted at the time I was making. I got rid of the windcheater, stuffing it crudely between the ropes—nearly falling off because I did it without dismounting—binding the bag to the carrier. I coasted down a long sloping flyover thinking how strange it was that I was cycling into a city. I had entered cities on buses, trains, cars, planes, lorries, motorcycles, autos and on foot, but it was the first time I was ever cycling into a city—and I had cycled all the way from Bengaluru to Hyderabad feeling all sorts of joys that no amount of writing could tell.

I was to meet Achyu 20 km outside Hyderabad, at a place where three flyovers converged. He called to say he wasn't going to make it on time. It was one o' clock and I was an hour away from a warm bath and a soft bed. Knowing how eager Achyu was to shoot the signboards, sights and the sounds as the highway took on the characteristic flavour of the city it was threading, I slowed. Taking the left beneath the three flyovers, I wound up on a commodious road so newly built it hadn't even been completed. On either side, there was no evidence of people living or working. I cycled until I met a quaint little chai shop constructed from tin sheets—the floor was gravel, the furniture, wooden modhas and cement bricks. I was hungry after subsisting on biscuits and tea the entire morning. Tired and happy, I wondered if I should carry on.

After half an hour or so of waiting, I began to cycle again. It was difficult to work up the incredible rhythms I'd churned out all morning. The frustration of not having Achyu meet me as planned added to the irritation brought on by hunger. The clouds threatened rain. I saw the grey filigree of a shower in the distance. The road was so broad and bare I made bets with myself about where I would cross dry land into the umbrella of rain. I could see the massive bulk of the rain-bearing clouds. I vaguely hoped I could make the Indian School of Business (ISB) without getting hit by them. I couldn't pick up the pace. I cycled slowly, persistently getting lashed by the winds gathering speed. In the distance, the curtain of rain came down in ragged smoke-strands. The sky darkened and hope dimmed.

Up ahead, the tarmac was painted two shades of grey by a line so sharp it could have been drawn with a thin paintbrush—one part was light; the other smoky-dark, sultry and agonizing. The dark grey strip began to eat up the light grey road with unhindered slowness and methodical precision. I took a few seconds to realize I was watching the advancing rain front. I nursed thoughts of waiting and watching as the rain enveloped me, but not wanting to stop, I pedalled slowly. The road blackened as the rain came speeding towards us. I was taken with an image of me manically cycling into the shower curtain of rain. So emboldened was I by this vision, I stood on Nataunki's pedals and rocked furiously from side to side. I was attacking the rain! It was the daftest thing I'd ever attempted.

I got closer and saw how heavy the rain was. It came down in thick ropes. Even before the rain rushed on me, I was frantically pulling out the plastic packet to cover my bag. In the few seconds it took to put on my windcheater, I was drenched. I tried to cycle more because I was already wet, but it was foolishness. There wasn't a place on either side of the road to take shelter. I veered in the wind, my glasses were smudged; Nautanki hardly moved in the driving rain and buffeting breeze. I had to carry on until I could find a place to stop. Pieces of leftover construction material were scattered at the edge of the road. I found an orphaned asbestos sheet and made it my poncho. The winds gusted. I was scared they would lift Nautanki off the ground and carry her away. I looked for something to anchor her to. Some distance away was a patch of guardrail I thought of using, but as quickly as the shower had started, it began to cool off and the winds simmered down.

Achyu and the crew arrived. Arjun scrambled to get the requisite rain shots. When the shooting was done, they offered me the solace of the car. I refused. I wanted to rough out the elements like I had originally intended. The rain slowed to a drizzle. I tried to cycle off the cold, my toes were wet and clammy, the skin frizzled inside my damp socks. I was soaked, cold and hungry and the absence of signboards made ISB seem longer than 20 km away. The persistent drone of the car began to bug me. All morning I had basked in the silence; now the monotonous chug of an engine I knew I would never get rid of had returned, and even if it fell behind, it would always come back to whisper like an irritating conscience. I was livid for not cycling with the same rigour as I had throughout the day instead of dilly-dallying over the perfect documentary. I had diddled myself with biscuits but now my stomach growled. I could have been lunching with Aarthi—instead I was haggling with Nautanki in the rain. Achyu popped out of the car, sat on the window and screamed, 'Brother, we're in business! Nidhi just called, Saina's on for tomorrow!' I stared at him glumly and pedalled on. 'You're going to meet Saina Nehwal tomorrow man!' Achyu yelled enthusiastically. He knew how badly I wanted to. But I was too cold to pretend, too peevish to care. All I wanted was to get out of my soggy clothes, have a warm bath and go to sleep.

So Much for Arriving Early

I decided to get happy again. After what seemed an eternity, the Gachibowli Outer Ring Road ended. ISB was a few kilometres away. I stopped to smoke, to celebrate, to soak it all in. I had made it to Hyderabad in what for me was an incredible time of five days, and done it easily enough to make me unconcerned about Nagpur. I had a day and a half to rest and I was going to meet Ms Nehwal the next day. But before that, I had to meet Aarthi whom I hadn't seen in years. We were all part of the same gang in medical college but had lost touch soon after as time and distance took their inevitable toll. I passed the Nimmagadda Pullela Gopichand Academy. I shivered; this was where the showdown was to take place. I spotted a Yonex Shop in the basement and relief rained. I didn't have to waste time shopping for a good racquet.

Strange how hunger unappeased can result in a peculiar distaste at the very mention of food. I washed all my dirty road clothes (in a laundromat that confused me and Aarthi no end, it was the first time I had ever used one), and had a slow long cold-water bath. I was finally famished. Aarthi rustled up a meal of egg Maggi noodles and leftover chapattis.

At dinner, I met Mayura (an old school friend of mine); I

had forgotten she worked at ISB. She was going out that night to a birthday party. I was unsure if I wanted to go. Mayura came to pick me up; I took her to meet Nautanki. Her eyes widened in surprise, 'You're doing it on *this* cycle?' she asked incredulously. I smiled at Nautanki proudly. We were making it across the land. 'Respect man, respect!' Mayura exclaimed.

Shikaari's diary spoke of Hyderabad being a city with 'no traffic sense'. I hadn't seen any evidence of his observations so far, but at night, I saw that in 28 years, Hyderabad's traffic hadn't changed. It was still nightmarish. People zipped, cutting across each other, everyone in a hurry to go somewhere; men stood at the edge of the road and advanced towards speeding vehicles with menus in their hands; when the cars didn't slow, they stepped aside glibly. Mayura drove as fast as the other lunatics, as crazily too. I braced in the seat and asked if she'd always driven this way. It was only after coming to Hyderabad that she had begun swinging a steering wheel the way she did, she said.

We reached the pub where the party was happening; the music was too loud to talk. Everyone asked me questions about the trip. I tried to make conversation. My throat hurt from the shouting and the cigarettes. I broke my resolution to not drink till Delhi and had a beer. As the night wore on and the group got progressively drunker and happier, I began to fade, withdrawing into the fringes and cursing myself. Finally closing time! It was decided to shift the party to someone's house. I was resolute; I would take an auto back home. Standing outside the back entrance of the pub (front door being closed because it was well past closing time), we heard the angry roar of a car's wheels. We turned and saw headlights enlarging as a car shot towards us. Instinctively, everyone parted, the car careened to avoid nudging someone. Someone from our group had been missed by a whisker. That silenced the crowd. Remonstrations followed. I was chilled to the bone; the driver hadn't once thought of stopping, forget slowing down. The path wasn't a broad one and after 30 m or so, it right-angled. The driver had shot through on screeching tyres, engine roaring, rubber burning black vicious skid marks into the asphalted driveway. The highway was infinitely safer than the nutcased alleyways of the city.

Aarthi rescued me. She had had enough of studying and asked if I would like to have a beer before she slept. I jumped at the idea. Aarthi and I sat around talking. I gushed about how this was the first time I was really travelling; how up until now I had only taken holidays, two or three days at a time, the greatest one being all of seven days—but now I was adventuring, journeying forth into our country, long and slow; and on the morrow, I was going to meet Saina Nehwal! Aarthi talked slower, softer, but gushed in her own way, telling me how she had finally found herself at ISB where the study was rigorous and the campus life adventurous, cosmopolitan, western. Once upon a time she couldn't stay awake at night, now she studied into the wee hours of the morning. I inspected her bookshelf and asked what she was reading. Like so many friends, she had switched to non-fiction too; she couldn't remember the last time she had read a novel. But her favourite book was still *Alice in Wonderland*. I was sitting on a chair; Aarthi lounged on her bed with her legs curled beneath her. I looked at the veins on her feet and began to think that memory was a terrific sham. She lovingly told funny stories about her husband; he was trying to make a fortune in waste-management. When they were courting, he had taken her on dates to garbage dumps. The smelliest dates she'd ever been on she said, and the easiest to dress for. In all her life, she never dreamt she'd know so much about garbage and shit. It was three o' clock in the morning and the night had turned to rust. Aarthi wanted to sleep.

I trudged back to my room, hoping to see some peacocks. Signs on the road warned people to drive slowly because peacocks crossed the thickly wooded roads of the campus randomly. The room I was staying in belonged to an ex-student who had quit a month after his course had started. Eventually, he had committed suicide. I thought about him, about how strange life was. I recalled how the previous afternoon when navigating the dusty underparts of the Trishul flyover heralding the left to Gachibowli, I had estimated I would reach ISB at 2:30 p.m., have a leisurely lunch and be asleep by 4 p.m. in the afternoon so I would be ready for Saina Nehwal the next day. And there I was on a window sill—a few hours before meeting the second best badminton player in the world (at that time)—watching the shadows of tall reed grass, listening to the peacocks' strange cries at 4:30 a.m. in the morning, smoking cigarettes relentlessly because I couldn't sleep, thinking tomorrow I would do it for Beesh.

15 September 2010

The Pièce de Résistance of the Documentary

When I first conceived the entire trip and thought of trying to meet Saina Nehwal, I wanted to interview her. When I would roll into Delhi, I would sell the article to offset the costs of the journey. But Achyu's advent had shifted my dreams to a larger canvas.

Nidhi had told Gopichand there was a guy cycling from

Bengaluru to Delhi for the Commonwealth Games who wanted to interview him and shake Saina Nehwal's hand. Gopi had agreed. Nidhi expressly told us that she hadn't mentioned anything about shooting with Saina. But Achyu and I planned on doing an interview with Saina on court while we tossed back and forth. I wanted to ask whether she minded her life being different from normal 20-year-olds; I wanted to find out how it was for her growing up when she had to deal with all her doubts and disappointments in the lonely recesses of childhood. Interview being done, I decided the best ploy would be to spring a game on Saina—challenge her on the spot. I was convinced I wouldn't have the courage to let her know in advance that I intended to play a game of shuttle with her, nor would she deign to accept the gall of my offer. And once the game was underway, I intended to play hard—hard enough to take one point off the (then) world's number-two badminton player. If I pulled that off, Achyu would recover his investment in the shooting of the documentary and I would have a story for my friend's children. This was the initial idea—grandiose and imperfect!

Seeing how we had limited access, we decided to play it by ear. Achyu woke me at 8:30 a.m. I rose surly and angry at myself, feeling like a conscientious sportsperson who's gone on a binge the night before a big game. We had an appointment with Gopichand at 11:30 a.m. but decided to go early. Achyu wanted to shoot the practice session; I wanted to see Saina train. We stopped to bedeck Nautanki with her customary floral necklace.

We were stopped at the gate of the Nimmagada Pullela Gopichand Academy by an old guard who didn't bother rising from his chair. Who was I there to meet? 'Gopichand Sir,' I replied. Did he give you a time? 'Yes.' The guard leaned back in his chair. We were through; the Yonex shop was still closed.

I parked Nautanki in the general parking lot where the cars outnumbered the bikes. We walked into the small entrance of the imposing facade of the academy. I spoke to the receptionist who replied in warm friendly tones. He seemed more like a man in his home than at his place of work. He asked if Gopi Sir knew I was coming. I said he had given us the time, but we had come in early to watch the practice session. I asked permission to shoot the practice session but the receptionist politely declined. The previous night Achyu and I had considered (and laughed off) the possibility of getting Saina to go for a ride on Nautanki.

Bargaining for anything, I told the receptionist we didn't want to take the cameras on the court, we had no intentions of disrupting the practice session; we only wanted to set up a camera on a tripod behind the glass panels overlooking the five courts where the training session was in progress. The receptionist softly, almost helplessly, said he couldn't help because he hadn't received any instructions from Gopi Sir. The academy seemed imbued with the same spirit of humility and congeniality that pervaded Timbaktu.

We contented ourselves with watching around 20 of India's top badminton players being put through the paces in the largest badminton arena I'd ever been in. Girls and boys trained together. Saina was easy enough to recognize. When I pointed out who I thought was Gopi, Achyu whispered back, 'Can't be man, he's too young…too fit.' The receptionist asked us to watch over the proceedings from the cafeteria on the first floor so the players wouldn't be disturbed. We translocated. The Yonex shop still hadn't opened.

I had no idea how we were going to swing a badminton game with Saina—that too without a racquet. I thought it best not to tell Gopi about the plan. We would finish the interview and ask to shake her hand. We'd be invited on to the court as she was packing up or cooling off, and when the handshake was underway, I'd ask outright and let her decide. Whenever I had imagined tossing with Saina, the only venue I had even remotely set the scene in was the makeshift badminton courts in Bangalore Medical College's auditorium. I had never envisaged playing out the dead heat on the wooden courts of the Nimagadda Pullela Gopichand Academy. Suddenly, I realized I wouldn't be let on the court without non-marking badminton shoes. I got frantic. I knew the Yonex shop would have racquets, but would they have shoes?

Naveen was sent downstairs to find out, the shop was still closed. I went downstairs to the receptionist. He said it stocked the entire range of badminton gear. I breathed easier wishing the shop would open. I didn't want to rush things when Gopi was ready. The shop opened. I walked around, looking at all the magnificent racquets that hung from the wall like showpiece treasures.

I told Achyu about an incident I remembered acutely because it was tinged with the ineffable sadness that accompanies a lost opportunity. It was the only time I was sent out of India on work. One night, finding nothing better to do, I went into an all-night multipurpose supermarket and wound up in the sports section. I was surrounded by gleaming sporting equipment, my pockets were stuffed with money; yet I couldn't find an article that seemed like a prudent buy. I fingered the badminton racquets longingly thinking about the only badminton racquet (worthy of name) I've ever owned—a fluorescent purple Yonex racquet that Aarthi had given me. It was a remnant of her childhood.

When her parents had enrolled her in tennis classes, the coach had quickly suggested that Aarthi's slim frame was better suited for badminton. This Aarthi had enjoyed until her parents enrolled her in Bharatanatyam classes; the racquet was exchanged with taals and *ghungroos*. When I had started playing badminton in medical college, the racquet was unearthed. I had used it well through consistent reguttings until the head had begun to warp like a less used guitar. It was finally put out of shape and commission by some fool who (in a fit of rage after losing a game) threw it across the auditorium. It was my final year in college and not having enough money, I had managed by borrowing racquets until it was time to set the nose to the grinding stone of work. Now when I had the money, there were no longer any avenues to play. That day in Mustafa Mall, I had thought about Beesh.

Beesh, the epitome of clumsiness with his ill-fitting clothes and his slow, slouching, crouched-at-the-neck and stooped-at-the-waist walk. We had christened Beesh 'Yeti' because of his walk. But all one had to do was stick a racquet in Beesh's palm, deck him out in a pair of shorts, put him on a badminton court, and sit back to watch the miraculous transformation. We didn't know how someone so ungainly could turn so lithe. Beesh would dance across the court, nimble like a goat, covering the length of it with short sure steps. He'd lunge and skip across the width of it, criss-crossing legs before regaining balance. Every once in a while he'd shift sharply across, curling his legs under his heavy backside to unleash all the dramatic power of a jump-smash, and his tongue would loll outside his mouth. And he always clenched his left fist, shouting to himself, 'Come on!' The strangest thing was that Beesh always punched above his weight. He'd upset higher-ranked players, play two people's game on a doubles court if his partner couldn't hold the pace, and carry the entire college team on his shoulders by the sole virtue of having an incredible ability to always play better than anyone thought he was capable of. Before every tournament, he'd troop away to borrow a racquet. I had thought about buying Beesh a racquet that day, but he was gone too.

At the Yonex shop, I bought a badminton racquet and a spanking new pair of badminton shoes. I thought about all the kindnesses I had received—the fluorescent pink, carbon-reinforced Vampire hockey stick that Shelly Raphael had gifted me in the eighth standard only because he was trying to woo my sister. I'd never fondled a more magnificent grip on stick, racquet or bat. It used to absorb all the sweat from my perpetually clammy palms and never frayed or cut. I had run that stick into the ground, playing with it for 12 years, until the curvature of the blade had warped into a thin strip of hooked wood. Then, there was Jordi Quintana's red hockey stick with no name, just a logo composed of a couple of elephants facing off with their trunks shaped like hockey sticks. My mother kept it within arm's reach to scare the stray dogs who peed outside our home. Aarthi's badminton racquet too.

We went back to the courts. The training session was drawing to a close; racquets were grounded, their owners lapped the courts. The boys started doing push-ups. I watched Saina—she was still tossing shuttles, juggling them with her head, arms, torso or legs as they floated across the net and were returned before they touched the floor. She joined the boys and bent into a push-up. This I wanted to see. I'd never seen a girl do a good push-up. At one point, I'd ask this regularly of every girl I knew because the results were so comical. I started to count as Saina began to rhythmically dip and rise from the floor. When she went beyond 10, my amazement grew. When she finished, I was stupefied—I had counted her do 60 push-ups, in two sets of 30 with a 45-second gap in between. The boys had done the same number. Gopichand was ready to have a chat.

He led us to his office. He wore training clothes like the

rest of his athletes. I watched as he walked in. He was tall, lithe, statuesque, majestic, fit and slow-moving; he had a walk underpinned by grace and a certain kind of strength—hidden, yet powerful and ready to be called upon. Achyu busied himself with the equipment. I introduced myself. I had to strain to hear him speak because he spoke so softly. He was such an elegant conversationalist—delivering sharp wisdom in murmurs grown tender with humility—you wanted to start from the beginning with him as your teacher. Hearing him talk about his mother being the drive that ran his engine put me in the mind of my own mother working ceaselessly for the last 35 years, without complains, except when anger made her truthful. That was the only time she was willing to recognize the terrible disparity of being a working mother saddled with an awful routine of wake, cook, work, cook, oversee studies and then sleep it all off, only to be the first one to jump on the relentless giant wheel in the grand circus of life the next morning. In truth, I wanted to speak to Gopi longer but didn't know if we were overstaying our welcome. Besides, there was also the small matter of challenging Saina Nehwal to a game of badminton. When the interview was done, I asked Gopi if it would be possible to do a small interview with Saina. He broke into a small regretful smile. I tempered my request to merely meeting her and shaking her hand. He said she was finishing her warm-up and I could meet her after. I was happy to wait.

Outside, I told Achyu it didn't look like we could pull it off. Then I silently began to muster up the courage to be 'devilish and daring', arguing with myself, telling myself to not be a coward, it was the one chance I would have to toss a shuttle with Saina—let alone meet her. What had I to lose except face and look stupid? We waited patiently, me getting more nervous by the minute. One moment I wouldn't care about the outcome, the next moment I'd be reasoning slowly, trying to convince myself that there was nothing wrong in challenging Saina Nehwal to a casual game of badminton.

From the flight of stairs that led to the entrance of the academy, we could see the cars parked. It had gotten beyond 11:30 a.m. Saina had walked off court long ago. We didn't know where she was, Gopi was nowhere in sight. We wondered whether she lived at the academy (Gopi had said it was a residential academy) or with her parents since she was from Hyderabad. We guessed which car might be hers. Achyu picked the Honda City (apparently the best car in the parking lot) —his reasoning was simple, 'She's the second best badminton player in the world, man. She's not going to drive around in a Maruti 800.' I was out of gear, frantic at the prospect of not meeting Saina, when suddenly we saw her walking towards the car park, ponytail bobbing, hair clips gleaming in the mid-morning sun. I calculated the distance she had left to cover. I asked Achyu if I should dash down and meet her. 'Let's...' he said, but something sank inside. Vanity overtaking my sensibility, I didn't want to leap down the flight of stairs and arrive breathless, explaining myself and trying to get her to pose with Nautanki for photographs—although Nautanki would have loved that. I had asked open-palmed and fate had not willed it. I was content to not meddle. I watched Saina walk past Nautanki, looking to see if she'd notice the garland draped around her handlebar.

But she calmly passed Nautanki by, slipped into her car (it was the Honda City after all) and drove away. There went our documentary's USP and there went a story for my friends' children—vanished within the doors of the car, sliding away in the dust. I felt a slow-dawning strange emptiness. It was supposed to be the highlight of the trip. The game had always been a fanciful scheme—an innocent dream, a blind ruse. But I had always wanted to shake the hand which gripped the racquet that, like some mad artist's brushstrokes, was captivating the imagination of an entire nation hungry for new sporting icons. After that, whatever happened, I didn't care about. The same all-is-lost hollowness and deep disappointment I'd felt when I had seen my name on the list of probable candidates for the school football team, I felt again.

I had put up a good show during the single trial game, pulling off a string of fake dives by moving away from the ball, when all I had to do was reach out a palm to stop it, and only because the defenders were so good I hardly got tested. I had a vague feeling I would be selected and had asked my father if he would buy me a pair of studs if I made it to the list. He had asked how much they cost. '400 rupees,' I had said. He had countered, 'What is the point of spending 400 rupees for one month on a football field?' Then, he had returned to reading his newspaper; he was a sensible man, a 'too practical' man. That day, I had stood shamefaced and quiet outside my neighbour's house after dinner. Ajay had come to the door and I had asked him, embarrassed, if I could borrow his football studs. He had given them to me. I had asked him to wrap them in a plastic packet. I didn't want my parents to know I was borrowing studs; they had a strange, easily offended, but not always easily fathomable, sense of pride. I had asked Ajay if I could keep the studs for the entire month if I got selected—but it was football season in Bengaluru then, and Ajay needed the studs too. I had wished my name wouldn't come up on the list. Better to not have a shot of making the school football team and enjoy the oblivion of failure, than get called up and show up for practice with no studs. It was my reason to become a goalkeeper in the first place, but none of the coaches seemed to buy the argument that studs didn't affect a goalie's performance. There was nothing left to do now but put all the ghosts to rest.

We went back inside the academy to hand over the badminton racquet to Gopi. When he came through the doors, he was apologetic that Saina hadn't been informed. I gave him the racquet, asking him to give it to an underprivileged kid of talent when he or his scouts went hunting around the country. He smiled and said he couldn't take it. I was insistent. I told him that it was all part of the plan anyway—to hand over the racquet after conducting an interview with Saina while tossing across the court. Gopi's face didn't betray any change at the audacity of our ambition. He accepted the racquet, but only after I told him that as a kid I was constantly gnawingly aware that my game wasn't as good as it could be because I didn't have the best equipment. Gopi gave me two T-shirts for my troubles, both bearing his academy's name. I was thrilled. I was going to wear them like a badge of honour.

The Greatest Massage of My Life

Achyu asked if I wanted to go to Osmania University as originally planned. I wanted to find out why the Telangana issue had so many kids committing suicide. I told Achyu it was too far away. He said I needn't cycle, we could take the car. But I was so dejected at not meeting Saina, all I wanted to do was be by myself and sleep. I had no energy to speak to anyone anymore. Osmania be damned, suicides be damned, Telangana be damned, documentary be damned, new cushioned cycle seat be damned.

After filling air, I cycled back to ISB. Aarthi was too busy to meet. I cursed myself for not bringing anything but Vivekananda to read. I read him anyway and realized there are only two times one should approach the itinerant mystic—when one is really happy or really gone. Only then there's clarity of feeling that allows for the seepage of tough knowledge. But he didn't do me any good and I passed up on his hard-earned intelligence. But I wasn't easily passing up on Gopichand's insights. I had asked for tips to make the journey easier; Gopi had said the one thing he would recommend was to get a deep-tissue massage on my rest days to clear the accumulated lactic acid. Even Ponappa's plan had included a massage during the cool down. I called Mayura and asked for the nearest place from ISB where I could get a massage. There was a hotel a few hundred metres away.

I pored over the map and plotted the route to Nagpur. I didn't want to nod off in the afternoon. I wanted to turn in early so I could wake up feeling fresh and new. I read Shikaari's 28-year-old diary for a while, then Nautanki and I wended down to the boutique hotel Mayura had recommended. The moment I got on the eternal driveway, I knew the massage was going to be expensive; I didn't care. It was my retail therapy. I ordered a deep-tissue massage for the frightening sum of 3,900 rupees. I was introduced to my masseuse, a comely slender girl from Northeast India. She led me to a large room and gave me my disposable underwear. I had never come across this invention. I knew about second-hand underwear and where one could buy it but disposable underwear required deeper study. I marvelled at it. It was made from the same material operating theatre masks and surgical caps were made of.

I asked if I should take a bath, she said that it was up to me. I wanted to suck the marrow out of my money. I opened up the shower without bothering which ran hot and which spewed cold and lit a cigarette. Standing under the steaming water that fogged up the large glass mirrors, I began to think about the second leg: 'Train the mind to not listen to the body'. I wanted to see how well I had trained my mind. I soon forgot the disappointment; Hyderabad was only a quarter of the trip, I wasn't going to let anything ruin my journey. I towelled myself dry and slipped into the disposable underwear that was surprisingly comfortable. I called to my masseuse. She came hopping in with short steps on padded feet and asked me to remove my towel, lie down and relax. I did. I prostrated myself on the bed and she began her work. She started at my Achilles tendons, repeatedly asking if she was being too hard. I didn't think such a thin woman could make me wince under the pressure of her fingers, but soon enough, I felt the delicious rivulets of pain snaking through my muscles as she kneaded them expertly. She started slow, constantly checking if I was all right with the pressure.

Once I had gotten used to the flickering spasms of pain, I asked her to increase the pressure. She shifted from the pads of her fingers to her knuckles. Initially, I tried to keep up a conversation. But as we got into the meat of the massage, I told her I was going to sleep and asked her to use all the strength she had to flush out the accumulated toxins in my muscles. I felt the pressure increase, I was certain she was using her elbows. At one point, the pain on my back and legs was so much I was convinced she was standing on me. I didn't bother to find out; I focused on the pain, imagining my body was a giant lactic acid press.

Gradually, the hurt of the day was erased by the good of human touch. My masseuse asked me to turn around. It was an hour-long massage and half was done. When she began to take oodles of time on my chest and stomach, I told the masseuse to forget the upper body, it was my legs that needed looking after. I closed my eyes and felt the quadriceps unkink. I thought about the money I had spent on the massage. It was the first one I'd ever gotten. I had always assumed massages were another wasteful way for rich people to spend their money. But lying on that massage counter, I was convinced I was getting my money's worth. It had been easy to look down on the rich when I was poor, but now when I had money and could occasionally partake in the hobbies of the rich, it was easier still to make peace with the pleasures that money indiscriminately bought.

I asked the masseuse how long I had left. She said I had 10 minutes, but if I wanted more, she would go on for longer. I turned over, and asked her to concentrate solely on my legs—my hams in particular. I closed my eyes and forgot everything. I asked her to go as hard as she could. It was such an intense composition of pleasure and pain, I unconsciously began to vocalize. Every time she'd take a long sweep of my legs from ass to knee, I would moan and whimper, 'Ummmm! Aaaaaaah!' She asked if I was okay. I jerked awake from my reverie. I said it was perfect, she was fantastic; she should carry on in the same fashion and give me more if she could collect the energy for it. She redoubled her efforts, I increased my moaning. I knew it must have sounded weird, but who cared—definitely not me. But maybe the masseuse did; not five minutes after I had started groaning, she stopped. The greatest massage of my life was over.

I stood under the shower for a long time. When I finished and went to the billing counter, my masseuse was there with a new customer. I paid my fare, fished out a 500-rupee note and gave it to her for the splendid job she had performed. She refused, but I insisted telling her it was incredible what she had done. I had never had a massage that good; I was a convert for life. I even asked her name to spread the word. The receptionist and the new customer looked at me suspiciously. It dawned upon me then that I was subconsciously propagating the stereotype of the masseuse helping her clients to an orgasm. I insisted my masseuse take the money and left feeling as awkward as everyone else—which was a pity because that massage was truly orgasmic.

Train the body to not listen to the mind, or Nautanki for that matter

Hyderabad to Nagpur

16 September 2010

Death of Momentum

It was raining steadily, a dull grey morning. I wondered if it was smarter to wait for it to stop. I readied myself for leaving while smoking a cigarette. Shikaari's diary recounted that the distance of 484 km to Nagpur was manageable. I thought the same. A little under 1500 km to Delhi—I wasn't going to dream about it. I thought instead of a shade beyond Nagpur, where the hills of Madhya Pradesh lurked. I wondered if I should complete the leg in four days instead of the originally planned five. The last three days into Hyderabad, I had clocked a steady 120 km each day and hadn't been too pooped. I felt fresh after the massage, like all the acid had been flushed clean. But the thought of whistling into Nagpur on a wild vicious wind, and flailing on the hills of Madhya Pradesh left me undecided. Achyu called asking what the plan was. There was no point waiting. It was time to stop picking the soft spots and see if I could be the all-weather man like I'd always fantasized.

I slogged up the small winding slopes of the many-treed roads of ISB in the slit-slatting rain; I hadn't seen a peacock the entire time I'd been there. Apparently, the easiest way to Secunderabad was via Jubilee Hills. Achyu and Naveen said the hills were too steep to cycle through. They had been there the previous day to shoot city shots. 'Jubilee Hills could be my training ground for Madhya Pradesh!' I thought. Besides, I would be saving 10 km. A few kilometres of bad road later, it was Jubilee Hills—steep imposing climbs, rising ghostlike and steady at a 45-degree angle to who knew where. I wished I had tested myself on the slopes of Kathriguppe.

During training, I had told Sachin I was a bad climber and was looking for tough slopes to harden my mettle on. A few days later Sachin had asked me to accompany him. He had insisted we go right then (it was early evening); he had taken me to a place close to his house and introduced me to some evil-looking slopes. I had memorized directions to the place. A few days later, I had introduced Nautanki to the hills of Kathriguppe. After one slope, I had had enough. Slopes like that were inhuman, made to order according to the demands of housing, with no thought for the necessity of gentle gradations that must accompany the construction of roads motorable enough for large transport vehicles. There wasn't a chance buses could go trundling up the baby hills of Kathriguppe that killed the calves of cyclists and made axles moan and chases wheeze.

Jubilee Hills had slopes triple the length of Kathriguppe's humble elevations. I heaved on Nautanki trying to keep a good rhythm, it was impossible. I concentrated on merely pulling through a revolution as smoothly as possible. Nautanki veered, I shifted to standing on the pedals. A few metres from the crest, where the road would surely have flattened if it didn't have the courtesy to dip, I stopped. What chance did I have against the hills of Madhya Pradesh when Jubilee Hills defeated me so easily? I decided this leg of the trip would take five days too. I humped the crest hoping for a flat, but it evaporated into another monstrous slope. I walked until I recovered my breath and jumped on again. I slavered as I slaved up plush Jubilee Hills, the dull cold in the aftermath of the rainy night doing nothing to stop the sweat drooling from my fingertips. I wrestled with Nautanki. I felt I was taking her hostage and she was an unwilling captive.

Three times I stopped on the murderous slopes of Jubilee hills, the last one bringing me the most discomfort because I was wholly intent on cresting it with pride when a school bus whipped in front of me. I pulled on the brakes as I cursed the loss of momentum—that magic carpet on which a cyclist makes love. Loss of momentum is sudden death to the cyclist's pleasure. It is anathema to the cyclist because it hacks his energies and saps his strength and spirit; it raises his eyebrows and tightens his lower jaw; and if repeated long enough, loss of momentum will make a cyclist dull and insipid until every welter of being shoved off the road, every bitterness of being run into the pavement, every uncalled for stoppage born out of selfishness and the instinct of self-preservation that comes so naturally to us all, makes him hateful on a slope like Jubilee Hills. As the weather improved, I resumed good rhythms.

To Build a Fire

Evening was setting in. Everyone was on their way home from whichever fields they worked in. The cattle and livestock were herded along the highway, choking it with their many hooves, starting little traffic hold-ups of two and three vehicles. Women balanced firewood for the night on their heads. The sun started to slippery-slide down the sky. A lake came out of nowhere when we least expected it. It was a large lake fringed at the back by rocky hills that once housed a quarry. Thoughts of camping entered our heads. Naveen was a self-proclaimed country boy. Having grown up in the mist-haloed verdure slopes of Chikmagalur, he wanted to sleep out in the open too. He promised us a fire that would last all night, he painted pictures of raw chicken and roast-fires; he began planning the night in infinite detail.

The crew had more pressing matters of transferring data, recharging batteries and making backups. Besides, Achyu had decided that the crew would always room at the nearest town because of their expensive equipment. All of a sudden I didn't want to sleep in the open alone. It was all right to sleep in a temple where I could take courage from the old caretaker couple who slept nearby. But to sleep out in the open—alone in the rocky wilderness, next to the large lake, close to the abandoned quarry, its ghostly offices long out of commission, with ferns mushrooming out of cemented parapets, the doors firmly fastened and the wood warped, the paint peeling; no protection from lake monsters, wild animals, snakes and scorpions—was a completely different thing. It had rained the previous two nights; and the clouds were on high alert, all golden brown and dark with omens of heavy rain. Nat Geo, ghost stories, and a roof above my head had made me cowardly. I quietly told Achyu, 'I don't want to sleep alone, man, I'm too scared.' And to think that I had wanted to do the whole trip alone!

Achyu asked me what could possibly happen. Snakes could crawl and scorpions could sting. It was decided the crew would room in Ramayampet—the nearest town. Achyu and I would sleep out in the open. When Achyu told Naveen he would have to sleep in Ramayampet with the rest of the crew, Naveen's face dropped. He was as eager to dream beneath the stars as any of us. I cycled to Ramayampet—a small town with one lodge and one movie theatre. Rooms were cheap—80 rupees a night for two. Naveen avenged himself by taking the crew to an Andhra Mess. He wanted a full meal where one could eat as much rice as one wanted. Prashanth, Achyu and Arjun preferred roti to rice; they meddled with their food while Naveen and I gorged. At the wood market, we bought 25 kg of wood at the ridiculous price of two rupees per kg. Naveen gazed wistfully at the wood, commending me on the purchase, saying it was excellent food for a fire—slightly damp so it would be slow to catch fire and last the night. We bought two litres of petrol for kindling (kerosene being unavailable) and returned to our lake.

Blackness was all around; a sea of fireflies lit our path. The humongous mat purchased in Hyderabad was unfurled; a grand fire licked the night. Naveen boasted, he called himself a man of the forest and claimed he knew everything there was to know about fires. Prashanth and Arjun ribbed him constantly. He took the bait. Their back-and-forth remarks riddled the air. Prashanth announced the bad news when a raindrop hit him in the face. Thick drops dimmed the conversation, a thin drizzle threatened to dampen the fire. We sat wondering, waiting for the rain to make a decision for us, but it was as confused and lazy as we were. Again, the weather was being kind, it could have poured and left Nautanki and me drenched. Instead it flirted casually, disinterestedly, only hinting at how dangerous things could get. The raindrops began to pelt us like little sharp stones. We headed to the lodge in Ramayampet; we had to buy a tent as soon as possible. The appetite for the open had been whetted, the promise of the stars was too great, and I felt funny going from lighting a fire to lighting a mosquito coil in the only lodge in Ramayampet, ideally located just behind the bus station, where an extra bed for the night cost a humble 30 rupees.

🚲

17 September 2010

The First Forest

By now, we had learnt enough about the sporadic nature of restaurants and dhabas to eat whenever we got a chance. We saw an Andhra Pradesh Tourism Development Corporation (APTDC) restaurant and stopped. A plate of puris and a masala dosa later, my eyes grew heavy with sleep. I felt the old familiar laziness taking over. I tried to evade it with all sorts of mental conjurations, but gave up and slept in a dhaba after a packet of biscuits and many cups of chai. I slept few minutes at a time, waking as if from a dream, not caring to swat the flies drawn to the wound on my leg. I was too lazy, the flies too many; I simply shook my legs.

Appalled at my penchant for laziness, I decided it wouldn't do to give in so easily and cycled on. I wasn't cycling at pace—the whole morning Nautanki had been groaning every time my left foot went through a downstroke. Earlier experience with these sounds convinced me I had a problem with the ball bearings. I had heard the same sound during the afternoon session the previous day and had paid it no heed. But the sound had grown louder and irritatingly regular. I pedalled slowly, paying attention to see if the sound came continuously. It did. I knew I would have to stop soon, but I wanted to cover as much distance as I could with the busted ball bearings, not only because it was clever but also because the next time this happened, I would have an idea of Nautanki's limits. I cranked up the rhythm, slowly building pace, until I found a speed that hovered excitingly on the tantalizing edge between effortless and excruciating.

The monotonous landscape gradually altered from open fields to thick bushes; the highway narrowed, its shoulders showed all evidences of new lanes being laid to rest. The trees got greener, thicker, taller; their branches grew longer, flew wider, more arterial; the air got crisper and the breezes grew bold with coolness. I could sense a forest coming on, and then boom! The forest started—trees arched overhead, dense foliage surrounded us, the mid-morning insects jabbered, monkeys by the wayside waited for scraps from passing cars—almost every monkey had a baby in its pouch. I saw the biggest spider webs I'd ever seen when I stopped to take a piss. We saw a spotted deer with a little fawn but she bolted when we tried to get close. We stopped next to an auto abandoned on a trail leading into the forest. The steering bar of the auto seemed to have stiffened with time. It was immovable. All of us tried to wedge it free. A general discussion into how long the auto had lain there ensued. We examined the tyre tracks and the caked mud rutted onto the wheels of the auto for clues. Opinions varied from a week to a month. An auto driver emerged from the forest, politely asked us to get out of the auto and sped away. He had parked it there two hours earlier.

I got back on and cycled quick and fast through the forest. What is it about cycling in a forest that impels one to fiercely feel (even if it's only for a few seconds) absolute faith in the reverie that one is truly free, that the essence of all life is movement, and the secret is to live in subservience to the earth? The forest ended as abruptly as it started, I was thrilled. I was 700 km out of Bengaluru, and finally, my first forest! I knew there would be more—after Maharashtra lay Madhya Pradesh.

A quick consultation with the map said the mighty Godavari cut across the highway around 70 km from where we were. We decided to halt on its banks. I would need to keep a steady rhythm to cover the distance that separated Nautanki and myself from the favourite river of my boyhood.

I set out at a good speed.

At Idulvai, I stopped to have Nautanki's busted ball bearings inspected. The sullen non-committal laconic man who manned the cycle-repair shop didn't even inspect Nautanki when I told him what the problem was. There was no diagnostic ear cocked to the pedal shaft like Rajanna would have done. But he seemed sure of himself.

He left what he'd been busy with, ventured into the small shop behind him and returned with a wooden stick as big as a small beam. To my horror, he wedged it between Nautanki's pedal shaft and her robust frame and proceeded to lever the pedal shaft outwards. I thought the pedal would come loose and he would fall backwards for his efforts. He turned the pedal a few times in the reverse direction to show me all was well, that the sound no longer existed, and said it was done. I told him Nautanki wouldn't whine if he turned the pedals in the opposite direction. He nonchalantly turned the pedal forward and it sounded fine; my doubts lingered.

Rajanna never dealt with Nautanki's groans this way—he opened her and slavered paraffin and grease on her, he'd show me the old worn-out ball bearings that looked like little imperfect balls of mercury as they whirled in his hand, cupping them the way the dentist gathers pieces of tooth after a troublesome extraction, before replacing them with spanking fresh ones that looked like buttons on a shiny new baba suit.

The length of the stop made it an even harder run to Doodgaon—the poetic village of milk. I was eager to make it in good time. Ever since we had left Hyderabad, I had seen people at regular intervals by the road selling *bhutta*. Never wanting to interrupt the rhythm I was constantly trying to build or sustain, I hadn't stopped once to eat corn. A family of three *bhutta*-sellers sat at the lip of the highway, the smell of freshly roasted *bhutta* lulled me into stopping. I ordered and watched the pods sputtering and crackling as the sparks from the coal jumped. The skies opened up.

In minutes, the steady downpour built to a shower. The family ran to protect the steaming coal beginning to fizzle and the roasted corn that threatened to get soggy; I busied myself with removing the rain gear from my bag and slipping a plastic packet over it. Shikaari had suggested a waterproof bag. 'Unprepared, unprepared, unprepared', I thought, but the rain looked beautiful coming down as I tried without success to take shelter under a tree while munching corn. Nautanki stood next to me, puddles of rainwater and rivulets of slush eddied about her wheels. It was tremendously romantic and as far as clichés go, it was straight out of Bollywood—all I was missing was a suitably bedecked girl. I laughed. Nautanki was my girl; she even wore flowers in her head.

Achyu, Naveen and Prashanth offered me the shelter of the car; I declined. Wasn't this supposed to be a solo trip? Achyu huddled under the tree with me in solidarity. A temple lay 50 m behind us. A quick sprint and we would make its shelter but still end up drenched. The rain came down in buckets. Who knew how long it would last? It would have to be the car. I was stunned by how warm it was inside the Innova. The family of *bhutta*-sellers huddled on their haunches in the rain under their single umbrella. The family had a little girl that was helping her father.

Doodgoan seemed an unlikely possibility, the Godavari got more elusive as the rain spanked the horizon. But the incessant luck I'd been having with the weather held and the shower passed. I changed into a new T-shirt quickly. Before I had my shoes back on, the charcoal was glowing anew and fresh corncobs were being roasted. The rain had come and gone, everything was as before—only wetter, greener, fresher.

A Dead Hand

Soon enough, I began to feel hungry. I warned Nautanki she'd have to go at top speed after lunch. Naveen suggested freshly slaughtered *nati koli*. 'Don't you still have another 40 km? If you are planning on putting in 120 for the day, don't you need the strength?' he prodded. But the great problem with having a farm fowl slaughtered and cooked is the time involved in the operation; an hour waiting, the better part of an hour eating (polishing off one chicken between three people wasn't easy), and another half an hour to laze around digesting the chicken. It was two o' clock and with 40 km left, it was touch and go, but I remembered Naveen's crestfallen face from the previous night.

The chicken was ordered; Naveen took great delight in inviting us to watch the slaughtering. A group of four men was involved in the capture. One of them who chased our meal as hard as the others caught my attention because of an immobile arm limping by his side. The hand stayed motionless as he ran, swaying slightly despite his left hand preventing it from swinging too much. Out of medical curiosity, I made a mental note to examine the prosthesis later. Fowl being caught, it was time for the fowl to be killed. Naveen made himself welcome in the dhaba's kitchen to supervise preparations—no doubt to give directions too. The TV was tuned to what the crew wanted to watch. I stretched on a charpoy.

When I was done, I invited the man with the motionless arm over. It wasn't a fake hand after all, it wasn't even a prosthesis; the darkness of the limb and its relative immobility had made me think so. The skin was tense, and it stretched over the swollen hand that had hardened by degrees. The skin shone ominously, it peeled in places; it was cold to touch. Where the man's shirt-sleeve ended, a soiled piece of gauze bound his broken wrist tightly to prevent the fractured bones from slipping. It was a foolish non-scientific way of alignment that would leave a permanent disability.

The man sat there impassively, his right hand positioned on his thigh with the palm facing upwards, his left hand supporting it. He moved his fingers slowly, gently, inquiringly, like an experimental cyborg testing out a robotic arm in a science-fiction movie. The hand moved, but not at the wrist—it moved above the wrist, but only fractionally and with the aid of the left hand. Any more movement and the man would scream with pain. It was a dead hand already, or maybe it was a dying hand; I didn't know. I had come too far from the vast shores of medicine to pronounce anything with any certitude. I listened, shocked at the man's ignorance, his naiveté, his gullibility.

His story was this: two months ago he'd been riding his scooter on the highway at eight in the morning when a Maruti 800 tried to overtake him. The side rear-view mirror of the car had clipped his hand as it overtook him. He hadn't been driving fast, maybe around 20 km/h. He hadn't even fallen off the bike; when he came home he had a terrible pain in his wrist and couldn't move his hand. He had visited a local medicine man who had applied a salve made from *jadi butiyaas* to the broken wrist. Thankfully, it wasn't an open fracture. Then, the medicine man had boiled two eggs and had bound them to the broken wrist; the treatment had been concluded by positioning the broken ends of the bones against one another and fastening them together tightly with supposedly sacred black thread. When the man had gone back in a month, the quack had told him things were fine, given him some more *jadi butiyaas* and asked him to come back after another month—broken bones took time to heal after all.

I asked the man, like we had been tutored in medical college, how much he had improved if improvement was measured on the scale of a rupee. 'Ten paisa,' he replied. It was the prototype of the sad story that must surely be replicated continually in the villages in our country because India's healthcare system is porous and poor.

As kindly and firmly as I could, I told the man that he would have to go to a hospital. He needed an operation, he would need to be admitted for a week, maybe two; but it was the only way he could save his hand. The man sat expressionless; the only time his face glimmered with emotion was when I told him if he left his hand that way it would get as useless as wet firewood—it was an expression I'd picked up from an attender in the government hospital where I had done my internship.

I watched the man's face and knew he wasn't going to take my advice. He had stopped watching TV, he was lost in his thoughts. When I repeated the advice, he looked at me with the same blank expression and asked, 'Where will the money come from?' Then, as an afterthought, he added, 'I'll manage, it will get better.' Blind faith had made him foolish, while poverty had made him obstinate and helpless. He left to go back to his work, his broken motionless hand hanging like dead weight by his side.

I marvelled at how (in two months) he had learnt to live a one-armed existence. I thought about the pain he must have suffered when the village quack had tied the fresh fracture. I should have asked how he had dealt with that. But the man was back in the kitchen earning his keep, mixing the curry with his left hand. Throughout the conversation, he hadn't evinced any anger, neither at the man whose car had clipped him, nor at the village quack who had rendered his hand useless, nor at the government hospitals where the bribes that turn the machinery scare away poor people. He was resigned; it was his fate.

Achyu said he wanted to shoot me chasing a fowl. I did a few cursory runs (laughing to myself), imagining I was Stallone in *Rocky II*, trying to get fit again. I was acutely aware of the fact I was wearing the T-shirt Gopichand had gifted me. Achyu's concerns were far greater. His was an orthodox Brahmin family who did things strictly by the book. 'If my parents get to know I am filming chickens being slaughtered and cooked, they might never speak to me again,' he said.

I set at a good pace. The quality of the road was patchy—all road markings and signage were gone, the road was rutted in places, potholed in others; the rain had whipped it to loose gravel, the elements had amplified the bruises of time and shoddy craftsmanship. I watched the road carefully, concentrating, senses alert, listening to the vehicles coming from behind, watching and waiting to see if they might run me off the road. We were on a two-lane highway with no median and the trucks and buses were looking to overtake, with Naveen driving at the same speed as me (which couldn't have been more than 20 km/h). I could sense the annoyance when the lorries had to tailgate him because the oncoming traffic was steady. They stalled at the speed we were going at, honking. We rode in this clamour for a while. It gave me tremendous thrill because to cycle in jostling traffic at a high speed demanded fervent concentration.

As a child, I'd stay awake at night when we travelled in buses, looking out of the windscreen at the road unfurling in the marauding light of the headlights. We always booked the front seats because they had the most legroom and my father's double knee surgery had left his leg bending only that much. I would imagine myself as the bus driver and try to negotiate the turns before they happened. I was always surprised when the road curved without me seeing it beforehand, and watched in awe at how close buses went to oncoming traffic without losing speed, negotiating all corners with the same nonchalance.

Now, I was riding with the same men I'd goggled at, negotiating the same curves as them with the same nonchalance, not letting up speed when they honked, but making them wait their turn because the roads were so bad I didn't want to impede my progress by cycling in the ruts at the edge. For one of the most gnawingly difficult things on a cycle is to go clattering through a persistently scratchy strip of road—the joints get rattled, the muscle fibres vibrate like plucked strings, the hands grip tighter, the fingers grow whiter, the shoulders hunch together as the road seems to administer an endless series of punches that brush the skin and bruise the muscles. I marvelled at Shikaari doing the same trip 28 years ago. I'd only had a few bad stretches of road: his entire journey must have been like this one—all 2000 km of it. I had to make it to Doodgaon in two hours; it was a fitting goal for a solid evening session.

Highways and Democracy

The NH7 adopted her original grand garb—four lanes, painted road-markings, big green signboards. By now Nautanki and I were in sync—it was like a training session all over again. Shikaari had impressed upon me that the harder I pushed myself in training, the easier it would be on the road. So I had pushed myself in training, but never as much as I would have liked, being lazy by nature and proud of it too. I thought of all the times during training when I had known I had energy in reserve but had not gone the whole hog because I always liked to think well of myself. Generally in life, I never wanted to discover what I was honestly capable of. I couldn't muster the courage to keep going when I'd already had enough.

When I was training I had promised myself one thing—I didn't want to struggle and heave, I wanted to have fun. If physically, I reached a point of no return, where I'd cycle slowly every day just to chalk up the kilometres for the mere vanity of reaching Delhi, I would quit. I'd call off the trip midway, apologize to the crew for wasting their time and enthusiasm, say sorry to Achyu for wasting his money, buy a train ticket to Delhi and take Nautanki with me to watch the Commonwealth Games.

But here I was—braced against the wind, steady on the handlebars, my heart booming, my breath slow as I tried to control it, the breeze fanning all parts of me that were exposed, the skin inside my clothes warm, the body warmer, and the legs hot, tight, firm, pounding, beating out rhythms of relentless precision. I began to speak to my legs, remembering all the writers who wrote about legs, their legs—Camus lying in bed for hours meditating upon his footballers' legs, Neruda likening his legs to the trunks of trees, Bob Marley singing about his legs like chariots. What is that strange happiness that comes to cyclists when they battle with their bodies while hardening the mind—playing games with it, telling jokes to it, cajoling it, berating it, urging it to stay with the rhythm? For how long can you really go? And if you really went as long and far as you could, you would end up going further than you had imagined you would. Surprises are always in store when you journey within.

The sudden proliferation of shacks and shops at NH7's edge portended a small town. I didn't want to slow, but I knew the teeming roads would entail a culling of speed. Making use of the town to rest my legs, I passed it sooner than I had imagined. The rhythm was back, so was Nautanki's groaning. The magician's sleight of hand at the cycle-repair shop had lasted half a day. I couldn't be bothered. Hadn't I already spent a week training the mind to not listen to the body—or Nautanki for that matter?

When the sun started her downward dip was when I loved cycling the most. It was the end of another day on Nautanki. I smiled as I watched NH7 unspooling in the horizon. The highways are the greatest symbols of democracy in our country. They alone are for everybody. The cyclist, the wheelchair-bound, the lorries, the trucks, the travellers, the corpses of roadkill, the vultures that feed on them, the bullock carts, the farmers, the livestock, the labourers, the villagers—everyone was going home on the longest highway in the country. Even the birds flew home at that time of day.

Sri Ram Sagar

Cycling slower, cooling down, letting a dull pleasurable ache subsume the tightened fatigue of my muscles, I took a detour from the highway to reach Pochampad, the village that houses the Sri Ram Sagar Project. I had never visited a dam before. I had always thought it would be a large stone repository of water with sluice gates at the bottom. But the Sri Ram Sagar Project was no reservoir, no dam, no river even; it was as large and unfathomable as the sea, and just like the sea, no one could tell where the water ended. The bridge was a stony beach high above the water that coursed and gushed. SRS was a tourist spot, and well, it was so.

People thronged the bridge under which the water pumped in one incredibly large white wave disappearing into curtains of spray as it leapt like a thousand jumping horses over the cement banks. I looked over the bridge's edge to see the individual pillars of white foam shooting out into a gushing swelling mass of water. The white wall of water dissembled mid-air into sheets of fine mist and invisible droplets. The orange and green tube lights fixed to the undersurface of the bridge made the sight more surreal.

And the sound of the water, that crashing booming roaring sound, as the lovers walked with the wind whipping their hair. I watched them look at the vast vista of water that pretended to be a sea; I imagined them talking about how the world was a big place, as beautiful as it was large; I could hear the promises they made to run through it someday, hand-in-hand, like kids running in a playground. The wind whistled, plastering clothes across torsos, fluttering dupattas like flags, lifting plaits and whipping strands, ushering hair into a bedlam of black smoke in the twilight. What is it about the immensity of water that convinces us of our humility? How does it hold us in thrall as it extends its giant white fingers across the earth to join the next water body and the next and the next until they all become one? Is it the constant stream reminding us that life is evanescent and fleeting; that we are of the water, like water, here one minute, gone the next, but going forever, coming out of nothing, from who knows where and who knows why but we must go, must flow, must blow until there is no more breath to be exhausted.

Dinner was at a highway dhaba. I ordered a glass of buttermilk; it came in a pink and white plastic mug, the kind one uses while having a bucket bath. Naveen couldn't contain his laughter when I tilted the protruding lip to my mouth. An inspection bungalow was our rooming quarters. They were Shikaari's first option for a night-halt on his trip. The bathroom floor was criss-crossed with cracks; a big hole lay helplessly in one corner where the cement and tiling had fallen through. Frogs jumped in the verandah. Ordinarily, I would be terrified of them, but when they jumped close to me as I smoked thinking about the next day, I didn't flinch or cringe. I was learning to be brave.

18 September 2010

Of Suicidal Fish, Harakiri Butterflies and Men Who Hold their Silence

From the time we'd left Hyderabad, Achyu and I had been talking about taking things a little slower. Shikaari's diary informed us that on some days, Basavva and he started as late as noon. We woke up late and had a leisurely breakfast of idlis and vadas served in green wax paper before checking out the majestic splendour of SRS in the crystal light of day. But instead of looking down on the water jumping ceaselessly through the sluice gates, we went at the base of the reservoir. Fishermen (bare-bodied except for their underwear) leapt from rock to rock, throwing nets as the Godavari foamed at their feet. We walked across a railed walkway, green with damp moss. I gingerly crossed crabs that were clamped to the steps of the walkway; as I got closer to the thousand white water horses, the Sri Ram Sagar drenched me in its flying dew. My glasses misted over. Massive fish sprouted from the water, some hurled themselves against the brick walls falling dead on the rocks and were carried away by the endless roar. It was attack, pillage and kill. Large rectangular pieces of thermocol had been lowered with ropes at the water's edge to catch the jumping fish.

I sat watching in mute humility. Achyu started in amazement at a suicide butterfly. He explained what they did. Soon enough, I saw my first suicide butterfly hovering at the edge of the white wall of mist that no man could survive if he attempted a phantom walk through. The black butterfly looked like a velvet Japanese fan framed against the white water horses. It fluttered, it hovered intelligently close to the man-made waterfall, it bobbed like it was dancing. I thought it was having a bath when suddenly without warning, the butterfly dived into the iron sheet of water. No one saw it again. Three more butterflies followed.

It was a bad time to start—near noon, the sun was overhead, head-winds lingered, the effort of the previous day's evening session began to tell; it was impossible to find a decent rhythm, I laboured through the revolutions. I took regular breaks. A slow-moving lorry rolled ahead. Immediately, it led to sudden acceleration, impromptu spreading of wings, and standing on the pedals to catch the end of the lorry. After regaining a degree of breath and covering a few kilometres through the largesse of the lorry driver, I pedalled on unaided.

Close to Neredikonda, we travelled uphill through freshly hewn mountains. There were gangs of stonecutters and loaders; women hammered rocky hillocks into boulders, men hoisted them into trucks. Some stared as we passed, most didn't look up from their work. Thick forests lay on either side of the highway. The slopes were gentle and long; I created fancies to keep myself going. I knew from conversations with a friend that we were travelling through alleged Naxalite country. I pretended I was a Naxalite cycling under the gaze of the law with a bunch of necessaries strapped to my cycle. The games I invented couldn't overcome the exhaustion I felt. Nautanki's ball bearings were busted again, except this time she creaked a lot louder. I wanted to stop but we had passed the forests and the open countryside didn't hold a tree in sight. All the days I had hardly wanted to train, when I had to summon every ounce of determination to drag myself out of bed at odd hours just to finish my workout for that day—all those days came in handy. I pretended it was one of those days and cycled like a mule. It was dull, unthinking, stubborn, helpless cycling.

Late afternoon, we stopped for lunch. I had only completed 50 km. I had two hours of cycling left; on a good day that meant 40 km, but it was not a good day—I set my sights at 30. I steeled myself for a good session. I settled into a good rhythm. The sun duelled with the clouds; I hoped no rain would slow me down. Nautanki's ball bearings were added incentive to cycle faster.

I knew the town of Adilabad was 50 km away. I was guaranteed a good cycle-repair shop there. I needed a man willing to get his hands dirty with paraffin and grease, not some sullen idiot who cured the capriciousness of ball bearings with long wooden beams. As the session progressed, I gloried at the distance I was covering. I pretended I was the man with the dead hand, if he could get used to the pain for two months, what were two hours? The forests reappeared; curtains of trees broke up into new patches of highway. The red disc of the setting sun sank slowly on our left. Up and down the highway went; Nautanki and I went with it.

A few kilometres from Adilabad, I stopped for an evening chai. If I waited any longer, the forests would stop and the chai stalls would get less pretty. A strange man by the side of the road looking blankly at the dhaba arrested my attention. The men in the chai shop said he was the local madman. Once he had been clever; some said he had been a teacher, others said an IAS officer, but whatever he had been, something had happened to make him lose his bearings or hold his silence. He wandered about, homeless, jobless, companionless and speechless. Occasionally, he stopped at the dhaba and waited in silence; he didn't even try to converse with his face, his eyes were mute. The cook rustled up some dal fry, packed five thick piping hot tandoori rotis in a newspaper, and gave them to the madman. I tried to speak to him but he looked away. I let him be and watched as he quietly walked into the distance, sat under a tree with his back to the highway, and started on his meal-packet.

'Where Is the Letter?'

I didn't mind cycling in the dark towards Adilabad. I was delirious with joy at having recovered all the lost ground in the final part of the day. Prashanth googled hotels, the first one that came up was in Subhash Nagar. We got off the main bypass that ran through Adilabad. The roads narrowed and were clotted with Ganapati pandals. Ganapati Visarjan was three days away, music blared everywhere. The street lights disappeared; people standing at the doorsteps of their houses told us grandly, 'Yes, all of this is Subhash Nagar, but there is no hotel here.' If we wanted a hotel, we would have to go back to the bypass. We backtracked another 5 km, changed plans and decided to repair the cycle first and hunt for a room later.

Achyu and I decided that I should try to sleep in a Ganapati pandal. We drove around Adilabad looking for a suitable match. Achyu wanted a big pandal, glittering with lights; we found one with women decked out to the nines, walking the streets with offerings in their hands, their children trailing behind and joining the young people dancing as the lights pranced in sequence down the street. Loudspeakers blared, a woman brayed bhajans into a microphone. Achyu thought the pandal was perfect. I refused. There was no way I was going to sleep surrounded by tuneless middle-aged ladies venting their devotion through songs.

We found a more modest, less crowded pandal that had been erected by the Professional Photographers Association of Adilabad. A bunch of men clustered around a chess game. After being given permission to sleep, I looked at the chessboard. I could ask to play a game once they were done. It was early exchanges; the opening gambits were plays I had never encountered before, either in the chess books I'd read or the games I'd played. White had opened both rook files, black hadn't advanced a pawn. He roamed the board with a devilish knight. Not being a great chess player, I wondered whether the players weren't budding grand masters playing out complicated strategies. We were in Humpy Koneru's backyard after all. I went for my night smoke.

The game had progressed to the middle stages when I returned. All had become clear—the chess players weren't budding anything, they were novices who made up the rules as they went along. White castled without the rules being adhered to, black's pawn jumped over the white queen; both began to rescind moves by the dozen. The game had fallen into a farce. The spectators laughed, the players giggled, the one who was losing scratched his head. It was best to not play. After wishing everyone goodnight I busied myself with my progressive relaxation exercises.

Ten minutes later, I was done. I was drifting away into sleep when I felt a rhythmic rapping on my feet. I opened my eyes, a young police constable was tapping my feet with his baton. I explained the situation, he asked several questions politely in reply: who was I, where was I going, what was I doing in Adilabad, why was I sleeping there? He asked to make a phone call, I gave him my phone. He called his superior—I could tell by watching him hunch and lean forward as he talked, eager to nod and ready to follow instructions. When he finished, he returned the phone and asked me to wait.

In 10 minutes, another policeman (middle-aged this time)

rolled in on a motorcycle. Just as politely, he asked the same preliminary questions. He listened more carefully, added a few questions of his own and proceeded to make a phone call. He put his phone down, grinned at me sheepishly and asked if he could use my phone to make the call. He had no balance, he explained. After he was done explaining to the person at the other end, he gave me the phone saying the inspector wanted to speak to me. I spoke to the inspector and answered the same questions telephonically. I was asked to give the phone back to the policeman whose nameplate announced him as Dasharath.

Dasharath finished the call and said I would have to accompany them to the police station. I asked why. 'Routine enquiry,' was the reply. For a second, I was scared. The endless cautioning of my father came back in a rush. Growing up, he had managed to instil a fear of the police in me by telling me stories about the various forms of torture they used while interrogating people. He would tell me repeatedly (especially when I went out late at night), 'Doma, don't get caught by the police, son, who knows what will happen before we get to know you've been arrested.' The good feeling of cycling was still with me, I decided to be unafraid. What could happen? I reasoned. I had done nothing wrong, I had nothing to hide. I told Dasharath I would follow him on Nautanki to the police station. He refused; I would have to accompany him on his motorcycle. We went back and forth until he spoke to me sternly. I gave Nautanki's keys to the constable; he would bring her to the police station.

The professional photographers of Adilabad had started another chess game. One of them told me not to worry. I asked if he was coming to the police station too but he said, 'No, I will be here when you return,' and he advanced a pawn three squares forward. All I had was my phone and my cycle.

I had left my bag in the hotel where the crew camped. I called Achyu and told him where the identification papers were. My voice was levelled, it was a good sign.

I sat on Dasharath's motorcycle. The pandal was at a brightly lit intersection. A few metres away, the dark shadowy roads to the police station began. I asked Dasharath what the routine enquiry was about. He said an anonymous informant had called the station to say there was a Muslim sleeping in the Ganapti pandal. It was a pleasant night and I felt no fear. I enjoyed the breeze feeling up the trees.

But as I approached the station, reality began to press in. With mild trepidation, I got off promising to make a brave front of it. Dasharath walked through the revolving gates interrupting the high compound wall running round the station. I followed. I hadn't taken two steps into the precincts, when a blood-curdling yell startled me; some madman bellowed in Telugu. I thought it was an unfortunate person in the lockup. But the voice carried on, shouting in short bursts, taking on the ominous notes of a martial command. I slowed to place the screaming. It was coming from outside the station, very close to where I was.

Slowly, I discerned the muzzle of a gun pointing at me from a man hidden behind a turret, only the tip of his head was visible behind the cement bags. I heard the sound of boots scurrying across floors as the yelling went on. Another man ran out from a corridor, knelt down on one knee like one would genuflect before God, pointed a rifle at me and clicked the bolt into readiness. I didn't move, I stood rooted to where I was. I was caught mid-stride. Not knowing what to do, I hesitantly began to pull my hands out of my kurta pockets. Remembering all the movies I'd seen, I wondered if it was a wise idea. What if the men with the guns thought I was pulling out one of my own? My hands froze mid-pocket. Dasharath had stopped and was motioning me onwards. But I wasn't going anywhere without taking permission from the men pointing guns at me. I pulled my hands out of my pockets in slow motion and half-raised them in the air, palms open, fingers splayed—I thought it was the best thing to do.

Dasharath kept asking me to move. I wasn't going to until the machine-gun toting, turret-carrying man gave me the okay. I wondered why Dasharath didn't order them to lower their weapons. I shrugged my shoulders questioningly at the gunner, he didn't flinch. I pointed to Dasharath and asked with my palms if I could follow. He lowered his gun and relaxed. Dasharath smiled broadly. Now, I was scared. Having never been to a police station before, I didn't know if it was a 'good-cop, bad-cop' routine. Inside the police station, Dasharath offered me a chair and turned on the TV to watch a Champions Trophy T20 cricket game.

The inspector arrived. He questioned me in English, the same questions I was asked previously, except this time there was a new one, 'Do you have a letter?'

'What letter?'

'A letter saying that you are doing this…cycling from Bengaluru to Delhi.'

'No, why would I need a letter like that?'

'So that people know you are cycling.'

'Who will give me this letter?'

'Anyone; the police station where you live, local MLA, any minister, but you must carry a letter with you so that people know you are doing this.'

I thought of Sammy—a kindred ex-doctor who was following his passion for acting. His first question when he had heard about my trip had been, 'Fucker, are you taking a letter?' I had laughed off his suggestions, they had come back to haunt me. We waited for Achyu to arrive with my identification documents. Why had I decided to sleep in the pandal while the rest of the crew slept in a hotel? Why had I chosen that pandal? Whose permission did I take before sleeping there? If I had taken permission, why had someone called the police station to say there was an unidentified man sleeping there? The inspector kept enquiring. I sweated, quietly waiting for Achyu.

Apologizing in advance, I asked the inspector if he'd been woken from his sleep. Unfortunately, he'd been dragged from the cinema hall during a movie premiere; it was Saturday night after all, slowly spilling into Sunday morning. There was a room with an open door covered by a curtain, above the entrance was painted, 'Writers Room'. I wanted to ask which writers used the room and was there a room like that in every police station in the country. If there was, I could go to the police stations in Bengaluru and write during the day. I imagined the innumerable stories I'd pick up, at least a tenth would be priceless. But the inspector was busy watching the cricket match that pitted Chennai Super Kings against a foreign club. By virtue of patriotism, everyone in the police station was rooting for the team from Tamil Nadu. It was a close match—Super Kings were chasing and had the upper hand. The slide started, the game began to slip away. Collective gasps grew, the policemen began to 'tch tch' and complain. I hoped for a miracle. I didn't want the inspector's mood to be ruined further. First to be called away from the climax of a just-released Telugu movie, and then to watch the Super Kings throw it all away! Where was Achyu? The air was pierced by the same blood-curdling yell. I wondered how Achyu would react. He would surely come with a camera. I hoped he wouldn't get shot.

Achyu came in and said 'hello' like it was the most ordinary thing to be summoned to a police station at midnight with someone else's identification documents. I was relieved. I gave my PAN card to the inspector. It was the only ID I carried but my father had foreseen the necessity of more universal forms of identification. I opened the plastic packet with copies of my election ID card. I watched the inspector flip the PAN card over in his hands and scrutinize it closely, 'Is this real or fake?' he asked. My first thought was, 'The inspector doesn't pay income tax'. I told him it was real and asked if he would like to see a copy of my election ID card. He seemed more satisfied.

He asked Achyu for his identification. Achyu gave him his defunct press card, explaining his role as director. The inspector nursed Achyu's card and asked, 'But why are you interested in this documentary?' Achyu was all professionalism, 'I think as a film-maker, you're always looking for an interesting subject to cover, and this...I think is very interesting... One man who wants to cycle across the country to discover what it is like.' I looked at Achyu with profound appreciation. For someone who spoke little, his articulateness when speaking about filming and what it meant to be a director was arresting. 'But what will you learn about the country if you travel on a national highway?' the inspector broke into a small smile. I hung my head in shame.

It was true—how much had I really seen? Not much. How much did I really know? Nothing. I was trundling through the country at 20 km/hr, and I was going too fast. Achyu was better prepared. He smiled indulgently, 'Actually, you'll be surprised to see what we've captured so far. I'm sure you'll find it extremely interesting. Would you like to see some footage?' he asked politely. The inspector chose not to reply. Achyu leaned forward, 'I was just wondering, inspector, if you would like to come on camera and say why Dominic has been brought to the station? It would be great if you could tell everybody why we're all here.' The inspector shrugged and threw open his arms in invitation.

Once Achyu finished, we all waited in silence for the circle inspector to come in. The Super Kings had catapulted to a spectacular loss. Again the blood-curdling scream; someone entered and whispered something to the inspector. He motioned all of us outside. The circle inspector waited in his jeep. He nodded off to sleep while he went through the inspector's explanations. Old-age had made him immune to the pleasures of late nights. He asked for identification. I gave him my PAN card. He asked what my name was. I told him; he looked at me and asked, 'Indian, ah?'

This time I had to laugh. 'Where is the letter?' he asked. Again the letter! I told him I had none. He told me I should have one. He explained how everyone was on high alert because they had received information that Police Commissioner A Q Khan would be assassinated during the forthcoming Ganesha celebrations. He commanded me to inform the proper authorities I would be sleeping in their town, and let me go, after ordering me to not sleep in the pandal. The whole investigation from the constable to the circle inspector had taken 30 minutes. I was free.

We had to write our names, fathers' names, addresses, telephone numbers and designations on a foolscap sheet of paper. Naveen was disgusted with the whole affair. He didn't want to leave any of his details with the police, he was scared of a false charge. He begged Dasharath saying he was only a driver, what was the need for his details when the entire crew was leaving theirs? Dasharath insisted he leave his car number too. Naveen frowned more, he cursed. We were readying to leave when we heard the blood-curdling scream again. No one flinched anymore, we were all familiar with it. Two young men were brought in; one of them looked drunk, the sober one had watchful eyes. The man who brought them in said something about pirated movies.

The inspector walked up to the sober one cowering in front of the lockup inside of which three men lay asleep. His hands were folded in supplication. The inspector asked questions as he approached. The young man shrank backwards while answering. Without warning, mid-answer, the inspector slapped the young man full flush in the face. The *thwack* resounded in the night. Instinctively, the young man brought his hands to his face. A neat punch caught him square in his unprotected midriff. He doubled up in pain. His bowed head received a hard fist. I cringed. Didn't his father ever warn him about getting caught by the police? The inspector ordered both men to be locked up. He turned around and saw us filming. He laughed and ordered us to stop. It was all in a day's work.

19 September 2010

Savitri Pimpri

We stopped for breakfast. We had reached Maharashtra; the signboards were no longer in Telugu. Naveen wanted to confirm. 'It is true,' the people at the dhaba said; it was Maharashtra. After seven days of cycling and slow-motion driving, we had travelled the length of the third largest state in the Indian Union and dipped into the great state of Maharashtra. We found it amusing that there hadn't been a single board or sign to mark the crossing over of imaginary demarcations and obscure squiggles on maps that are righteously guarded in real life; nothing to indicate how suddenly, miraculously, everything had changed. Breakfast was different—aloo *bondas*, *pakodas* and samosas instead of puris, idlis and vadas; the tongue was different; the people looked different and dressed differently too.

Just like that, from one Indian state to another, we were in a new world, another foreign country. Possessed with all the irony that marks good poetry was a puncture shop located next to the dhaba, it advertised itself in chalk scrawled on a lorry tyre balanced atop a stack of spent tyres—Bihar Tyre Works.

I stuck to bananas and an aloo *bonda*, avoiding oily food in case it precipitated heartburn. I wished for *poha*. I drank tea and smoked, thinking about the bad stretches of road we'd encountered. My body had taken a battering because I'd decided that good road or bad—I was sticking to a steady pace; the slower I cycled the more tired I got. I sat in awe at the foot of Maharashtra, thinking if the roads were this bad here, it didn't augur too well for Madhya Pradesh. My respect for Shikaari had deepened with every jagged pothole I'd bounced through.

After lunch, the heat continued unabated. I focused on keeping a steady rhythm without pushing too hard. I read the names of the villages and rolled Yavatmal over in my mouth because I loved the way it felt on my tongue. We stopped for tea. Nagpur was 120 km away. I wanted her under 100 before I stopped. I lolled on a coir charpoy perusing the *Eicher India Road Atlas*, when Pankaj Tate came upto me. He was the sarpanch of a village called Savitri Pimpri. He sat next to me, 'I know this car is an Innova, I have that much knowledge. I saw you coming on a cycle and them in the Innova, I wondered what was happening.' I told him the drill about the dream of cycling across India. He repeated everything I said as if he was trying to assimilate it. He was a farmer who'd come to the dhaba to celebrate a friend's birthday. The rains had been good that year and there was money left to celebrate. The village they lived in was 3 km away.

Pankaj pointed out to a canal that cut perpendicularly from

the highway to the village. 'Now because of the canal, we can bring our vehicles onto the road...even in this rain,' he added as an afterthought. 'Before, if there was any emergency, we had to wade through ankle-deep muck to come to the highway.' The canal was still in the process of being constructed—the earth had been deepened and the containing walls had been inclined. 'After 20 years, we've started coming to the highway once a month again.' From my perusal of the map, I knew a river ran past Pimpri. I asked Pankaj where it was. There were four Pimpris in the area, he said, and the village with the river running through lay further down. 'You won't know all this. Only the ones who live inside will know.' The conversation flowed like rivers and ignorance.

'When was the highway built?' I asked. It was there from the time he'd been born. Pankaj remembered his teacher telling him stories about the pre-highway days when he would take a bus to where the highway stopped, then walk the remaining 25 km to school. To arrive at 10:30 a.m., the teacher would leave home at seven every morning. 'He must have been a teacher exactly like Shikaari,' I thought.

One morning, Brojo and I had arrived early for hockey practice (we were always early because we had to catch the first bus of the day to make practice in time). We had watched as our teammates had filtered through the stone arches. Practice always started at seven; at 6:45 a.m., Skikaari would trot in, helmet hanging by its strap in his hand. His walk bordered on a slow jog. That day, as we had watched Shikaari grow by degrees in the distance, Brojo had mused, 'What is his motivation? He's always on time, every day. He's never missed a single practice session. It's okay for us. We're kids. He has kids and a family, and he's still more consistent than all of us. Every year, for the last seven years, he's the only guy on the team who hasn't missed a single practice session.'

Pankaj grew garrulous. That year the rains had been so good, he'd never seen so much rain since his childhood— 'It was more than 100 per cent'. If the rain kept pouring the crops would get damaged. If it stopped, the farmers would eke out a profit, but even if it didn't, they would still get by. At least the rain had come this year. The previous year, the land had gone bone dry. 'What did you do when the rains failed you the previous year?' I asked. 'What could we do, we couldn't do anything!' Pankaj exclaimed helplessly. He had spent 20,000 rupees trying to deepen his well but nothing had come of it. 'The biggest problem in Maharashtra is load-shedding. Last year, we had load-shedding for 12 hours a day. This year, because of the rain, it's only for three hours.'

Pankaj gave me a concise geographical outlay of Maharashtra's power supply. The names he mentioned didn't spur a wisp of remembrance. 'If the line meant to supply Vidarbha stayed that way, we would have electricity 24 hours a day; but Sharad Pawar has favoured Marathwada. He has forgotten about Vidarbha. Over here, we don't say anything. There is no one to question anyone. There are reservations for the Panchayat—that's how elections happen over here. Who gets elected as the panchayat head? An adivasi woman who doesn't know how to read or write. What is she going to ask anybody? The Secretary—the one who pays her salary—he comes once in a while and says, "This is your salary, these are your funds. Sign here." She signs,' he said stabbing the air with his thumb. 'And he pockets all the money. How else can a government secretary who gets paid 3000 rupees a month have a two-storeyed house, two wells and forty acres of land? That man has amassed crores!'

Not knowing what to say, I stayed silent. Pankaj rattled on about the problems his village faced. There wasn't enough water so they couldn't farm the entire year. There was hardly any irrigation; they sowed soya bean in June and prayed for rain. The Diwali celebrations (or the lack of it) depended on how well the soya bean crop did. Then they planted wheat and chana that were harvested in March, and there was no work and no money until the next monsoon. 'If we don't have water, how can we farm? But the canal is being built,' Pankaj reiterated. In a couple of years they would have water the whole year round. It was what had been promised. They would have to wait and see.

I mulled the steady stream of information on agricultural solvency. Pankaj began, 'But let's see what happens once the canal is built. If we have no land, what will we get?' he wondered. 'If you cycle from Bengaluru to Delhi, you won't know anything. If you want to learn anything about our country, go inside. Along the highway everything is *taka-tak*. You won't learn anything by looking at the road, and this is true for any big road in the country.'

We decided to go to his village. The recent rains had indentured and folded up the ground, the wheels of Naveen's Innova rotated helplessly in the slush; when he had navigated that, the car skid each time he accelerated. The wet slush gave way to the caked solidified muck, temporary little land masses grated against the chassis. Naveen put his foot down on the brake and refused to go further. It was decided that Arjun would ride on the birthday boy's motorcycle, I would take Nautanki. After scouting Savitri Pimpri, we would call the crew to take the longer tarred route to the village if necessary.

It was past five. I watched the canal as we rode alongside. The hope was that it would become the village's bloodline. Pankaj sat between his friend and Arjun, who sat back-to-front to film me. Pankaj kept turning to sneak a peek at what was being filmed. His friend trundled the bumpy route too quickly for the camera to be held still; '*Aaram se, aaram se,*' (Easy, easy) Arjun kept repeating. Pankaj became the director and told Arjun he should film the fields too. Arjun fended him off saying if he saw the footage he would see fields and nothing else. Pankaj manoeuvred himself so he could see the viewfinder in the rear-view mirror. 'Take my village also,' Pankaj complained again, to which Arjun laughed, 'First let the village come.'

Achyu called to find out what was keeping us. We told him to find the tarmac road to Savitri Pimpri. Arjun, in deference to Pankaj's wishes, sat the right way so that he could focus on the fields. At one point the motorcycle braked; to avoid losing momentum I rode around the motorcycle instead of braking. I looked to see what lay around me; framed in the viewfinder of the camera as Arjun panned the landscape, I saw the beautiful ruinous farms of Vidarbha. It was the first time I had looked at the footage and was startled to see how beautiful things looked focused within a frame. The fields were greener; the sky looked greyer, clearer too. I promised I wouldn't look at any more footage so my own perceptions wouldn't get diluted. Arjun was caught in his own dilemmas; he still hadn't stopped shouting '*aaram se*'. Pankaj waved his arms proudly over a few huts that loomed, 'This is my village!'

'Take my village now!' Pankaj harangued Arjun. The bullock carts came home with their families of farmers. Pankaj pointed to a middle-aged man who was squatting. 'Take this too,' Pankaj said, 'in the village we have no toilets, so people shit near the village itself.'

Savitri Pimpri, with a population of four hundred, was a stone's throw away. We passed the main thoroughfare of the village. Where the thatched huts and stone walls stopped, the unpaved road started. People lived their lives outside their houses on the road's edge. Bullocks were untethered, goats grazed, girls played *bucch aata*, boys ganged, men lounged with their backs against the houses or around the shaded arbours of a banyan tree or under the awnings of a small *kaaka kade*, women washed clothes, litters of puppies rolled in the muck. We stopped outside Pankaj's house.

In a few seconds you could notice the buzz the camera drew. The children were the first to come in with swinging arms, giggling and running towards the camera. Then, the adults appeared without the disarming exuberance of children, but with as much curiosity. Arjun reeled them in like he was the Pied Piper of Pimpri. I took the chance to walk around. I wanted to scout out the village temple to see if we could use it as our sleeping quarters. When I came back, half the village had surrounded Arjun. Even the bullock carts coming home to roost were stopped so the cattle could pose for the camera. Everyone vied for the camera's attention, jostling and pushing one another. Pankaj Tate brought his father out to be introduced. The father wanted to know where I would spend the night. I waved his concerns aside saying it was never a problem, all we had to do was find a temple. Immediately, the offer of staying at Savitri Pimpri was made; I accepted just as easily.

I met Babban: he had seven acres of land, he had sown cotton but the rains had finished him off, he said. The previous year he had suffered losses because of the lack of water; this year there had been too much rain. He looked like a defeated man—helpless against fate, circumstance and the vagaries of the monsoon. A little child tugged at my shorts. It brought a smile to Babban's face. The child's name was Saarang, he was Babban's son. He was one and a half years old and had eyes only for me. He didn't care about the camera. As the light was fading, we moved into Pankaj's house. I was surprised at how big it was, much bigger than my house in Bengaluru. We were served tea. Pankaj said, 'Everyone in the village lives like this—together. You saw for yourself. Everyone came out to meet you when you came, to ask where you are from. Your language is different from ours, so I explained who you were. But everyone still came out to meet you. In villages, everyone mixes with everyone else.'

I told him this sort of communal living was difficult to find in the city. Babban joined in, 'In villages, whoever comes, there is always someone to ask, "what do you have, what don't you have, where are you staying, can we make arrangements for your food?" In the city, it's every person for himself. Over there, there are big people with money who mix with other big people with money. The small people live by themselves.' I agreed with Babban's assessment. 'What do you want for Saarang when he grows up? Would you want him to go to the city or would you prefer he remained here?' I asked.

In a levelled voice, speaking slowly and picking his words carefully, Babban replied, 'I will educate him. When he is 11 or 12 years old, I will gauge how his mind has developed. If he turns out to be naughty and stubborn, I will make him a Naxalwaadi.' I instinctively laughed out loud at the suggestion, but Babban was unfazed. He hadn't meant it as a joke. I fell silent. He continued, 'It all depends on his mind. If he studies well I will send him out.' I asked if there was a Naxal problem in the area. 'No, no, there is no problem like that,' Pankaj said, but Babban cut him short. 'There is no problem with the Naxals,' Babban retorted. 'They are around because the farmers are poor. So it all depends on how Saarang's mind develops. We are OBCs, and there are no facilities for OBCs over here.'

I asked him about the reservations for OBCs. He said that the people from his village weren't clever enough to get into the reservation lists.

'The life of a farmer is terrible,' Babban said.

'Why?'

'Because our biggest problem in Vidarbha is that we don't have water. All the water gets directed to Western Maharashtra. And the politicians from here who get elected to the State Assembly either get useless posts or are induced to move over to the other side. The farmers' situation in Vidarbha is very serious.'

'What will you do now?'

'What will he do?' Pankaj snorted. 'He will work in his fields. If that doesn't help, he will work in someone else's fields. He's married, he has children, he has to do something for food and water for his family. Everything depends on the weather. Last year it was too dry, this year the rain won't stop. Everything is out of his hands. He has nothing to work with. What can he do?'

I was tired of the questioning. I wanted to watch the sun swishing her kaleidoscopic skirt around the village. Pankaj introduced me to a man as we walked through Savitri Pimpri's streets. I asked him what he would do if he had a choice between the city and the village. His answer came back quick like a punch one doesn't see coming. 'I'll stay in the village. We were born as villagers, we'll stay villagers. Without villages, there will be no India.'

'Why?' I demanded. 'What about all the other people who come to the city from their villages?'

'What are they doing there?' Pankaj retorted. 'They go to the cities and they live on footpaths and in slums. The ones who have money, the ones with jobs, they build houses and stay in them. The ones without money are in a worse condition than we are. At least, when we come back home there are people asking us "How is your field?" If a lot of work falls on someone, he tells the village and we divide the work among ourselves. We rely on each other. In the city, who will we turn to? If we go to the city we won't get jobs there. What will we do in the city?'

Darkness had fallen, load-shedding was on. There wasn't enough light to shoot. A kerosene lantern was procured. I asked Babban what he would prefer. He spoke slowly, choosing his words as was his wont, 'A village is better than a city. That's what I feel. Who lives in a city? Educated people live in a city. No one else lives in a city. We are farmers, and farmers stay in villages. Have you been to a village?' I didn't want to confess my ignorance, but Babban kept up the drill. 'Have you been to a village?' Pankaj rescued me by saying it was why he had brought me to Savitri Pimpri. Babban continued, 'You may have been to a city but only when you go to a village, you will know what it is like, how the people are, what their living conditions are.' He pointed to a child and said, 'That boy's parents' desire is to educate him in a *canvit. Lekin majboori hai ki uske paas paisa nahin hai*. (But he is helpless because he has no money) Where will they get the fees from?'

'What is a *canvit*?' I wanted to know.

Pankaj helped me out. 'It's an English-medium school.'

'How much is the fees in a *canvit*?'

'It is 20,000 rupees per year,' Babban replied. 'So we put them in our school. We have a school in our village that goes up to the seventh standard.' I turned to a bright-looking boy scarcely in his teens and asked him what he would choose—city or village? He wouldn't answer. He stuck his tongue out in abashment and smiled embarrassedly, as everyone prodded him to answer. Pankaj egged him on, '*Sang, sang. Marathi mein sang.*' (Speak, speak. Speak in Marathi) But the boy was tongue-tied with shyness, he wriggled between the crowd of kids who poked him from behind. A voice spoke, 'This is the condition of the village.'

Achyu tilted the lantern to see who had spoken. A middle-aged man in a pink shirt with curling hair greying at the roots said, 'This is the difference between the city and the village.' Achyu asked him to step forward. The man became sheepish with self-consciousness. He smiled in discomfort, smoothed back his hair and stepped in front of the camera; the moment he started speaking he sounded like the Prophet of Pure Reason. 'This is the condition of education in the village. He's in seventh standard and you ask him a simple question in Hindi, he can't reply. In the city, even a small child speaks both Hindi and English. What is the difference? There is no money in the village to send them to *canvits* and English-medium classes. So he has to stay in the village because he can't go to the city, and this is his fate,' he proclaimed before fading into the blackness from which he had emerged.

Babban breached the silence that followed, 'The food you get in the city, you get in the villages too. But what you don't get in the city is the weather you get in a village.'

'Why? What's the difference?'

'In the city, you have smoke and dust and mosquitoes and gutters. But one problem with the village is that people do *sandaas* outside their house.'

I heard sun dance, so I asked him to say it again. I whispered to find out what *sandaas* meant. Achyu whispered back, '*Potty*.' Babban continued. 'In the city people have toilets in their house, so it's clean. In the village, people shit by the fields. Some people in the villages have toilets, but not all. If this could change, then the village will be better, the surroundings will be cleaner and there will be less disease. But the people here don't understand that, they're stubborn and don't change easily.'

Arjun had been whispering from behind the camera that I

should keep plugging Babban with questions about the Naxals.

'Is there a big Naxal problem over here?' I repeated.

'There is no Naxal problem over here.'

'Who are these Naxalites?'

Babban started falteringly, 'The big people...'

'Which big people?'

'Imagine there's a trader and something is being sold for 30 rupees. He sells it for 40 rupees, that's how he becomes rich. Then there are politicians and government officials. If they don't look after the welfare of the people, or if they do anything to harm the villagers, then the Naxals try to finish them off. That's why they are called Naxalites. People like you and me don't have to be afraid of them. The ones who have studied and haven't got jobs, they have training for them in Gadchiroli.'

Achyu asked where Gadchiroli was. It was 150 km away. I mulled over it and realized I couldn't afford the detour. I cursed myself for not having started earlier. I made a mental note to tell Achyu that Gadchiroli was out of the question before he even asked. Babban continued. 'MA, M. Com, B. Com...these are the ones that become Naxals.'

Night had descended, the electricity was out. All the interrogating and interviewing had made me tired. I preferred slow conversations with many digressions—not questionnaires conducted under the arc of an emergency study lamp with people crowding around a camera. But we were getting substantive footage. I wanted to slip away with Babban. I left to find smokes. There were no Gold Flake Kings in Savitri Pimpri. I asked in three shops—little window-like establishments with the owners sitting cross-legged inside, surrounded by their humble array of essentials. No Smalls either, the only cigarettes they had were Four Square and Bristol. I settled for Bristol and chanced upon Babban in the street. I asked to go to his house. We escaped the crowd and walked through the narrow unlit streets of the village. Saarang followed us with his rolling baby steps, his smile unfurling relentlessly like waves on a beach.

In a few minutes, we were at Babban's house. It was much smaller than Pankaj's house. The outside walls were unadorned with paint or plaster. Babban called to his wife as I took off my shoes and played with Saarang. Babban's wife looked quiet and submissive. She invited us into their home. I was made to feel comfortable on the only bed available in the single-roomed house, Babban's elder son had to be roused from it to make space. He didn't have half the delightful impetuosity Saarang did, but Babban said he'd been sick the past few days. A small passage led into the kitchen where Babban's wife disappeared to make tea. The wife too had been falling ill since his mother's death three weeks ago. Immediately after the bereavement, Babban's wife had grown lacklustre and disinterested. She had suffered from a fever. Now when she was getting better, the son had fallen ill. Their cow had died a week ago. I asked Babban to show me the medicines his son and wife were taking. He pulled a plastic packet off a nail on the wall, I looked through it. All the medicines were as they should have been, but when I added up the costs it came to 361 rupees.

'Poor people can't afford to fall sick,' I thought. Babban's wife came in with the tea. She was demure, beautiful, slim, wiry and sick. When she offered the tea I could tell she had strong hands, like my mother. She stood in the corner of the single-roomed house with its solitary bulb. Babban apologized for the tea not having milk. 'The cow died,' he explained. He apologized for there not being sugar. The tea had been sweetened with jaggery. It made the tea tastier, healthier too, he said. Until I insisted Babban's wife sit down, she didn't budge from her downward-gazing place in the corner. When she did sit, she promptly sat on the floor. I pointed out a stool for her to sit on and it was the first time I saw her smile. It made her look even more enchanting than before. The elder son began to brighten up because Saarang wouldn't let him sit still.

A battered trunk lay in one corner of the room, a radio reposed in the other. There was still no altar for Babban's dead mother. Under the bed were two cardboard boxes, a few clothes hung on a nail. Apart from that, the room was bare. There wasn't even a television. It was the first time I had ever entered a home that lacked a television due to helplessness, not choice. We sat silently until Babban's wife began to respond to my questions with clear lucid answers. Babban proudly said she was more educated than he was: she had finished her twelfth standard and knew better Hindi than he did; she could write it too, he boasted. He went back to staring into space while the wife spoke to me hesitantly and clearly. I was stunned at how beautiful she was. I stole a glance at Babban to see if his pride in her education extended to her beauty. But he didn't even glance at her, forget that faint side-smile of possession or love. He was a man lost in his own misery.

Pankaj came looking for us. I had sensed earlier that he didn't like the excessive interest I displayed in Babban. I half-suspected he had come to see what we were doing, but he only wanted to show me around the village. Pankaj asked more people to reiterate what he had already told me; he puffed out his chest telling the village people how he had brought us 'all the way from the highway' so we could film the conditions in Savitri Pimpri. He was a very clever sarpanch. He showed us the village temple—a small one-room affair; it had a red stone icon for a deity. The icon's nose ran to the ground, as did the cheeks and chin. It looked worthy of worship. I leaned over to Achyu and said the icon was straight out of the *Pirates of the Caribbean*. Achyu said in a shocked voice, 'You fucker, that's Bajrang Bali,' and he laughed repeating *Pirates of the Caribbean* disbelievingly to himself.

At the fringes of the village, we met the village drunk who put me through the drilling of an interview for a change. He only spoke Marathi and I knew from the peals of laughter that he was making fun of me. But the laughter had been absent the whole evening and I didn't mind. The drunk quizzed me, I kept fumbling with my answers. He passed comments as the village rippled with laughter. When it looked like the drunk was getting out of hand, Pankaj insisted we leave. The drunk gripped my hand firmly, pulled me closer and said conspiratorially, 'Tell me, what is your education?' I was glad. I knew my answer would make him see me in a new light. 'I am a doctor,' I said softly and promptly the drunk whispered, 'Despite being a doctor you haven't been able to buy yourself a pair of long pants.' The village erupted, I cracked up too. I turned around and everywhere was the laughter I loved. Achyu jumped and lassoed the air wildly. He had a perfect shot for the documentary.

It was time to wrap up. We went back to Pankaj's house where a humble yet delicious meal awaited—rotis, dal and a sabzi. We sat in a circle and ate. I was famished. The rotis were cut into quarters. I marvelled at the simple ways in which the village folk cut corners. I was the last to finish eating. Arjun began his dinner once I'd finished. I walked away gingerly, my legs numb from sitting cross-legged on the floor. I blamed my Anglo-Indian heritage for this 'unindianness'. Two sharp piercing wails split the tranquility of the night. I made my way towards the sound. Two swarthy boys, their heads wrapped in scarves, cupped their hands to their mouths and were shouting as loud and for as long as they could, '*Maharaj Tukaram ki Jai!*' (All hail Maharaj Tukaram!)

Pankaj said it was a quotidian ritual in Savitri Pimpri. Every night the singers walked around the village singing the praises of the village deity. At the four corners of the village, they bellowed the deity's name. I suspected it was a way to keep wild animals at bay. I liked the singing so much, I followed the singers around. Poor Arjun was called away mid-dinner. The four singers belted it out in the temple, keeping time with a couple of castanets. It was mesmerizing music. I sat at the doorway listening with closed eyes, trying hard to remember the refrain to hum to Nautanki the next day. One of the singers added the ringing of a little bell to the sounds of the castanets. Achyu asked me to get up. It wasn't difficult because I was so moved by the music. I would have worked myself into a trance if he'd asked me to. When the singing was over they spilt sugar around the temple and gave me prasad. The guest room in Pankaj's house had been made up for us—five beds in all—and it wasn't long before we were all knocked out, sleeping the sleep of the dead.

20 September 2010

Mindful of Shree's warning—if I was lucky enough to sleep in a village, I wouldn't be allowed to leave easily—I woke up at six. We went to Babban's home. The wall was caked over with cow dung that peeled like aged scabs of a chronic disease. I had wanted to shoot inside Babban's house but even at seven in the morning there wasn't enough light. There was only one bulb; setting up more lights would take too long. I was all for canning the shoot when it was suggested. Thoughts of my run into Hyderabad were still fresh. I wanted to roll into Nagpur the same way—on a high with the legs pounding steady, arriving early on a fast breeze I had created with no unnecessary stops, so that instead of resting for one day, I could laze around for a day and a half instead.

Babban refused to let us go without having chai. I tried to wheedle my way out of it, but he insisted. He pointed to his wife sitting on her haunches kindling the firewood. She turned to dazzle us with her morning smile of reticent warmth. I bought another Bristol cigarette. Naveen suggested I slip a hundred-rupee note in each of Babban's kids' hands, '*Adde bestu.*' (That's the best) He shook his head in disbelief and horror at Babban's home. The tea came. Saarang played with his brother as we talked. Babban apologized again for the chai not having any milk in it. He would set out in a few hours with 2-4 rotis to try and save his crop. It would take him four days to clean up the *keechad*, he said. I looked at the two-and-a-half-year old potential Naxalite and wondered what fate had in store for him. There was nothing left to do but move on. I stuffed five hundred rupees in Babban's palm under the guise of a handshake. I was embarrassed at the futility of the gesture. He tried to return it but when he saw the denomination on the note he wavered. I extricated my hand and beat a hasty retreat.

Back at Pankaj's house, Apoorva, his baby daughter was all made up and beautified with the dark spot to ward off the evil eye; we filmed her in all her glory. Pankaj's address was simple—his name, his village, his taluk, his state, the pin code. We promised to send copies of the documentary when it was done.

Faith

Thoughts of Madhya Pradesh were already with me. It was my last day of undulating flats before I hit the hills where the real examination lay. I decided to test myself one last time; I wanted to sweat into Nagpur around mid-afternoon with my confidence intact.

Passing a board that pointed to Chandrapur and Butibori (it lay en route to Garchiroli), I wondered whether Saarang would find the course of his life marked at that crossroad someday. Nautanki breezed through Hinganghat which turned into a big disappointment—the name sounded enchanting but it was only a little industrial town, pepperd with tall smoking towers and not a single dwarf ghat I'd hoped for. We stopped at Wadner Pimpri to have *poha* for breakfast, all of us musing over the unoriginality of having four Pimpris in quick succession. There was a problem with the car. I headed out alone while the rest of the crew tended to Naveen's beloved car. It augured well for the ride. Going into Hyderabad too I'd been freed of the drone of the car and ridden well. Making swell time despite the sun firing arrows, I employed the same strategy. No unnecessary stops except every hour of riding was broken for fifteen minutes when I stretched, drank two cups of chai, smoked a cigarette and ate a two-rupee packet of Glucose biscuits.

A sign proclaimed Delhi to be 1,014 km away, I patted Nautanki; we were halfway there. Before the day ended, Delhi would slip under a 1,000—another milestone to chuckle over. We passed a couple of blank milestones painted white, black and yellow with no number prophesying how far you had come or how close to elsewhere, and they were my favourite milestones throughout the entire trip.

By noon, Nagpur was less than 40 km away. I wasn't feeling tired, but not wanting to overdo anything, I stopped at a highway dhaba for another chai. Achyu and I talked about the sheer futility of having tried to plot the trip. Achyu said, 'I've realized one thing man. A documentary like this…there's no point planning. Look at everything that's happened so far. Timbaktu—unplanned; getting arrested—not planned; spending last night in the village…wouldn't have happened if Pankaj hadn't come up and spoken to you.'

A man with a martial moustache approached and asked in English, 'Are you on an expedition?' I nodded. He introduced himself as Sunil Shinde. I told him my name, his eyes widened like he had met an old friend. He grabbed my hand and pumped it like a borewell. I didn't know why he was so effusive until he proudly declared, 'I am also a Christian!' He was a man of deep faith, I told him so. 'It is our testimony,' he replied. Sunil Shinde was an ex-army man. I told him my father was an ex-army man too. He launched into an inventory of the places he had served in, 'Leh, Bhutan, Shillong, Sikkim, Siachen, Meghalaya, Dwarka, Assam. I was there.' 'All the beautiful places,' I said. He began to list a bunch of his comrades, and just like my father did, he appended their registration numbers to embellish the stories.

Foolishly, I assumed Sunil was a convert; he corrected me by saying that he'd been born a Christian. Apart from owning and managing the dhaba we'd stopped at, he also ran a charity in Nagpur called Faith, Hope and Love Society that organized eye-camps (the last one had administered treatment to 80 people) and medical camps for the Adivasis who surrounded the area. When I asked him where the money came from, Sunil gently said, 'Charity'—like it was the most obvious trait in humankind and the easiest to arouse. He loved the Adivasis of the area whose main occupation was keeping goats. He averred that he talked, lived and dressed like them. In fact, some of the workers at his dhaba were Adivasis.

'They are good people, just a little bit backward. We have to give them support.' The Adivasis in the surrounding areas had Sunil's mobile number. If anyone was sick he would ferry them to the hospital. 'I love to stay with these people...they are good people,' he beamed. 'We should stay with them and help them. Otherwise who will help them?' he asked jerking his head at me. 'If everyone decides to stay in the city, who will help them?'

Sunil lived in the dhaba. He was 56, and once in a while, he spent a day with his wife and grandchildren who lived in Nagpur. His family didn't mind him spending his time in his dhaba. They were coming the next morning after church to spend the day, and would return to Nagpur in the evening. I was amazed at the peaceable arrangement of affairs. I had always believed one of the great drawbacks of marriage was not being able to run away on a whim to chase some crazed dream for as long as it seemed important.

One of the common threads running through the documentary was to figure out what made people tick despite the hardships they faced. Achyu asked Sunil. 'What drives you to give up your family to come live with the Adivasis and work with them?' He took a few seconds to ponder over it. 'Faith,' he said quietly. 'I believe in God; and what does he say?' he asked me with a knowing smile.

'Blessed are the meek,' I offered, knowing my answer was partially right.

'Do for those who are needy,' he corrected. 'When I see that a patient is getting better, I feel good. When I see a person feeling happy, I feel good.' I knew this to be true. I'd had similar feelings long ago when I used to be an intern, and not a particularly good one either. When a patient I'd taken care of was being discharged, they'd come with small gifts to thank me. 'For what?' I would ask. 'For curing us,' they claimed, when all I used to do was oversee their recovery. Now those simple pleasures were lost to me, but I wasn't prone to mixing nostalgia with sadness.

I watched Sunil, feeling ashamed. Every time I had done something vaguely charitable it had been out of a sense of discomfort at being more fortunate than most. I was always embarrassed by my own smallness each time I slipped money to someone. Here was a man who did much greater things out of pure faith—sheer and simple faith—because God decreed it. God had ordained it; therefore, Sunil Shinde would do it. I had lost my faith long ago in the face of everything I had seen. I had a notion that if there actually was a God he'd come down to earth with an army and the guns wouldn't stop until there were very few people left, and then they'd start building anew, because the present model was too flawed to warrant saving; no one could heal what we'd become. But I knew there was no God and I hadn't yet found a war worth fighting. I'd go to sleep thinking that at the end of the day one had to believe in something, or if that didn't exist, then someone—one had to have faith in something or else life threw too many questions at you.

About 20 km from Nagpur, the trees lining the road threw large shadows which made cycling a greater joy. In a space between the lorries—grown grimy with road dust—all massed together in a relentless line, I found a bum shack chai stall for the last break before Muir Memorial Hospital. The chai seller asked where I was headed; Delhi, I replied. Where from? Bengaluru. He arched his eyebrows, 'Adventure, ah?' I looked fondly at Nautanki. When I had first thought about the trip, I had never referred to it as a cycle yatra, or Bharat Brahman, or desh darshan like I did with the people on the road. Back then, it had always been 'the expedition' or 'the adventure'. Now after 10 days on the road, I heard those same words again, except this time, it was people saying them to me.

🚲

21 September 2010

It's All Tied Together?

Although I hadn't planned to, I woke up at five. I lay in bed for an hour dreaming about the hills and Shikaari. When the light came rushing through the windows, I went to get chai. I watched in silence as the old banana-seller cajoled the cycle-stand attendant of the Young Men's Christian Association (YMCA). The previous night I had seen the banana-seller—his face wrinkled like sand dunes, hair scraggly like a piece of white coir, chasms in his mouth where his teeth should have been, his limbs like canes, struggling and heaving over the pavements with his cart half-stacked with bunches of bananas. For a small fee, he paid to use the precincts of the YMCA as his sleeping quarters. His bed was a sheet strung tight across the frame of his cart to fashion a hammock between the wheels. He was trying to get the attendant to let him leave a little later every morning. He haggled, he coaxed, he beseeched; he complained about no one buying bananas so early in the morning, he kept up the entreaties until the attendant raised his voice to ask the banana-seller if he knew the grave risks he took in letting him sleep there in the first place.

The banana-seller shuffled and bowed and put forth his reasons until the attendant exasperatedly told him there was nothing he could do—if he couldn't leave by six he would have to find a new sleeping quarter. The banana-seller apologized, he was only asking, he told the attendant. He promised to leave early as always and tottered away. I had a leisurely cup of chai and found out when the cycle-repair shop opened. I strolled back, eager to read Shikaari's diary.

I started reading from where they had left Hyderabad. I

was stunned—Shikaari too had roomed at the YMCA. I had completely forgotten. I was convinced he had stayed in the same room I had woken in. Shikaari's diary made no mention of a room number. He hadn't even taken a break in Nagpur; he'd shot out immediately the next morning 'after receiving a breakfast of eggs and bread from our friends in the hostel'—and the friends had met Shikaari and Basavva the previous night. They didn't stick around because they'd been forced into losing a day when Shikaari fell ill with an upset stomach.

I thought about Shikaari's journey and the things he had had to overcome—accidents (he knocked down a woman carrying hay across a highway and a car clattered into Basavva a mere 100 km from Delhi), illness, a cyclone through which they managed to cycle 50 km because they didn't know it was a cyclone (they thought it was heavy rain), lack of money, and what surely must have then been punishing roads. In comparison, I'd lucked out. I had avoided the heat, the rain had been sparse (if not welcome), I hadn't had an incident that caused me to doubt Nautanki or myself, and my health was at its best.

I came to the part in the diary where Shikaari had climbed the 11-km ghat section I was so nervous about. I was assailed by the feeling that tomorrow was too close for comfort. But as in a dream, I could hear Shikaari's soothing voice, sense his smile, as his fatalistic humour took over when I asked him what I should do if the slopes were too difficult. 'Push the cycle to the top of the hill and start cycling again,' he said. Nervousness gave way to calm. 'Prepare well, and leave the rest to God.' I breathed slowly. Even if the hills were a day away there was nothing I could do and though I didn't believe it, I convinced myself I'd done all I could to scale them with a modicum of decency. I remembered the original plan—when the going got tough, the lazy got off and walked. I cast the diary aside and dreamt, imagined, wondered, conjured up what the morrow would bring.

It was eight, the cycle-repair shop would have opened. I asked for a new seat. With all the tossing and turning, Nautanki's voluptuous bum had been ripped at the crotch; the seat rode up the hard plastic saddle like a very short skirt on a long-legged girl each time she climbed atop a high bar stool. I was halfway to Delhi and the padding had been pummelled into the flatness of a dosa. I cursed myself for ignoring Shikaari's advice. He had suggested a four-inch thick cushion so I could ride 'like a maharaja on the road'. I had asked whether four inches would be overdoing it. His response was a wicked smile, 'Anyway, by the time you reach Delhi, it will be flat'. I looked at the available seats covers. They were flimsy pieces of rexine stitched around thermocol as thin as tissue paper. I asked for one to be put on anyway. The new seat cover looked precarious. I slapped it to flatten the creases, I smacked it to check how comfortable it was; I wondered whether I hadn't been better off in the first place. The new seat cover was deplorable, it lacked nothing to not recommend it. A 1000 km on that! I mused thoughtfully. I had no other choice but to slither and slide.

Nautanki gleamed and had grown silent after the overall, she thrummed as I rode her back. The crew stirred. I lay down to pore over Shikaari's diary although I knew it well already. He spoke about the '8-km ghat section' and how he went over it 'with ease, all thanks to the training of Mr Subbaiah. It was a fantastic experience.' I thought about the import of that line—it was a fantastic experience. I had always been nervous about the hills of Madhya Pradesh. The first time I had met Shree, the first thing he had said when I told him the route map was, 'The good thing is there are no hilly sections. So that's one thing you don't need to worry about.' But I was worried. Every time I had heaved up a slope, I had wondered how I would get over the 8-km ghat section Shikaari's diary spoke of.

The challenge too had changed complexion. Earlier on, I'd been content to train for it. The thought of sailing over it had never crossed my mind. If the slopes were too tough, I would get off and wheel Nautanki, until we could swallow-swoop down. But considering the documentary, I didn't want to look silly panting up a slope. If I was going to collapse from tiredness, I wanted to do it alone without being watched. I wanted to savour my defeats, exult over my inadequacies, glory at my failures and laugh at my failed ambition in solitude.

It took too much effort to be myself in front of a camera. Being natural didn't come naturally to me. From the time I was young, I had always been too scared of being myself, too scared of other people's perceptions. I had once wanted to be the best at everything—best friend, best son, best boyfriend, best disciple of God. I'd even wanted to emulate certain Christian saints. I'd pick up gravel from construction sites and put it beneath the mattress to make sleep uncomfortable. And another aim for the trip had been to conquer vanity. I was ashamed at worrying about being embarrassed by a slope. I blamed Nautanki for my pettiness. I didn't want her to look bad. We had worked well in tandem and finished half the trip with more ease than I had feared we would. Now to go over the slope with a huff and a stiffled guffaw would be bad form. My friends had always insisted Nautanki was a bad idea. Midway through training Sibi had realized I was serious and had offered me his Trek for the trip. Arjuna, in a stroke of tardy generosity, had offered me the money to buy a geared cycle two days before I headed out. But I wanted to go on Nuatanki. If it was good enough for Shikaari and 90 per cent of the country's cyclists, it was good enough for me. I was sure that if anyone saw me slaver up the slope, rather than thinking that it was because I had allowed my body to rot over the years, they would blame Nautanki for being too heavy.

One of things that frustrated me most when reading cyclists' blogs was being unabale to find a single site that spoke of adventuring on an ordinary cycle. The way some people went on about the specifications of their cycles! I felt like throwing a spanner at the laptop. It was all gears, rims, frames and equipment. Some days I'd jump from the chair in disgust at reading how much some cycles cost; I'd take Nautanki for a spin belting out the anger beating down on her pedals. When I was spent, I'd stroke and whisper to her while spinning back home. She had behaved immaculately thus far through training and on the trip. It would be a terrible thing to show her in a bad light, I wouldn't be doing Nautanki and her ilk any favours. I put Nautanki's name at the head of my ever-expanding Litany of Petitioners.

But it wasn't only for her I wanted to do well. The second time I had met Shikaari, I had taken Nautanki along. He had ridden a circle under the tamarind trees at the head of the circular highway of school. 'From now on, this is your travelling companion, your mate, your best friend. Take care of it well, and it will take care of you.' He used to say similar things about a hockey stick, forcing us to respect and love it until we came to feel that it was an extension of ourselves. If I was going to scale the hills in style it was as much for me as for Nautanki, because where one stopped, the other began. It would be good to have a massage before the slope. It would flush out the massed lactic acid.

Nas, nas

After failing to find a massage parlour on the Internet that didn't sound dodgy, I enquired at the mall close by. I was directed to a unisexual hairdressing salon. My first massage had lulled me into an overarching sense of luxury. The Nagpur salon was in the basement of a two-storeyed office complex. I opened the door and the cool of the air conditioning hit me as quickly as the formica-topped table, threatening to fall out. An ample woman in her mid-twenties manned the saloon; evidently she was the owner, or the manager. I told her I wanted a full-body deep-tissue massage.

She called; a young man emerged from the depth of darkened partitions with a shaving brush in his hand. I refused to judge a book by its cover. I waited my turn. I was ushered into a small cubicle occupied entirely by a bed covered with a white sheet, grown particoloured with stains in various stages of decay. The oil blotches were in a winning battle with the fading white areas. I scaled down my expectations of the massage. I asked for my disposable underwear. The young man didn't know what I was talking about. I explained—the use-and-throw green underwear made from the same material that surgeons' caps were made of, and whose seams were made of elastic—all in broken Hindi. It didn't help.

I finally showed him some tissue paper and asked for underwear made from it. He bowed his head in embarrassment and said they didn't keep underwear like that. I told him every massage parlour I'd ever been to in my life had disposable underwear. He wanted to know where in Nagpur would he find underwear like this. I told him he could see it in Hyderabad. He smiled like I was a fool and said, '*Bade bade sheharo mein milta hoga.*' (You might find it in big cities) I told him I wasn't wearing any underwear; his smile grew wider at my audacity. I asked what was to be done, he told me to go back and wear my underwear. I didn't want to back-track and asked if he wouldn't mind giving me a naked massage. The smile disappeared. I told him the hostel was 2 km away, I had cycled far and had nearly as much to go. I could see him soften and weigh the decision in his head. He shook his head firmly and said no, he couldn't do it; he had never done it before, I should wear my underwear and return. On my way back, I stopped at the Regional Transport Office to enjoy the bedlam and confusion that accompanies any large government office with a constant influx of the *aam janta*. I remembered the day so easily as it was akin to being transposed into a reverie from the past.

It was a day exactly like this one—hot and sweaty amidst the stone columns grown stale with the circulating eddies of dust and people as they learned in unscrupulous detail the corridors of power. I needed a domicile certificate from the *tehsildar's* office to prove that I had lived in Karnataka for seven years to get into a government medical college. Till then I had never heard the word 'domicile' or '*tehsildar*'. I had seen my father bribe the official earlier that morning. It was our second day at the office. I heard him supplicate, 'Sir, please do the best you can.' The official nodded his head. 'Sir, I had taken leave from office only for this, today is the second day I have come.'

'It will be done,' the clerk said, in Kannada.

'Sir, I have arthritis, Sir, in both my knees. It is difficult for me to walk and stand for a long time.'

'Then why are you standing? I have told you to come in the afternoon,' the official said in a tone of exasperation.

'I will definitely come Sir, but please Sir, please make the sure the certificate is ready,' and we walked out. What incensed me was that despite paying a bribe, my father had demeaned himself before the official. We bought bhelpuri to pass the time. It tasted as dry and stale as the air; I blurted out, 'Why did you act like that Pops?'

'Act like what?' he asked chomping on a mouthful of bhel.

'Why did you have to grovel?'

My father chewed slowly until he swallowed the bhel completely, 'What's the meaning of grovel?' At the time I'd look up every word I didn't know the meaning of in a dictionary. I abandoned 'servile' and 'obsequious' as a means to explanation, 'Why did you have to act like he was doing us a favour? Why did you have to bow and say please so much, like he was superior to you?' My father looked at me thoughtfully and responded like it was the most normal question in the world, 'Bugger, you're young now. When you come to my age you'll understand why I act the way I do. I hope you never have to, but someday you'll understand why I folded my hands before that man.' It was the first time I came close to understanding the unbearable predicament of the Powerless Man.

As we sat munching our bhelpuri on the stone slabs ringing in a little mud sports field on the premises (the oddity of it all), I thought about how my father must have once been like me—young, impassioned, principled, filled with faith and foolishness. Somewhere along the way, time and knowledge of the world had forced him to betray his idealized innocence. That day, I had promised myself I'd watch carefully for the first instance when I would have to grovel. Thankfully, life hadn't yet served me such a bitter pill (grovelling with lovers being excluded). I told myself that if I had to suffer in the hills, I would suffer with the same gracious ease my father had exhibited that day in the *tehsildar's* office many years ago.

I walked back laughing at how the masseur's face changed contours as he deliberated giving me a massage in the buff. I was glad my masseur was a guy and not a girl; I remembered the swiftness with which the lady had wrapped up the massage when I'd started moaning. Now when the masseur would work my thighs, I would groan until my throat went sore. I reached the parlour. I stripped and lay on the dirty bed. The young man started with my back. I wanted him to start with my calves like the girl had. He turned in the opposite direction. He kept bumping into the partition that housed the bed. I listened to every bump as we conversed, my eyes closed, muttering amiably as I felt the impress of his fingers ripple the muscles from knee to calf. Nothing was going to deter me from enjoying the calm of the massage. I told him specifically I wanted him to do a tremendous job on my legs, in particular my thighs.

When he finished my calves, he returned to my back. I decided against directing. Leave him be, I thought, he knows what he's doing. Suddenly, I was roused from my dreamlike state by the masseur's elbow grating forcefully against my backbone. I ordered him to stop and massage only the sides of my back. He insisted that he continue with his technique, he even offered to do it slower. After a short trial where I couldn't stop wincing, I told him to forget it. I was sitting on the bed threatening to leave if he insisted on carrying on. I lay back and his widening strokes reached my shoulders. He squeezed my shoulder and elbow joints until they hurt. I asked him to stop, but he was adamant, 'If I don't do it like this, how will your joints get loose?' I told him to forget about my joints and stick to kneading my muscles.

He started with his elbow on my backbone again. I asked him politely whether he had gone to any school to learn the techniques of a massage. He said this was the way massages were, if he didn't massage my bones what good was the massage? I told him to forget all the massages he had given or seen. I promised a good tip if he managed it. Then he stuck to the sides of my spinal cord. When he started kneading my hamstrings, I gritted my teeth and squirmed at the pressure. I asked him to switch from his elbow to his fingers; it was all I could do to prevent myself from jumping off the bed. I kept arching my back and crying out, 'Aah, aah!' as I imagined every last drop of lactate being milked out. He began to find the knots in the muscles, I asked him to untie them. He redoubled his efforts commiserating, '*Nas bhar chuka hain.*' I tried to get him to explain. It was as futile as me trying to explain disposable underwear. I imagined that the '*nas*' he spoke of were the hardened muscular excrescences, one little microscopic tear in an individual muscle fibre being heaped on another, until they all began to tear in unison leaving a firm little muscular knot of imperfection. My legs were filled with *nas*.

When he started unkinking my quadriceps, I was shooting up on the massage bed like a jack-in-the-box. Every stroke he went through, I came up for air, like a reflex, grimacing at the pain scurrying up and down my thighs. I begged him to go slower so I might get used to the searing strands of fire his fingers wrought. I was on the verge of tears, I settled on my palms to have the lactate pools cleared. My thigh trembled after each stroke, the masseur kept slapping it, '*Dheela chodiye, dheela chodiye,*' (Keep it loose, keep it loose) until I was calm enough to let him work his magic. I lay back and groaned, long and hard, eyes crinkling and face grimacing, repeating aloud, '*nas, nas*'. I was beginning to like the word and all it symbolized.

Tomorrow I was starting my third leg of cycling. And what was the motto for the third week? To failure. '*Nas, nas.*'

Tomorrow I was going to cycle to failure on the dreaded slopes of Madhya Pradesh and if I had to get off and walk, I would do it with the same dogged determination my father and the old banana-seller lived their lives with. '*Nas, Nas.*'

I thought of Muhammad Ali, speechless and gasping, so devoid of energy after dancing deftly for 14 rounds with deadly

Joe Frazier, he couldn't be lifted from his stool either by his will or someone else's strength. When they had asked him later what that fight had been like, he had whispered, 'It was the closest thing to death'. *'Nas, Nas.'*

I remembered Lance Armstrong writing eloquently about schooling his son in the ways of the Tour de France before he set out to win it for the seventh time. Lance was carrying his one-and-half-year-old son and asked, 'What does Daddy make them do in the mountains?' and the little boy replied without batting an eyelid, 'Daddy makes them suffer in the mountains.' *'Nas, Nas.'*

I didn't have Lance's self-confidence; as the masseur's fingers riveted me to the bed, I asked myself, 'What is Daddy going to do in the hills of Madhya Pradesh?' and deep down within, a baby voice whispered back, 'Daddy is going to suffer in the hills of Madhya Pradesh.' *'Nas, Nas.'*

To Failure

Nagpur to Gona

22 September 2010

I woke at five, nervous after a series of dreams that revolved around cycling. A bunch of friends and I were cycling to some place; we sat on our haunches in a circle. When it was time to leave, one among the assortment of friends (I wasn't sure who he was but knew that it was a 'he') got on a tricycle parked beside him. It had materialized out of thin air. It was no ordinary tricycle either because once my friend sat on it, it sprouted spinning rotor blades and he left. With my jaws agape, I watched as he gently wafted into the air, adroitly swerving to avoid an old lady walking down the street. She too had materialized out of thin air. When I woke up I remembered thinking in the dream, 'What a tremendous form of transport!' I had a vague foreboding that the climb wouldn't go well. I lay awake and stretched silently until all that was left was the sound of my breathing getting deeper, each breath being drawn serenely to a height before it came floating down like a dry leaf in a breezeless free fall. There was nothing left to do but go on.

I strapped my bag extra tight so there would be no unnecessary stops thinking this was the day I would find out how well I had learnt to cycle over the past seven weeks—that, or I would get shown up. Either way the hills of Madhya Pradesh had to be negotiated. My butt and hamstrings felt tight. True to his promise, the old banana-seller had left. I drank a cup of chai staring steely-eyed at nothing and thought of the first 100-km cycle ride. It was when I had begun to believe I had a chance of making it to Delhi; it was also the first time I thought about the hills of Madhya Pradesh as something to be cycled across and not walked through. How clearly I remembered that ride, not just every inclination and perverse dip in the road, but the multitude of thoughts and feelings as I had climbed.

All the plans were in place. I had a made a mental note of all the long rides and every place I had wanted to stall but had soldiered on; I would replay them in immaculate detail when we hit the hills. The Litany of Petitioners had been arranged in various platoons—doubters first, parents next, lovers after, immediate family, friends in India, friends overseas, acquaintances, madmen, poets, doctors, colleagues. There were innumerable categories to remember every person I'd ever met; when the hills got too steep, each one would have a revolution plowed in their name. These and several other schemes I had devised to make sure I went over the hills in style.

An hour into the ride, the tightness disappeared. Breakfast was at a rundown shack in an army cantonment. The scenery changed from city brush to bright green foliage. I had good form. I knew from the map that Mansar was 40 km from Nagpur. Immediately after was Pench National Park. It was where I assumed the hills would begin. I had forgotten that coming out of Nagpur, Shikaari and Basavva had set a blistering pace, cycling 129 km to reach Seoni by nightfall. I didn't plan on going that far. Once I scaled the hills, I would look to sleep.

I stopped at Mansar for chai and bought some fruit for the hills. Shikaari's diary warned of desolate stretches for kilometres on end. Shree had said that in some places in Madhya Pradesh, I was liable to cycle 30 to 40 km without meeting a soul; those were always the tough phases, he added. The previous day when I had googled Pench, I had learnt that *Jungle Book* was based on the immense biodiversity that once studded the area like living diamonds.

At Kandri, the trees overarched. Chandrabahuli and Mogra

passed. The undergrowth on either side of the highway grew from a fence to an endless curtain, a backdrop across which Nautanki and I passed for a brief moment in time. In a while, we were in Pench, the board proclaiming it as 'India's First Interstate Tiger Reserve Project—Maharashtra and Madhya Pradesh'. But where were the hills of Madhya Pradesh?

The Hills of Madhya Pradesh

The confusion had been cleared. In my eagerness to reach the hills, I had neglected the scale of the map and assumed that Mansar and Pench were a few kilometres apart because they bedded down together on the map. I asked everyone where the hills were. I remembered Jubilee Hills, I wanted to set myself this time. As Nautanki ate up the kilometres, the forests grew dense with thick-trunked trees bearing exceptionally broad leaves. Ordinarily, anytime I saw a plethora of green I'd admonish myself for not knowing the names of trees—I'd poke fun and wonder if I was serious about being a writer.

But that day, I simply enjoyed the waterfall of leaves cascading on either side of the road. If Moses could part forests instead of seas he would make a killing in construction. The trees flung their arms around each other above me, I was glad for the shade. When the canopy wasn't trellised enough to create a tunnel, the cool was a sensual delight. I let it wash over the sweat falling and flying. How does 75 km into the country wring such a drastic change in the weather? The body thrummed like a finely-tuned musical instrument. Trucks were parked by the side of the road; their inmates settled on mats and bedsheets in the shade of the jungle with unpacked stoves and packets of raw rice. How I envied their lives! At least the parts where they dined in jungles when driving got boring.

I clattered along the bad roads. If there was a sliver of smooth tarmac slim enough for Nautanki's robust wheels, I'd thread her through it. When she rode rough in a slipshod manner, I didn't grip the handlebar tightly anymore, but gently rolled it between my fingers so that every gentle vibration from the bad road, through the stock, past the shocks and up the spring-loaded seat was absorbed and defused through the jerky train of slack-jointed, firm-muscled limbs. I stopped to take a piss and saw spider webs as large as garden umbrellas. At the centre were massive spiders weaving masterpieces of their own perfection. I was intent on not losing time. I wanted to make the lead-in to the hills after a small lunch and a calm rest. Spotted deer dotted the landscape; I glanced them through the trees, they watched with fearful eyes. I didn't stop; the crew did. Langurs appeared and charged the crew as they filmed. The forests of Pench were bursting with life. A board announced '*Seema Prarambh*' (Journey Begins)—and what a reception it was! The whole road was battered and bruised. I parked Nautanki.

We were in Madhya Pradesh, the hills were close at hand. We asked about them. I loved how everyone called them 'ghat section'. It was just beyond Kurai, 4 km away. The day had been planned to perfection. It was time to forget, rest and meditate. Naveen goaded me into ordering chicken. It was an oily mess, it didn't taste too good either. Arjun spared his taste buds which left Naveen and me a sizeable portion to polish off. I couldn't believe how full I felt. I had wanted to relax for a bit post-lunch but slept instead beneath the boughs of an eloquently rooted tree.

Achyu finally resisted all pleas for five more minutes. I put on my socks as of yore, like I would the blue and white stockings in the Sports Room smelling of sweat and boyhood dreams. Guys would be cracking jokes and describing funny incidents from class. And though I romped in the arena of their thoughts, I was always steeling myself for the game ahead. I couldn't simply turn on the juice like Joseph or Brojo or Karthik. Before I could swim easy in the ocean of doubt I had to still the mind and shut everything out. It was all clear in my head. I averaged three minutes to a kilometre, the ghat section was half a kilometre from Kurai. In 15 minutes, I would hit the slope. Depending on whether the slope was 8 or 11 km long, I would crest it within 60 minutes (assuming I climbed a slope at five minutes to a kilometre).

We passed a board saying Kurai. I leaned into the pedals. The roads were out of shape and traffic surprisingly regular. Nautanki began to jolt, I bounced with her. I plowed through each curve and shook through every pothole. The breath was calm, the legs were strong, the mind was rock-jawed—there was nothing to worry about as yet. There was rarely a sharp curve on those generous slopes. My hands gripped Nautanki's handlebar as I searched for the smoothest, slickest, softest way through the badgered roads. This then must be the infamous roads of Madhya Pradesh that everyone (Shikaari, Shree and Gopi) had warned me about. I steered by centimetres, holding up a lorry until he wouldn't stop honking, so I could ride a clean passage for longer. We took the curve together, my head bent towards the lorry cleaner waiting for abuse, but he gave me a thumbs up sign and smiled.

Everything seemed to give some hint of encouragement. I looked at the stop clock I'd started at the foot slope. It was past 20 minutes, my breathing was still unscattered. The ghat section didn't wind on itself like a snake unfurling loops as it slithered languorously uphill but was composed instead of a sedate array of mild slopes coupled with wide-sweeping curves—easy on the legs, easier on Nautanki. But none of this stilled the good feeling within. These were the hills of Madhya Pradesh and I was scaling them with ease.

The feeling of wanting to take a shit grew by degrees. I spied a large lake through a break in the walls of the highway. It didn't matter anymore if I scaled the mellow ghat section in one go. We stopped to inspect. As the threat of twilight grew, the sun streamed through the gaps in the dense forest, the lake sparkled like diamonds. A little wooden house nestled in the background of the vast grassy edges rimming the lake on the far side. It was a place only a writer could dream up. Achyu wanted to take a crap too. 'What is with you guys? You see a lake and you want to take a shit,' Prashanth commented drily. We squatted on the side of the road opposite the lake, me glorying at the serenity with which I'd climbed. I felt light; the bowels had been evacuated, the pipes were plumbed clean. But it was more than just the crap. I was no longer encumbered by any nervousness about the ghat section.

I tried to set the same steady rhythms thinking about Shikaari. He had climbed these same hills with different emotions, though the essence would have been the same. A lengthy carrier lorry stacked with long flats of iron lumbered past, the clamour of it was tremendous. I could hear Shikaari's diary being read in his own voice in my head, 'Now this journey was changing from plain land to thick forests and ghats. We crossed the border of Maharashtra into M.P. The forests were thick and dense. We had to cycle with some difficulty. At one place, we had to pedal 11 km on steep ghats. It was a fantastic experience. I climbed the ghats with great easiness and of course with extra strength and energy. I am sure I could do this because of the excellent training by Sir MP Subbaiah.'

With each revolution, my confidence mounted. As my legs thumped on the pedals, I thought in awe of Shikaari —he had taken me from a pasty mound of flesh and moulded me into something I could be proud of. He had made me larger than my limitations. Every Monday (when I chatted with him after Sunday's long cycle ride), he would say, 'Don't push yourself, don't overtrain. This is not the Olympics. What is going to happen when you reach Delhi?' I shrugged my shoulders. Back then, I hadn't had the temerity to look that far. 'If you reach Delhi, is someone going to give you a medal?' I knew the answer to this and shook my head. 'No one knows your body better than you do,' and he had helped me rediscover my body.

It was time to explore. I had held back long enough. Half the slope must have fallen away. It was eventide, the winds were a tonic, the sun was a sliver in the sky—and the blood running in my legs was molten lead. I ratchetted up the revolutions, thundering down on the pedals, staying rooted to the saddle; it was no longer enough to stay focused on the road, measuring the ride. It was time to see how much I really possessed. What were the limits of my endurance? How far had I come, how quick could I go? It was time to let the body loose and allow the mind to soar to new heights of surprise. I began to lean into Nautanki, willing her to work in tandem, heaving my hips into each stroke, grinding out the force. I didn't bother keeping shy of the potholes, I aimed my front wheel at the smallest stones. It was time for reckless abandon; it was time to cycle free—without thought, without doubt.

I felt I could swallow everything the road threw at me. I flew over potholes and clattered through craters but didn't pull on the brakes. It was flat out bust till my lungs burst or my heart exploded, until a muscle tore or a tendon snapped; full throttle ahead with nothing to lose and nothing to gain except the exhilaration of gathering pace while climbing a hill slope. I let myself go holding nothing back and cycled as fast as my legs allowed. I didn't want reserves of energy anymore.

As Nautanki and I clambered up the battered slope at top speed, or at least to my mind we did, I pretended I was Alexander Vinokourov leading the assault pack onto the slopes of the Alps for Alberto Contador; I was Andy Schleck getting hit with no teammates around and that was where I lost the race; I was Ale Jet shooting off like a rocket; I was Marco Pantani snorting cocaine; I was Big Jan Ullrich who put on too much weight during the off-season because his appetite for life was too big; I was Eddy Merckx; I was Emil Zatopek—the human locomotive—his face made hideous by a fake grimace; I was Boris Becker flying across the grass of Queens; I was Steve Waugh with a stone face in an inexhaustible arena of self-belief; I was Rahul Dravid in the dungeons, writing moving masterpieces because even he knew history was kind to kings; I was Dhanraj Pillay, swarthy and agile, with the wings of the devil trapped in my heels as I streaked a white flash of uniform down a green Astroturf conducting the ball in an orchestra of my own making; I was Shelly Raphael, short and stocky-limbed, thundering across the hockey fields of Bengaluru; I was Shawn Michaels acting stupid and making everyone laugh; I was Saina Nehwal clambering up the Peking order—I was every single sportsperson I had ever admired as I blew myself out on the middling slopes of Madhya Pradesh.

I heard Shikaari telling me over and over again, 'Do your best in training. And leave the rest to God. Ask for his graces, he will help you. Believe in him, he will give you the strength and belief.' Every time he'd mention God or ask if I believed in him, I'd nod my head, unsure about what I believed in anymore. Not wanting to get into dead-end conversations, I played along, saying that I was Roman Catholic, when years before I'd insisted that I was a 'follower of Christ'. Now I had stopped that too, never praying, never asking for anything except when there was no other option.

When everyone was helpless I'd say prayers that demanded more than they cajoled, prayers that were like challenges to God to prove his existence, prayers that were more like promises extracted under the threat of eternal defiance. Out there on the hills of Madhya Pradesh, I realized I had found my God. There could only be one God for me—and he had to be human, a flesh-and-bones God. My God was the best the human race had to offer. Shikaari was my God. I thought of 20 more people who could be fast-tracked into the pantheon. The sky clouded over, big diamond drops roused the earthy smell of rain, and the sun came out. We were awash in it; the drizzle splattered my body as I stomped on the pedals, wanting to crest the slope before the rain came down. I imagined the down-swooping curves of the descent, I wanted to hug them before the rain made brakes imperative.

I barrelled along knowing I had never cycled harder or faster. I was heaving now, riding on the opposite side to use the well-tarred strips. In the distance, a lorry loomed, I was thrilled. I took the speed up a notch knowing I had plenty in store. I wanted to attack the lorry but it wasn't necessary. The load of the lorry and the degree of the incline reeled me in. It was the same flatbed with the iron flats that had passed me earlier. It was my proudest moment when I passed it, beaming at the driver. He grinned at me and shouted something I didn't hear, I had gone deaf with pride and disbelief. The rain came down. In the distance, I could see what looked like the crest of the slope. I cycled faster. If I could only crest it, I could take the descent when the rain stopped.

What is that feeling when a raindrop falls to the tarmac and the edges splinter as it splashes its shadow across the road two feet from where your eyes stay peeled? What is that feeling when your body is wet with sweat as the rain sweeps the first flush of cool across your skin, yet inside you can feel the heat radiating? I could feel the rain wet my legs and exposed arms. I could hear the patter of it on the peak of my cap, and through it all, the fourth breath accompanying the fourth revolution—the exhalation coming out in one long, prolonged, controlled, steady whoosh.

Half a kilometre before the 8-km ghat section ended (or 11—the number didn't matter anymore), I stopped. I didn't want my socks to get soggy. I changed into my tracks and covered the bag with a plastic packet. I started a slow spin to the top, ecstatic at doing so well. Three boys on cycles just like Nautanki crested the slope in the opposite direction on their way back home from school. I chuckled and smiled—they were like the three wise men. It was good they arrived when they did and humbled the excessive pride I was bursting with.

Daya Ram

At the top of the mountain was a dhaba. I was so delirious from the myriad emotions, I felt like I had reached Delhi already. The shop next to the dhaba arrested our sight. It was closed but looked like the typical *theka* shops in Delhi, with the customers fenced out from the shop by iron bars. A large signboard adorned the shop: 'Post, Bhukki and Dod Shop'. We asked the dhaba owner what it was, he wouldn't say, he walked away. A trucker who sat alongside remarked, '*Driveron ke nashe ke liye hai.*' (It is for providing drivers with drugs) We asked what the drug was but he couldn't explain clearly. 'It makes your eyes red and doesn't let you sleep for 12 hours,' he said.

Naveen jumped at the information. He quizzed the trucker

about the drug. He was desperate to try it—something that delayed sleep for so long was pure gold for drivers, he said. He didn't mind buying a sack and taking it back for his friends. It would come in handy on our journey too—driving in second gear on the empty highway naturally put you to sleep. We all laughed. The rain stilled to a drizzle. In a clearing were a bunch of schoolboys.

The sun was dropping like dead weight and Achyu wanted to shoot. We wandered over; a middle-aged man joined us out of curiosity. His name was Daya Ram. He asked where I came from. He had been to Karnataka too to teach people the art of conservation. Madhya Pradesh was Number 1 in conserving its green cover with the aid of local forest conservation groups. Daya Ram headed one himself. Whatever we need, the forest can give us, he averred. First the idea had been to preserve ecology, now the focus had shifted to creating a vibrant ecology. And so Daya Ram and his village had decided they would build a forest. 'What?' I asked in surprise. 'It isn't difficult, it is a lot easier than constructing buildings,' he replied. 'All you have to do is plant a tree and nature will do the rest.' His group had curated a forest for the past 12 years.

He asked if I wanted to see it. He began to take the names of herbs, plants and medicinal shrubs. I couldn't keep up with the easy dispensation of knowledge. He spouted statistics—when a tree died, 40 human beings lost their natural sustenance. We had ruined the country by blindly following western traditions of culling forests to set up industries; now we were paying the price. 'But at least, we have realized our folly and the government is waking up,' he said. When he was young, it used to rain five to six months in a year; now it rained only for a month or two, and even then rain didn't come on time. 'The rain has to eke out time to fall,' Daya Ram said drily. We laughed. Daya Ram's intelligence and confidence were impressive.

He paid us no unnecessary deference, he spoke to us as equals. 'You keep reading in the papers and seeing on TV... everyone is talking about the big bomb that can destroy the world. We don't need to worry about that bomb. We already have another bomb created by our enterprise that will blow up the world just as easily.' I doubled up with laughter. We promised to meet Daya Ram early on the morrow, he promised us a tour of his forest. I didn't want to cycle further. The dhaba loaned out rooms with beds, we took it.

23 September 2010

A Man-made Forest

Despite the good intentions, I woke marginally late to see the man-made forest at dawn. I didn't want to rush the morning. I ordered a cup of chai while Arjun set up a time-lapse shot of the sun climbing Nautanki's frame. Two trucks rolled up, five men got out. One of them was the fabled Punjabi truck driver—turbaned, long-bearded, broad-framed, with a massive hulk he carried fearlessly. He settled down on the charpoy. 'Nothing can daunt him,' I thought. He looked the oldest and wisest of the crew. The youngest of the lot drank water and made for the Post, Bhukki and Dodd shop. The crew of truck drivers called the dhaba owner over. They wanted to have a full-blooded meal at seven in the morning. They were disappointed with what was on offer. They were even more disappointed on hearing the fare wasn't ready.

One of the truckers asked roughly why they couldn't order

since everything was being prepared from scratch anyway. The fabled Punjabi trucker stilled him. He ordered chai. The youngest driver came back with three packages rolled in newspapers. He gave two to the others, and unrolled one. A coarse white powder was inside. All of us were keen on watching the imbibing of the drug, we huddled around our table discretely. The young man tore a piece of newspaper from the edge and using it like a scoop, he took a tablespoonful and funnelled it into his mouth. After passing the powder on the newspaper to the next person, he drank water from the jug on the table and sat back. Everyone did the same thing. We wanted to see the drug take effect. The man-made forest paled into insignificance.

The truckers' tea arrived. We ordered another round. The truckers got a little more talkative, a little louder. When they started on their second hit, the dhaba owner said that if they wanted to do *nasha* they should do it elsewhere. This incensed the younger members, they raised their voices. The owner said it was a family dhaba. The argument got heated. The old trucker stepped in to calm everyone. He asked the dhaba owner how he could call it illegal when government-authorized shops were selling the drug. If the police found the white powder on him they wouldn't arrest him, he pointed out. The dhaba owner lowered his voice but insisted he wouldn't have it in his dhaba. The youngest of the lot rose threateningly but the old trucker motioned him down. He asked how much the tea cost, finished his chai and left taking the entire crew with him, telling the dhaba owner he would spread the word about the dhaba atop the hill; it was the first dhaba of the new highway too, he said dangerously. It sounded like an ominous threat, he looked like he knew every truck driver in the country. The dhaba owner came over to complain about the truck drivers. We paid and left too.

Daya Ram's village was 2 km away. Arjun and I waded into

the streets. They were broader than the ones that led to Savitri Pimpri. The houses were *pakka* too, cemented and whitewashed. As I expected, Daya Ram had left. He had no time for people who overslept. But his associate from the previous night had waited eagerly. We piled into the crew-car, he pointed the way to the forest. He showed us a runway being constructed in a large clearing. 'Madhya Pradesh is going into ecological tourism in a big way,' he said. 'What else is there in the state?' we asked. 'A few fields and plenty of forests,' he answered.

The clearing gave way to dense vegetation, the *kachcha* road wound into bare tyre tracks with small clumps of ferns between the wheel-treads. It lost its gravel-topped flatness; we bumped across the earth, Naveen complained. The tyre tracks were obliterated by bushes. Naveen asked how much further. The guide gazed around vapidly. He seemed to have lost his bearings. He told us he hadn't been to the forest for some time. By the looks of the wheel-tracks, it had been a long time since anyone had been there. We entered the cool shade of the forest. The man made us backtrack. Naveen grew irate. When the chassis of the Innova grated across the forest floor, he refused to go further.

We footed it into the slender-trunked forest. It was 12 years old but the sun struggled to shine through. It came in like knives through the leaves. I had never seen such slim trees. I could encircle them with my fingers. But the forest floor was awash with green. You could see it spreading wings, growing upwards, outwards, downwards, inwards, burrowing in and flowing out. The man climbed trees and pulled the branches, but he lacked the easy erudition and the calm confidence of Daya Ram's tutorial ability.

'In this same forest that you are standing in...certain people have walked through—I've seen them and have thought to myself, "I don't know anything about them, and they don't know anything about me."'

'*Bahaar ke rahne waale the kya?*' (Were they from some other country?) I asked.

'*Mujhe toh waisa hi laga*,' (That's what I thought) he nodded. 'They didn't understand anything I was saying, and I didn't understand anything they were saying. One lady insisted on walking. We told her to take the jeep but she insisted. She was so fat, we needed two men to carry her through the jungle.' We laughed. I was enthralled at the vastness of man's ambition. To build a forest! I had never conceived it before, never imagined it, never dreamt it. All through my childhood, I had only heard of concrete jungles, and there I was—in a man-made forest of fledgling trees, with an airstrip being constructed a few kilometres away. The foolishness was astounding—first raze nature to the ground to build and after realizing the near-sightedness of it all, commend oneself to the creation of forests with the same cracked zeal that had accompanied their destruction in the first place. There were peacocks, deer, wild boar and other animals in the forest.

Our guide pointed out a clump of ferns. 'Daya Ram could have told you the names and uses of each of these,' he said pointing out the differences in the leaves. 'We were all waiting at six in the morning. That's when you see the maximum number of birds.' He pointed to a clump of trees with bare patches in between. 'This is where the peacocks come in droves. It's like their adda.' The morning sun filtered through the slats in the leaves. We dropped our guide to the village and headed out.

I took stock of the conditions—a sheer blue sky without a cloud in sight. A cycle-repair man from the previous day had insisted the rains were done, I believed him. Now that the hills were behind me, I was no longer nervous. The bad roads had bloomed into an immense four-lane highway: spanking new, flat and evenly grained like a good carrom board. I built up a good rhythm against a backdrop of steady climbs and declines. I focused on keeping a good pace. I wanted to really enjoy the ride from then on. Where would I next break my journey—Jhansi or Gwalior? They were 100 km apart. Jhansi was 300 km shy of Delhi and the promise of flying to Delhi in three days was compelling. But Jhansi was still 600 km away; if I rode strong, could I make it in 5 days?

Nandu Baba

We passed Amagaon and Gopalganj. After Seoni, I stopped at an isolated shack for chai. A medicine man had set up shop in the fluttering morning sunshine. On a table on the highway, he had spread out his wares. He had all manner of dried stems, leaves, roots, twigs, seeds, fruit, oils, powders and splinters of wood arrayed in used quarter bottles, plastic containers and wicker baskets. The medicine man's hair was dyed deep russet, its roots were orange. The moustache was also orange but flecked with white. A *rudraksh* mala hung around his neck. I examined the medicines. All the bottles were labelled with printed stickers. First the labels invoked God, then listed the ingredients; last came the instructions. He offered Arjun a therapy for gas. This one was for hypertension, he said pointing medicines out in quick succession, that one was for infertility, another was for diabetes; he had something for every ailment.

'What Nandu Baba's medicines can't cure, no doctor in the world and no medicine on earth can.' That was his guarantee. He showed me some seeds in a glass bottle—five of them a day for seven days cured a dog bite. He pointed to a powder that purportedly glued bones together.

I asked Nandu Baba how one took the medicine. 'With boiled eggs,' he said. I told him I knew a man who had his wrist broken and went to a doctor exactly like him, who then gave him a powder that needed to be mixed with boiled eggs, had his wrists tied for a month, and three months later the bones were unglued and the hand still useless and dying every day. 'Tell him to take this medicine,' Nandu Baba shot back, 'he was given the wrong cure; otherwise how can it be that his bones didn't get stuck again?'

He told me his knowledge had been bestowed on him by Devi Bhagbati's blessings in reward for many years of meditation and tapas. 'I myself am an *angootha chaap*,' he said, jabbing the air with his thumb. But his knowledge was divine. He brought his medicines from the jungle—he spent all day there scouting for the right herbs. He searched more and sold less, he averred. His shop was right there, in the same place, every day. He had even bought some land in the village across the highway and had been living there for three years. I wanted something that would make me powerful, superstrong. He gave me a bottled powder. The label proclaimed it as *'mardangi takat'*. I burst out laughing and bought a bottle. As I left, he called after me, *'Pyaar se khaana, Dilli aisi he pahunch jayoge'* (Eat with love, you'll reach Dilli easily).

Goodbye NH7

I thought about the man with the motionless arm. He would have had his hand wrecked by someone exactly like Nandu Baba after being taken by his impressive confidence. Maybe he had even gone to Nandu Baba. I remembered all the people that came to the government hospital after getting fucked up by quacks and medicine men; I remembered all the people I had seen getting fucked up by doctors in the hospitals I'd worked in. Where would it all end? Or was it all happening from the very beginning? I put it out of my mind. All around were fields, signboards, mixed-up distances. Another forest swallowed NH7.

I stopped for chai at a wood-and-thatch chai shop. People walked by carrying faggots of firewood. On a rusted board in faded paint was this piece of wisdom—'*Bible, Gita aur Quran, sab bolte hain Vraksh Mahaan*' (Bible, Gita and Quran, they all say trees are great). I consulted the map. I couldn't understand why I was so tired. I wanted to know where I was. I stretched, I lazed, I sucked the air, I tried to forget everything and become the forest. In the oven of the day, the forest was jewelled cool.

The closer we got to Lakhnadon, the worse NH7 got. Everything seemed to get poorer—the people, the houses, the villages. I stopped at a few shops scattered around a roundabout at Lakhnadon. The one shopkeeper that stocked Gold Flake only had three packets. I bought all and smoked a cigarette in honour of NH7. It was a magnificent highway and it had been kind to me for over 1,200 km. Past Lakhnadon, the road had been air-raided into a dustbowl of gravel. I took the turn onto NH26 surrounded by vast clouds of dust. For a kilometre or so, Nautanki and I tottered uphill, me gripping the handlebars tightly out of caution mixed with fatigue. The sun blazed, I lolled on the cycle.

The roads continued to slope uphill. I wanted to stop, but stop and do what? There wasn't a tree in sight, only vast pasture lands. I couldn't see a house or a shop. Occasionally, a Luna or a car passed blowing more dust in my nostrils. I couldn't believe I was struggling so much—it frightened me. Delhi was 800 km away. At the first chance at a dhaba, I stopped. I asked if there was chai. There was; I parked and sat down staring at the heat that flickered in glowing transparencies outside. Little red circles floated before my eyes. I was too tired to shake them out of sight. I tried to blink the floaters away. They changed hue to blue, then green; they danced slowly like the plastic rings in the pseudo video game water toys I'd played with as a child. I sat there motionless and weary, cockeyed with disbelief. I couldn't understand why I was feeling so shitty. I had intended to enjoy the ride. This was far from enjoyment. It was crack-brained effort, the will of a fool.

The crew car appeared. Arjun came out with a camera, Prashanth waddled in with his boom mike, Achyu came striding in like Groucho, Naveen sauntered in swirling his key. The five men in the dhaba got stiffer. When Achyu asked for chai, they said there was none. Achyu asked me why I was sitting around if there was no chai. I exploded. I asked the man again if there was no chai, he confirmed. A few minutes ago I could have sworn he said there was. I got into a slanging match. Naveen asked where the next dhaba was. I was too tired to leave. Chastened, I sat there drinking water.

When I felt better (and calmer), I decided I had been gotten cocky pretending there was nothing left to the ride. I returned to the old philosophy of taking it a humble 100 km at a time. The sun was no longer shooting at us directly. She was slipping slowly. I vowed to forget the day and ride steadily—neither slow nor strong. The road turned immaculate again (so new at several places only half was built); traffic trickled both ways on a single lane, the highway swallow-swooped across the land. All day I had taken interminable climbs. Now in the deepening cool of sunset, I reaped the rewards. I hunched over the handlebar, turned my cap around, and tried to make myself as small as possible. The slopes ran for metres on end. In the distance, I could see the road rise sharply again. It was time to redeem myself. The clouds gamboled, the sun splashed through the trees. The walls of the road bled green. I could see the lines where the cutters had spliced the stone hills. I stood on the pedals and sailed gently over the slopes. The moment Naveen said I had crossed the 100 km for the day, I looked for a place to stop.

The Ghosts of Suspicion

At a crest in the hill was a sparse dhaba, its charpoys strung with coir rope. Three young men were shutting shop for the day but the god-blessed chai was available. We ordered large ones. I swung conversation around to the possibility of sleeping there. The young men were all agog at the equipment we carried, as was everyone else along the way. Small children returning from school gathered around. It was safe to sleep there, they said. No one ever came by. They lived in the tiled roof house across the road. They asked how much the equipment cost. We quoted under. I had seen a small stream running beneath a bridge over which the highway was being carried by a crew of men. Prashanth could linger around the dhaba while the rest of us would bathe. Arjun set up a time-lapse of the sunset. I stopped to speak to a road gang labouring.

They were closing up too. A labourer wanted to know how much they paid for *mazdoori* in Bengaluru. I didn't know; I led such a sheltered protected life, wrapped up in the bubble world of my books and my parents growing old, I didn't know simple things like this. I told him it must be about 110 rupees. He shook his head and clicked his tongue. 'No, no,' he said, 'it's a very big city, it must be a minimum of 150 to 160 rupees over there.' He was from Bihar, earning 90 rupees a day and still sending money back home. I asked if it was safe to sleep at the dhaba. He said it was. Then, he wanted to know who all were sleeping there. I told him five of us, a cycle and a car. He nodded and said it was safe, but one never knew, after all we had a car. Prashant was left behind to watch over the car. The rest of us found the stream and jumped in. The sky ran purple.

Achyu couldn't believe I was still using soap in a running stream. He was of the opinion that nothing cleansed like running water. I couldn't get rid of the countless scrubbings of childhood. Naveen yelped, something had bit him underwater—on his thigh no less. We told him to thank god that it wasn't his balls. He scrubbed his leg furiously. His face had darkened after the initial laughter. He was fair and got red easily. He examined the bite. It was getting redder. Naveen got out. We all got anxious about getting bitten by underwater unknowns; we climbed out and walked home in the dark. A hut was nestled in a small clearing in the forest.

Naveen made small talk with the old man who sat inside. He came out beaming saying it was all arranged. What was arranged? I wanted to know. The two of us could sleep on the dung-caked clearing in front of the hut. The old man and his wife would sleep inside. I marvelled at Naveen. He was definitely taking on the role of a jungle boy. He was desperate to sleep out in the open. In the stream, he had insisted we pitch a tent on the banks. Achyu asked him how he intended to bring his beloved car to the banks through the overgrown fields; Prashanth and Arjun could sleep in the car at the dhaba, anyway, they usually slept in it at night, Naveen reasoned. He offered Achyu a slice of the experience too. The idea was shot down. Naveen didn't want to waste the arrangements he'd made. He whispered as we trailed behind, 'I've told you right now…you and I are sleeping in the hut. Let them sleep in the car. We'll buy a chicken and cook it by the stream. I am from Chikmagalur. I'll show you what fun it is to sleep in the forest.' I told him we would see.

Back in the shack, I pulled a charpoy out of the dhaba and lay down to watch the sky. Achyu came and sat on the charpoy. Prashanth had told him that the three young men who manned the dhaba were very persistent about knowing who would be sleeping there. They had wanted to know specifics—how many people, would the car be there? I knew what Achyu was getting at. He asked if I thought it a good idea to venture a little further. I told him I was too tired. He called Prashanth. We mulled it, Prashanth was all for moving. I wasn't going to budge—besides being too tired, I thought the crew was overreacting. I asked Achyu what he thought. He said if it was safe, then he was fine, but what if it wasn't?

He reminded me how the three young men had kept asking the cost of the camera, the cost of the car, the cost of everything. I told him it was simple curiosity. Achyu reminded me about Shree getting robbed in Dwarka after a financial stock-taking of his goods. I got tetchy. I stupidly asked, 'Is all the equipment insured?' Achyu waved me aside as he contemplated, 'It's not the equipment I'm thinking about, it's 12 days of footage man, 12 days of work.' I realized the entire trip was as much Achyu's documentary as it was my own meanderings. His concerns were larger than mine.

I told him that he could do what he wanted, I was going to sleep there that night. Deep within, I was mortified at the thought of sleeping alone in the shack in the forest with the night slowly blanketing me in. Achyu knew that I was nervous about wild animals, snakes in particular. He said we would think it over. I lay down again and watched the sky studded with stars. The clouds were sheer, flimsy and few; the darkened sky began to glitter and gleam with millions of electric blue eyes. I thought angrily about the purity of the trip being ruined. I had wanted to cycle alone to rid myself of that horrible city suspicion that defined the Indian middle class.

There too I was always concerned about people stealing my things. Now it was the same story although the only things I had, I didn't mind being taken. I didn't want to suspect the three young men of planning a heist. Achyu was on the phone with his father. He came back and said we would have to leave. His father who'd done a fair amount of travelling in central India said the place we were at was lonely and poor. Anything could happen; it was unadvisable to sleep at an unmanned dhaba with no one around for hundreds of metres. The next dhaba was 6 km away in a clearing of forest with an entire village a stone's throw away; more importantly, it was open all night for lorry and truck drivers. I told Achyu they could carry on without me, I wasn't cycling anymore that day. Arjun offered to cycle. Petulantly, I said I was going to cycle every single kilometre to Delhi.

Naveen jumped in; he suggested he and I could sleep there while the rest of the crew slept at the all-night dhaba. Achyu refused saying it would complicate things in the morning. Naveen faded away irritated at not having his way. Finally, Achyu said he and I would sleep there while the rest of the crew could sleep at the all-night dhaba. I heaved an inconspicuous sigh of relief.

We drove down to the all-night dhaba. The charpoys were strung with broad strips of tanned leather. At the far end of the dhaba, a framed painting of Shiva was the centrepiece of an altar. It was the best painting of Shiva I had seen. It was black and white like the negative of a photograph—all shadow and interpretation. The black scales of his snake hung like beads on his neck. His white hair flowed like a mountain of snow—he looked benevolent and dangerous, apathetic and comical. He gave a tremendous impression as the garland of lights wound around his face like a worm.

The cook, Govind, asked us what the camera was about. Govind came over. When we told him I was cycling to Delhi, he rocketed around like a doll on a spring and pointed to a cycle languishing in the corner of the dhaba. It was his cycle, always close at hand, ready to go where he willed, when he willed it. He had been working in the dhaba as a cook for the last two months. When he got bored, he would take off, he didn't know where. He would ask for the money that was owed to him on the morning of his departure and cycle away. He didn't know when he'd get bored, but the cycle was always ready, like Black Betty.

I was full of rapt admiration. In college, I was convinced the perfect life involved changing professions every three years. I thought about an old lover. She had wanted me to write her a fairy tale. I wrote one called the 'Princess and the Drifter'. Even then, I had vaguely imagined myself as a drifter. In truth, that was the sum of my ambition—I wanted to be a mote of dust, a shimmer of star, a bubble of spume—here one minute, gone the next, like dry leaves tossed in the wind. I wanted to be a piece of pulp—amorphous, nameless, shapeless and unrecognizable, and here was a man who had never dreamt but simply was. All my life I had dreamt and never done. Now I was confronting the harshness of doing, and although I envied the men I spoke to, I quailed at the thought that I didn't have the strength or the single-mindedness, the wit or the wherewithal to live the life they led. I was too firmly schooled in security and family ties.

On our way back, the crew car weaved on the lampless highway. Two men waved their arms for us to stop. Blackness was all around; their silhouettes grew lengthening shadows under the bobbing beams of the headlights. Achyu consulted with the crew—did we want to stop? The bug of suspicion had infected me too. 'Stop man,' I whinged in the backseat. I was sick with the knowledge of giving up what had kept me happy for 30 years, sick with disgust for never having lived life the way I had dreamt, sick at the thought that time was escaping and hastening into the never-recoverable beyond, sick at all of us donning the garb of suspicion the moment the highway got lonely and unpeopled, sick with myself for never having drifted like stray logs of wood, sick because I had never tried to swim against the current of the tide I had grown up in.

Naveen pulled over, the two men were young village folks coming back from a drink. They were so ecstatic at having gotten a ride they wouldn't stop their profuse 'thank yous'. They tried to start a conversation. I wanted to beg them to stay silent. They were reeking of liquor. Their house was 2 km away, they said. 'Where are you staying?' I told them. 'All of you?' they pushed; I nodded. When the drunks realized none of us were talking they lapsed into silence. They gabbed quietly amongst themselves instead. Two kilometres came and went. I began to wonder whether they were in on the plan to mug, rob and rape us too. I closed my eyes, leaned my head on the window and wondered whether the ghost of paranoia had in fact walked by my side like a shadow my whole life. From believing firmly in the supremacy of the individual, I had started to write in my mind the philosophy of the powerless man.

The drunks motioned us to stop. They thanked us again and didn't stop waving until we turned to the road. They stumbled onward into the darkness, happy to be let off. We were happy to be rid of them and the silence they had wrought. It was so strange and stupid. We were dropped off at the dhaba. Naveen was sullen and bitter. All I wanted to do was watch the stars wheel as the trucks bawled.

Achyu and I shifted the coir rope charpoys out of the dhaba. We were at a winding curve of a rise in the highway. The first truck lumbered through swishing headlights like search beams through the darkness. We watched the truck pass, lighting us up and lowering us again into the tremendous blackness of the forested night. It was like being in a disco with the strobe lights swaying in ultra slow motion. I lay down and gazed at the sky shot through with stars. I thought about Beesh telling me on the terrace of his hostel, 'Imagine how it would be to sit on top of a star and smoke *marm*.' It was a sheer night with translucent clouds.

The winds ushered the clouds gently across the stars. I was surprised at how the number of stars had dipped. The moon was resplendent, she overshadowed everything. The slow-trailing clouds sent the moon scudding among the stars in a slow whirling dance you wished would go on forever. It was the most magical night I had witnessed. I was goggle-eyed at the immensity of it. I saw one little incomprehensible star that hadn't been named, I imagined I was it. I smiled as it twinkled, and then—it dropped out of the sky. It disappeared without as much as a puff of dust, a trail of cloud, a swirl of smoke. The star was definitely me. I thought about Govind and his innumerable nights like this. He must have gotten tremendously bored of it. The magic would have been driven out by the regularity. What he would have given for a night in the bejewelled city? I must have stayed awake for an hour watching the party in the sky and the disco on the highway. It made up for all the chaos of the evening.

The trucks showered the colours over my closed eyelids. It was a deep, dreamless, unbroken sleep. I began to hear dogs bark; I thought I was dreaming. The barking got louder, I shook off the sleepiness. The barking approached. I lay motionless and calm. When I heard the dogs close by, I opened my eyes and raised my head. Three dogs were accompanied by two of the young men from the dhaba. They didn't show any interest in me. As one of them passed, he said, 'Don't worry. It's nothing. We heard some noises and people.' I looked to see if Achyu had woken. He hadn't stirred. About five minutes later, they came back, 'Where are you friends?' they asked. I told them. They went away with the dogs skipping about their feet. I stared at the sky for a little while and went back to sleep, thinking about the guardian angels of the road.

24 September 2010

All in A Day's Work

I woke before the stars began to dim. I stared at the sky wondering if it had all been a dream. The night of the surreal had made me doubt its existence. The sky raised its eyebrows. While Achyu performed his ablutions, I set the course. After the shambles of the previous day, I was eager to get on the road. In the stillness of the previous evening, as the suspicions had mounted, I had sat apart from the crew picking Shikaari's diary for clues as to why I felt so miserable on Nautanki. On the third page after Nagpur, was the line—'It was a fantastic three days climbing in the ghats'. I had always assumed it was a single 8-km stretch that needed to be scaled. It was my last day cycling in the ghats but I was unhappy because I was setting larger goals for myself. I thought about Gwalior.

It was a good early start, I vowed to take whatever came my way. The stiffness of the morning slowly peeled away. The sun was out but I was in the thick of a forest. In a few kilometres, the forest was over; we were back on the open highway with its immense clearings and vast fields. The highway grew another lane with a median so gentle it was only a threshold; I rode on the wrong side because people threshed their dal on the right lane. Traffic was light and no one minded. An hour and a half later, we stopped for breakfast. All I wanted to eat for breakfast ever since we had entered Madhya Pradesh was *poha*; each time it got more delicious and was garnished more intricately. The crew ribbed Naveen about his sunglasses. He swore they were Ray-Bans; the crew insisted they were fake and weren't worth even 200 rupees, let alone the 2000 rupees he had dished out. Naveen turned to me for help. This was a recurring theme on the trip: Achyu, Arjun and Prashanth—the three North Indians ranged against the lone South Indian—and Naveen always leaned to me to bolster his case. I must have had three plates of *poha* as we kept up the charade.

At Narsinghpur, I stopped to ask the way to Sagar—the next big town on the map. There was a Chhoti Sagar and a Badi Sagar. Two paths were pointed out; one through the maze of rush hour traffic, the other through the highway skirting Narsinghpur. I took the centre of town because it would lop 10 km of the journey. I searched for the crew in the crush of vehicles. They were nowhere in sight, I threaded my way through traffic alone. I felt like I was giving them the slip. I didn't want to unhitch my bag to make a call. I was on my own on a single-track tarred road that cut a swathe through fields and villages. A slim ribbon of road, barely enough for a small car, and it was as empty as a sick man's heart. Occasionally, the shade of a tree fell. All around were fields. In a sanded clearing, boys in school uniform thronged, Nautanki slowed.

Sports Day was being conducted in a freshly harvested field. The discus throw was underway. The thrower's face was a picture of concentration; he tensed up and threw. They marked out his distance with a sketch pen on yellow nylon rope so new it spangled as it caught the rays of the sun. Arjuna was right—a cycle was the only way to travel because it was slow enough to really see. It was supposed to be a 20-km stretch back to NH26; after a while, I began to ask directions from people.

One man got tremendously excited when I asked the way to Sagar. He confirmed if I wanted to go to Badi Sagar, threw his arm in the direction of the road, pointed far into the distance and said, 'Go straight on this road. It goes all the way to Sagar. You'll hit the highway soon enough.' He looked at me and beamed beatifically, 'I built this road,' his chest burst with pride. Carried by the breeze, I heard the man's voice after me, 'I built this road…and it goes all the way to Sagar.' And what a road the man had built—arrow-straight and slim. Unwavering like a bolt of truth or a jet of ecstacy, it flew through fields that fluttered in the wind as it dipped and humped into culverts spanning drains and streams in the villages it traversed.

A man with a bundle of grass beside his cycle gesticulated; he wanted help hoisting it onto the carrier. I looked at the old tyre tubes that would hold fast the sheaf of grass. 'I need to fashion something like that for myself,' I thought. Strapping my bag to the carrier took five minutes every day. I stood astride the bundle opposite the man. He must have been in his mid-forties, he was thin and strong. I heaved mildly at my end and stopped a few centimetres in my rise to the heavens. The bundle of grass hadn't budged. '*Thoda bhaari hain*,' (It is a little heavy) the man smiled. This time I braced myself and we heaved the bundle onto his cycle. I asked how much the bundle possibly weighed. 'Around 40 to 50 kg,' he said. He had spent the whole morning cutting it for his buffaloes and the goats. His home was 6 km away, I marvelled at the man and the work he did.

I jumped onto Nautanki, the sky had been bleached by the hot sun. I was doing my own work for the day. It was my first stretch of road that cut loose from the highway—how novel and different these little village roads were in comparison to the monotonous regularity of the changing scenery on a national highway. I felt bad at not having called—Achyu would have gone demented with joy at how beautiful India's innards were.

When the little ribbon of road ended, I stopped for chai. I struck up a conversation with the five men who sat in the little shop's shaded thatched arbours. I looked like I had stepped out of a shower of sweat. They asked where I was going. One of them said, *'Toh zaroor Naram-da ko jaana'* (Then definitely go to Naram-da).' I didn't know what he was referring to and probed. As they explained, I figured they were talking about the Narmada. I loved how everyone at the chai shack called the river Naram-da; they spoke of it warmly and reverentially—like it were a goddess—saying it was a miraculous river; people came from far and wide to pay homage and pledge obeisance to its mighty powers. Would the river take me to Delhi if I took a dip in her fabled waters? One man said I would reach Kashmir if the Naram-da wished it. I called Achyu. They were already waiting at the bridge where the highway swooped over the Narmada.

Nautanki passed the bridge, I gazed at Narmada's swirling muddy brown waters. The Innova was parked in the shade of trees. I was surprised when Naveen declined to take a dip. I had always thought he was just like me, eager to jump in to stare at the clouds swirling from our little island of water. He pointed at the brown waters and told me I would get even dirtier if I bathed. He tried to talk me out of it, but I was too eager to escape the heat. Besides, there was no point taking any chances by not invoking the river's blessings.

When we returned, the sun lashed the road but I was rejuvenated. On either side of the highway, there were neither fields nor forest—just empty stretches of flat land without a tree in sight. I set a good pace imagining I was riding a course in the Tour de France. I passed a smashed snake, its body flattened against the highway. Its eyes were open. Achyu later told me how he had been so disturbed at the sight of the dead snake, the crew had stopped and spent 20 minutes finding someone willing to remove the snake for a little money.

Far away on the horizon, the hills were ranged like giant shadows, their shoulders hugging each other the way friends stand in photographs. The road began to hump softly, the shadowy interior of a forest loomed large. The sun was baking. I hadn't yet gone over a slope in style. Even the 8-km ghat section that I had skimmed through with little discomfort had been broken in two by a shit. I stood on the pedals and scaled the humble 2-km slope with a modicum of dignity and mild elegance. As soon as the slope finished, the landscape went from foliage to flat nothingness as if it were a magician's trick—I couldn't understand the mystery of it all.

The Seed of an Idea

I looked for a place to stop. All day my pace had been steady if not stodgy. The usual discussion with Naveen about chicken or eggs ensued. I had dipped under 400 km to Gwalior. If I could finish another 40 km, I'd leave myself a steady 120 a day to make it to Gwalior in three days. The man who ran the dhaba told us about his ex-cycling days. He no longer cycled since his foot had been wrecked in an accident.

Once upon a time he had cycled from Agra to Delhi in a day, he smiled to himself as he reminisced. I was astounded—the distance was a flat 200 km. I asked him how he did it. '*Bas, truck pakadte pakadte...main pahunchta tha,*' (I simply used to grab trucks and reach) he replied. It was my turn to smile. I thought about the magnificence of a 200-km ride. Achyu saw me thinking, 'Maybe we also should try it?' I asked if he was mad. He suggested we pick a day and do nothing but cycle and see how many kilometres I clocked. I shot the idea down, it was too late in the trip to attempt personal bests. It should have been attempted in the first two legs of cycling, preferably in the second leg.

The sky started her slow shimmy down the slopes of the sky. I wanted to blow myself out for two hours. In the distance I saw a lady seesawing gently on the carrier of a cycle. She wore a blue sari that shimmered in the afternoon sun like a patch of sky that had come down to earth to dance and proclaim—'I'm much bluer than you think'. A travel bag was precariously wedged under her arm. Her left leg was stuck out for balance; she supported the weight of the bag against her thigh, her arm snaked around the waist of her husband or her man or her brother as he weaved on his seat while slavering up an incline.

As I passed the two, I was even more surprised to see a teenage girl sitting on the cross-bar. They were living out their lives on a cycle whereas Nautanki and I were travelling through. I'd been foolish to presume I could learn so quickly. There was no way I could know the deepest thoughts the man had, I would never know the smallest iota of his experience with this float-through-the-day travelling. What was the point of stopping and speaking to people? I was merely skimming the surface; but could I feel like they did, could I say for a fact that I knew what they felt? The answer was a resounding no. There was no way to know anyone unless you went and lived with them, or more importantly, lived as them.

The session was winding down, I crested a small slope. I stopped to oversee work at another of the numerous bypasses cutting through hills and shooting through forests. All day I had seen road construction. Apart from that and the threshing of the dal at the side of the roads, there was nothing else to speak of. I saw the little girls of Madhya Pradesh returning from school and their sky blue pinafores looked even prettier than the salwars. I took off my shirt and watched the slope I would go down. It was a sharp steep slope, rotted and rained in with pebbles and loose gravel. 'I am going to go down at top speed,' I thought.

I told Achyu we should film. I watched the road gang working far down below. One of them waved to me, I blew kisses. He grew angry and began to curse. I waved back, he threw rocks that wouldn't reach. When I shirted myself again, Achyu flung open the dicky of the Innova and readied the camera. Arjun settled himself amidst the luggage, his legs on either side of the tripod. Then, for a minute of absolute and indescribable joy, I clattered down the slopes looking for the path of least resistance through the bad road. I could see Naveen's eyes as he watched in the rear-view mirror, Nautanki's front wheel threatened contact with Arjun each time Naveen gently eased on the brakes. At one point I gathered so much speed, I hoved right to overtake, and Naveen skillfully swung back in front of me, quick enough to not make me slow. We all thrilled at the prospective danger of having an accident.

When the slope finished, I could hear Naveen talking happily to the crew in his broken Hindi, 'If I applied brakes even slightly...*dhamaar*! He would have flown into the car, Arjun would have flown out of the car, and the camera would have flown into the forest.' It was true; I was very impressed with Naveen's driving skills.

The sun was setting, the map hinted at a small river stretching languidly across the highway. We stopped at a slimy green lake instead. It was darkening too quickly for a dip, swarms of mosquitoes masqueraded. I decided to spend the night in the dhaba adjoining the lake. I saw a jazzed up cycle reclined against a tree and went to inspect. It was fantastically overloaded with all sorts of intricacies. Its owner was a young man who said his cycle had seen better days. He had even given her a name—Night Queen! She had a dynamo in the front and a brake light at the back. There were indicator lights and a musical horn. A large heart was pasted onto the stock of the handlebar. In it were lights that ran like an army of iridescent ants crawling across the perimeter, but they had ceased to function. He pointed out fancy flaring mudguards that he had welded on—they had fallen off with time.

Night Queen sported a battery-operated radio that no longer worked. He had spent nearly two hundred rupees on all the fittings, he said. Sibi had often told me to do the same with Nautanki—'pimp the cycle,' he'd goad, 'make it wild, like a cycle that Rajinikanth might own'—that was the reference. But I had been so nervous about my abilities, I had wanted to travel as light as possible. I asked why the cycle was going through a period of neglect. The owner smiled proudly and said he was focused on modifying his tractor.

Soon, the crew said goodbye, I settled down to thinking what a fantastic day it had been on Nautanki. I had spent seven hours in the saddle and covered 140 km—I hadn't done either before. It was all in a day's work after all.

25 September 2010

A New Plan

I wondered about the strangeness of my sleeping place. I was thrilled at the regularity being imposed on my body. I woke at five without wanting to. Where once I'd turn over and curl up, hugging the last snatches of sleep to myself, now I didn't feel the pull to stay in bed longer than was necessary. I wanted to be up and about, watch the sky change colour as the sun removed her cooling glasses. It was early morning childhood joys again, where every day you wanted to wake up because everything was imbued with beauty. I took a delicious crap thinking back to the last time I had risen steadily every morning at an appointed hour, and worked. I had to go all the way back to my fifteenth year! When had I lost the faculty of waking early and why? When had life overpowered me enough to make me want to sleep a little longer every morning? I marvelled at my shit too. Even that had taken on a remarkable consistency. Every morning, aided by a cigarette, I had the most complete evacuation of my bowels, like I'd just been administered an enema. The remnants of my previous day's work lay there in two neat blobs: one turgid and tubular with all the magnificence and exact girth of a perfect cock, the other, a subtle little squiggle like a flourish at the tail end of an autograph, and well it was so, because the two pieces of faeces had begun to acquire the unerring sameness of a signature shit. They were getting to look as trustworthy as a fingerprint.

By the time I reached the dhaba, the crew had come in. Arjun captured the sky mounting Nautanki for another time-lapse shot. I changed into cycling clothes. Achyu was ecstatic, 'Delhi's so fucking close man! It's only 660 km away. If something happens…we can make a few phone calls and someone will come get us in what? Eight hours.' I thought about the 660 km. For a moment, I was assailed by a sudden desire for the trip to be over. It was still seven days of cycling. I had begun to nurse the confidence that I was going to make it to Delhi after all, but Achyu's assertion that Delhi was within touching distance made me wish it was. I thought about the first seven days, it seemed a distant memory; every part of me had protested during those first seven days. All of a sudden, Delhi seemed too far. I shook the feeling and hit the road.

I was eager to find out how my body would react to the previous day's exertions. The sun was a blinding searchlight, the road so indented it looked shell-shocked. Women walked by with faggots of wood balanced on their heads. The faggots were longer than the women. They stared at us without breaking stride or moving their necks. In less than half an hour, we passed a series of treeless rolling lime-green pasture lands unfurling as far as the eye could see. It was the perfect place to pitch a tent. I felt sad for Naveen. He must have been ruing another missed opportunity.

I laboured through the first half hour convinced I wouldn't clock a 100. I took solace watching a boy, young enough to be on either side of puberty, standing atop his pedals as he wavered on a mild slope with two 10-litre plastic containers filled with water clanging against the sides of his cycle. I was far better off. Nautanki's rear wheel began a ceaseless rat-a-tat-tat. I stopped to inspect. A spoke had come loose. Nautanki was beginning to fall apart. I tried to push the spoke back in, but it kept getting unstuck. It refused to behave. It was a free spoke with a free spirit. I started cycling again but the clatter drizzling on the rim was impossible to ignore. After many experiments, I figured all I had to do was thread the spoke back into the groove. We stopped for chai and a rest. It was spanking hot, I needed a new goal.

Nagpur to Gwalior was supposed to have been seven days. I decided to make it in six. News had come in that I had all the tickets I wanted except two—the Opening Ceremony and the Badminton Finals were sold out! I thought about how popular Saina was becoming; she had sold out the finals 10 days before the Games had started. She was making people sit up. People wanted to watch her as much as they wanted to watch an India-Pakistan hockey match. That was sold out too, but I hadn't requested tickets for it. I decided to make Delhi a day ahead of schedule to see if I could wrangle a ticket for the Opening Ceremony. The Ayodhya ruling had been postponed to 28 September. If I timed the ride into Gwalior, I could kill two birds with one stone by scheduling my rest day to coincide with the Ayodhya ruling. If the country burnt, I could sleep it all off in my room. Who knew what protests I would have to cycle through in the aftermath of the ruling? There was nothing left to do but clock a steady 120. I pedalled on stoically. Children walked the highway's lip with chunnis strung across their heads.

The car headed back into Sagar to pick up some leftovers. I took the bypass that skirted the town. Sagar was a big town in Madhya Pradesh. The pride of Sagar was its colleges. In the span of a kilometre, the colleges were gone and it was the empty highway with the dust swirling in the sun. I wanted a break. I was beginning to feel the heat. I wondered if this was what Shree had warned me about 'the closer I got to Delhi'— the soreness setting in, the lack of motivation making me tired. My body was protesting, my thighs quivered when I stepped off Nautanki.

Sunny Deol ka Mandir

I set out again on a single lane highway that was the perfect bed of gravel. It was a long stretch too. I had learnt that if I stood on the pedals, my body didn't take as bad a hammering. It was slow going, but the mental alertness this required broke the monotony of the heat. The heat was making me crack-brained. At a railway crossing was an interminable wait. I welcomed it. Traffic had swollen, everyone was cursing and raring to go, wondering about the extra-long stop—I relaxed, thankful for the extended unplanned break.

I struck up a conversation with the man next to me. When I told him I was going on a Bharat Darshan, he asked me whether it was a Mandir ka Darshan. I thought of all the temples that I had been sleeping and kneeling in, and told him he could think of it like that if he wanted to. He leaned over and told me that a few kilometres away was 'Sunny Deol ka Mandir'. I was stunned. This was worth recording for the documentary. I asked him again if he was sure it was a temple dedicated to Sunny Deol. He nodded his head vigorously and said it was a very famous temple—great miracles took place there, presided over by a powerful *murti*, and there was guaranteed to be a crowd of the faithful. I had to see it, he insisted. I wanted to be dead sure. I asked him whether he was sure it was Sunny Deol—the famous star—whose temple it was. He looked at me, grinned and said I could think of it that way if I wanted to.

At the end of the road, the temple came into sight. The grey cement of its facade hadn't yet been painted. Scaffolding was tied together with ropes of thick coir. Men worked the facade, devotees queued on the floor. The temple was still being constructed and it was already a full house. People perched on the stone fence of the premises, several devotees were being tonsured, slippers milled like flocks of pigeons. People sat and prayed on the cemented floor of the temple yard, some knelt, others rolled their beads. Two steady streams of people waited patiently as they trickled to the deity before unravelling. I sat next to one of the newly tonsured devotees. '*Ye Sunny Deol Ki Mandir hain?*' (Is this Sunny Deol's temple?) He nodded his head.

I had seen so many different renditions of so many different Gods, I wanted to see how Sunny Deol was portrayed. '*Murti kahaan hain?*' (Where is the idol?)

The devotee pointed to an empty space where the two lines converged, 'Right there,' he said.

'I can't see anything.'

'You won't see it. It's a very small *murti*.' I was amazed. I had loved *Ghayal* as a child. I thought it was a tremendous way to portray Sunny Deol—in miniature. 'It's a very powerful *murti*, that's why it's so small, so that people have to kneel before it.' This was in keeping with my memory of *Ghayal*: everyone knelt before Sunny Deol. 'The *murti* is so powerful, people don't have the courage to look at its eyes. It's also not good to look at it,' he counselled.

'Why?'

'If it looks back at you, then you're ruined. You can look at it…and many people have looked at it, and it hasn't looked back at them. But if it does look back at you, then it's the end of you,' he cautioned. 'That's why it's so small, so that even by mistake people don't look at its eyes.'

Across the road lay another temple, more majestically fronted with superior carvings, painted and better-maintained than the Sunny Deol Mandir, but only a few devotees lingered there. I asked him why this was so.

'That's Narasimha's temple. Over here, people have a lot of belief in Sunny Deol. That's why more people come here. Do you know how this temple was built?' I shook my head.

'All the devotees got together and contributed one rupee for the construction. That's why it's still being constructed.' I was stunned by the popularity Sunny Deol still wielded among the faithful. I was amazed by the fascination that Bollywood has for so many. I scanned the devotees. I expected to see shapely women with long flowing hair in tracks or tight kurtas or gleaming saris, and thick-wristed men with biceps bulging beneath T-shirts that hid flat boards. But it was the typical temple crowd you're likely to see anywhere; wives and husbands, college kids and working folk, old people and children. 'No matter,' I thought. There weren't too many who came close to emulating the Gods they professed to believe in. 'And this is Sunny's day too, that's why there's such a big crowd,' a man said.

'What do you mean by Sunny's day?' I asked.

'It's Sunny day,' he averred, shrugging me of. I was confused. I took off my shoes and stood in one of the queues to pay my respects. More than anything, I wanted to see the idol—how had Sunny been rendered? Did he still ripple when shrunk or had they left a carving of him as a suckling child? I was delirious with the myriad possibilities. I peeped over heads and stood out of line to watch the devotees pray. I wanted to see how they worshipped Sunny Deol. Very reverentially it seemed — everyone knelt, bowed their backs, and touched their heads to the floor if they could. No one dared to look Sunny in the eye. I decided I was going to give him a frank stare full flush in the face. I tried to glimpse him but the bowed backs prevented me. The darshan was taking a long time, I felt foolish and went back to the devotee who had told me the story. 'Are you sure that this is the same Sunny Deol?'

'Yes.'

'The film star?'

'Yes, yes.'

'The Bollywood actor who acted in *Ghayal*?'

It was the devotee's turn to look confused. And then he kept repeating as if he had been accused of telling a lie, '*Sunny Deol ka mandir hain, Sunny Deo ka mandir hain, Shunny Deo ka mandir hain.*' (It's Sunny Deol's temple. Sunny Deo's temple,

Shunny Deo's temple)

I couldn't believe my idiocy, my gullibility, my Anglo-Indianness. I was a credulous fool. I rejoined the line vowing to stare Shani Dev in the face just as I would have stared at Sunny Deol, but when it was my turn to genuflect, I chickened out like everyone else. I merely touched my head to Shani's feet and left for the chai stall across the road. The devotee followed and asked for a cup. I bought him samosas too. We sipped chai watching people crowd around an elephant walking across the road, its trunk was painted with coloured chalk. Business perked up at the chai stall. I rejoined the crew. I expected Achyu to find the Sunny Deol temple fiasco funny. His face darkened, 'Shit man, we're missing all the good stories.'

At Bandri, I had my first cold drink of the trip. The heat had dried out my mouth like the aftermath of a joint. I stretched righteously, slowly, painfully. 'It was work,' I thought—the work I had chosen—and I had six more days before I could bust up and drop out. The sun came down like a thousand hot ice picks. I was a sensualist no longer. The mind was playing tricks with the body. It was time to play tricks on the mind. I thought of the many wars, and what the forts and statues of Jhansi Ki Rani we cycled past spoke of. I imagined the infantry walking the roads in the dusty heat. The horses clip-clopping along, their armours clinking gently in unison with the hooves. There must have been elephants too. What were the thoughts of those men as they walked in the heat in full metal armour with their weapons in tow?

I pretended I was one of them and soldiered on. I was transformed into a messenger bearing urgent important news to the Rani regarding imminent danger, except I was a bicycling messenger and had to reach Jhansi in a day and a half. I thought of Rani waiting anxiously for the messenger she didn't know.

I imagined her relief when she saw the guards edging past the filigreed curtains billowing in the evening cool as they ushered me in. So happy and impressed would she be at my having cycled all the way from the southern ramparts of India to bring good tidings of the Maharaja of Mysore offering unstinting support for any adventure she might consider, a walk to the queen's chambers with her leading me by the hand wouldn't be out of order.

Then, I was a professional cyclist training for the Commonwealth Games. In 10 days, I'd be barrelling down the slow loping caressing curves of the Greater Noida Expressway, hammering on the pedals in the glittering North Indian plains heat. The sweat would be fizzing off my body, evaporating in a sizzle as soon as the drops fell—better to practise now in the heat. I ploughed through another 10 km.

I thought about Gopi's heroic mother toiling quietly through the day to make life smoother for her son. I thought of my own mother and her uncomplaining unerring toil as she went about the mundanity of life with grit and determination that made the very act of living with honour and dignity an enormous act of profound heroism. I watched people walk their cycles up a long interminable slope. All of them were dressed in everyday fashion, unlike me in a T-shirt, shorts, with my cushy running shoes beating out hopeless rhythms on a sun-boiled slope.

For a kilometre or so, all the cyclists walked. And then came the slow floating descent like we were all leaves in a mild breeze that promised to last forever. I made up my mind to not cycle back. There was no way I could go through the whole rigmarole again. These endless slopes I was floating down, was I mad to think of cycling back against it?

The flats arrived with a hundred gentle headwinds, each one blowing casually in my face, making me sluggish. Nautanki rolled unsteadily. The road was bad in patches, the passing wheels vomited flying dust. A carpet of urad dal waiting to be threshed occupied half the highway. A tractor wound round in circles at top speed separating grain from the husk. The heat, the husk, the dust, the dirt—everything began to tire me out. I was desperate for a stream. I hadn't had a bath in two days. I was running out of clean clothes and cycling is high-friction activity. I was convinced a dip in a lake would do me good. The rushing waters would invigorate me.

The map had the Mahavir Wildlife Sanctuary scattered across the NH26 at Gona. It was 35 km away. I thought I might stop there. The evening would be beautiful in the wooded forests. In the gathering cool of the evening, army trucks loaded with personnel flew by in convoys. We assumed preparations were afoot for 28 September. We asked about sleeping in the open, everyone said it was a bad idea—*ek sau chawalis* had been imposed. Gona was at the southern tip of Uttar Pradesh. I had thought every forest I had cycled through was my last one in Madhya Pradesh. After four days in her belly, I was leaving her, with her rusted red and green Forest Department boards and her sky blue government school uniforms. She had it all—rolling hills, forests, man-made jungles, immaculate four-line highways, tremulous stretches of road, gushing rivers, slimy lakes, shushing streams—she was as beautiful as she was poor.

I had thought Andhra Pradesh, with her rocky hills and stocky trees, was beautiful, but Madhya Pradesh was a love affair to remember. At a bypass cresting a slope, I stopped for my last cup of chai in Madhya Pradesh. Hundreds of plastic tents had been erected in the fallow fields adjoining the road. People were massed at the edge of the highway. It seemed a mini exodus. Women fluttered in their brightly coloured saris, kids played, infants mewled, men sat around smoking. Achyu wanted me to ask a few questions. I was too tired to play anchor. I sat against the asbestos shed of a shack reading the sign painted on the highway *'Sab Padhe toh Sab Badhe'* (If everyone studies, everyone will grow). I was cockeyed with fatigue but the sun had lost her sharpness and Gona was a few kilometres away.

A long climb led us out of Madhya Pradesh. Ramshackle unmanned toll tax booths abounded. We wound around barricades of loose stones. My cross-border co-passengers were cattle going home. I stood on the pedals and mooed in their faces. As we crested the slope, a huge signboard spanning the highway announced: *Uttar Pradesh Aapka Swagat Karta Hain* (Uttar Pradesh Welcomes You).

'And what a welcome!' I thought. I licked my lips at the prospect of coasting down such a delicious slope. I hunched over Nautanki as we ducked under our welcome banner and immediately the road went to pot; I had to pull gently on the breaks and weave to stay on the asphalted bits, it was the end of my free-flowing ride. I decided to spin to Gona, it was 4 km away.

Van Vihar Dhaba

It was past five when we saw a dhaba advertised by a gleaming tractor standing to attention at the highway's head. In a clearing backed by forest, stood the Van Vihar dhaba with a well-maintained garden in front. It was the first dhaba we'd seen with a garden. We stopped for chai and pulled charpoys onto the highway's shoulder. We made enquiries. There was a Bajrang Bali Mandir 100 m away where travellers could sleep the night; there was a tank in back of the dhaba where we could bathe; we could also sleep in the dhaba if we wished: all of this was told to us by Pappu Yadav—a gruff-toned, hefty man who was neither welcoming nor unfriendly.

He made it seem like he needn't trifle with us if he didn't want to. I was done cycling for the day, we were all in love with the dhaba anyway. Achyu told me how Prashanth, when passing under the sign welcoming us into Uttar Pradesh, had heaved a sigh of relief because he finally felt safe. 'The most unsafe state in the whole country, and he feels safe because he knows some politicians,' Achyu cracked up. Arjun time-lapsed the sunset, Pappu grew friendlier on seeing the camera. I washed off the grime and the sweat of the day's work with a long luxurious bath.

Pappu took the crew on a tour of his grounds that included a visit to his bedroom where he showed them the gun he slept with. Clearly, he was not a man to be trifled with. He asked if we wanted liquor, it could all be arranged.

Prashanth, Arjun and Naveen settled in the car to watch a movie on the LCD display set. They could watch any of the movies he stocked so dutifully: Telugu, Kannada, Malayalam or Tamil, but Naveen wouldn't let them play a Hindi movie. The show for the day was *Mungaru Male*. Achyu and I sat and talked. We traced the stars falling into the sky. It was suffused with millions of glittering sequins, who knew how many sparkled up there that night? The air grew cooler. Naveen eyed a space in the garden's lawn between two trees. He wanted a hammock to swing about in. When Pappu came around, I asked him '*Bali Barshan ka darshan kahaan hain?*' (Where can one do Bali Barshan's darshan?) meaning '*Bajrang Bali ka mandir kahaan hain*'? (Where is Bajrang Bali's temple?). He looked at me like I was mad. We went to the temple. I learnt that Bajrang Bali and Hanuman were the same God, only different avatars.

The idol sculpted on the wall was different too. He looked nothing like Hanuman, or the *Pirates of the Caribbean* Bajrang

Bali in Savitri Pimpri. The strangest thing about the sanctum sanctorum was the presence of three clocks mounted around the red idol whose legs were both turned the same way. All three clocks showed the same time. I cursed time and how it slipped and shifted like money changing hands.

We drove back to the dhaba where Pappu had tied tube lights wrapped in blue cellophane paper to the smoke-funnel of his tractor to seduce customers. The dhaba itself had no electricity, he lit the tubes with wires running from his tractor's battery. He was all invention. A retard with unnecessarily tight half pants scurried around, Pappu constantly abused him. He turned to us and said, 'He's a new boy, he has to be made to understand. No one thought him worthy of employment, but he's working now.' The retard mumbled, he spoke unintelligibly in a garbled way using a sort of word soup instead of sentences. We ate by a kerosene lamp. I was happy at having done my work for the day—101 km.

I thought about Gopi saying if one could work hard at something for four hours every day for 10 years, one would surely accomplish something great. I had only been working for a month and already my body felt stronger, lighter, leaner. Now if only I could bring the same devotion to my writing. I went to sleep realizing that stars are the most numerous and shine brightest at the beginning of nightfall, before the moon rises and blots them out as she beams like a freshly minted coin gleaming in the sun's light.

Suffer

Gona to Agra

26 September 2010

Pappu Yadav

I was alone at the edge of the highway. Somewhere in the depths of the previous night, Achyu had moved his charpoy back inside the dhaba. Pappu milked the cows at five. He bellowed in the predawn hour. Even the crows of the morning roosters held his stamp. I listened to his harsh voice roughly barking orders. '*Utho behenchod, utho!*' and he let out a string of curses. The retard whimpered. Pappu got louder, the retard grew restive; he stayed unyielding though. They kept this up for some time.

There was a rustling of clothes as the peacocks gave up their yammering calls and the insects tweeted ceaselessly. Pappu's voice roared to new decibels of rage, '*Pant kyu nahin pahna behenchod?*' I heard thwacks of flesh on flesh and the sounds of a struggle as a charpoy gently thudded against the walls condemned with cracked pots. The retard yelped like a dog that had been struck. I sat up to watch, the retard confessed helplessly through tearless sobs, '*Pant se dikkat hota hain.*' I laughed silently as I saw the dark shape of the retard trudging towards the water tank, swinging a torch ahead of him. I lay back and listened to the contending sounds of the peacocks and the rush of water from afar.

Imprisoned in a haze of drowsiness, Arjun sauntered a few yards away from the dhaba and readied himself to sink into a sleepy shit. Pappu yelled as Arjun lolled on his haunches. He told him to go far away, didn't he have any sense, shitting outside a dhaba. Arjun had to suit up all over again and find another spot—as an extra precaution, he crossed the road too. I watched Pappu in the immensity of his early morning bustle. He insisted we visit his house further down the road to shoot, we were guaranteed beautiful pictures. He left to make preparations. I didn't want to pander to Pappu's vanity or fall prey to the humongous hospitality that would most certainly be breakfast. He returned, he had traded his motorcycle for a bright red open-topped jeep. He could have been an illustration in a children's book, with his prosperous paunch contained by his strained T-shirt, reclining against his blue-and-white tractor with its steaming sliver pipe glinting like a blade in the rising sun. I thought about his full-blooded, able-bodied life. He had always had a singular ambition, he had said the previous night—he wanted to own a dhaba, a dhaba that people visited to eat the food he personally cooked, and he wanted everyone to talk about his dhaba.

In between keeping the dhaba spotlessly clean, he administered his fields and attended to his duties as a successful landowner. I commended him again for the Van Vihar Dhaba and thanked him for his hospitality. He tried to extract a promise that I would be back for breakfast in his house; preparations were afoot he said, a sumptuous spread was being laid out. It was exactly what I was wary of. It had been getting progressively hotter and I wanted to cycle light.

The highway was the nation's threshing ground. People threshed whichever side of the highway their villages fell, the non-existent traffic shifted lanes accordingly. There was no sign of the forests that I assumed would be Mahavir Gona Wildlife Sanctuary. I hadn't even seen a sign announcing it but I was learning that the *Eicher Road Atlas* was not the gospel truth of our country.

I slowed my speed to take on a cycling partner. Around 5

km flew and it seemed much quicker than my normal rhythm. I missed Sibi as I sunbathed with my companion cyclist. How good it is to cycle with someone else and not make conversation with milestones! The next time I went on a long ride, I was definitely getting a partner, even better a gang, preferably with a few girls thrown in. I was getting tired of myself. It was too late to start thinking about my whole life and everything I'd jumbled up. My companion turned into a side road to go home, I was alone with Nautanki in the cauldron of another boiling day. I cycled steadily, pretending that all I was doing was practising to get better on Nautanki. Delhi wasn't even my destination, I was merely training for the next trip. Now that I knew Nautanki and I danced well together, I wanted to become a strong cyclist, a good cyclist, an indefatigable cyclist.

Lalitpur

I was wearing my last set of clean clothes. Purely by instinct, on seeing the land hump to a height that prohibited the landscape, I swung onto the mud track that led to a bund of some sort. I wandered down, slipping along the slopes of the embankment. The water was motionless and green with a thin film of slime fringing the edges. I would get dirtier than I already was if I washed my clothes in that water.

In the centre of the rock-hewn pool, the water was clean. I had wanted to take a break and wash clothes; the thought of cycling on didn't appeal to me. I walked over to a bunch of boys studying beneath the shade of a large tree as they swished a stick at their cows grazing by the little reservoir. Three men made their way over. They worked in the cement-brick factory that sprang at the highway. The factory churned out 2000 bricks a day. How much does each brick sell for? I wanted to know. 'That you have to ask the company people,' the youngest one said softly and harshly at the same time. Another man ventured an answer, 'Seven rupees a brick'. The one with the most cheerful face of the lot ventured forward. He had no interest in things he knew too well. He wanted to know where I was from. I told him. 'Over there you won't see things like this,' he surmised, throwing his arm generously across the slowly undulating expanse of land. I smiled and said it was true—it was difficult to find large open spaces in the heart of the city. The man added with a rueful smile, 'And we...we don't get to go anywhere. We are farmers; all we have are the fields, the trees, the bushes, the environment. In your country, you must throb to see places like this.'

I laughed at the word he used—*taraste*. It explained the emotion well. 'And we...we throb to see big buildings and bright lights.' I ventured it was in the nature of mankind—to always want what we did not possess. How was the factory working on a Sunday? The sharpest man of the lot stepped forward. 'It's privately owned,' he explained. The wages at the factory were 800 rupees for 1000 cement bricks made. Three to four men could fashion a 1000 bricks a day, but it would take all of 16 hours. I turned to the children and asked the eldest kid what he wanted to be when he grew up. He smiled bashfully; one of the smaller kids shouted, 'Doctor!' In all the villages I went to, everyone wanted to become a doctor, and very few would achieve that. I was mildly ashamed. I went down on my haunches to examine his textbook. It was a thick book with small print—too large for a 12-year-old. I asked which subject it was. The boy grinned mutely. The sharp man started, 'You see. He's in the seventh standard, but he still can't answer a simple question. That's the problem with an education in government schools. It's all corruption. What will he do when he grows up?'

Lalitpur was the most backward district in education when it came to Uttar Pradesh, he opined. Nestled at the southern tip of Uttar Pradesh, cradled between the two eastern pseudopods of Madhya Pradesh, Lalitpur had slipped under the radar of politicians who showed their face every five years, got elected and made their money. There was no one in Lalitpur who could question the politicians about their neglect. 'We couldn't study because we didn't have money; now when we want our children to be educated, we have no time to make them learn because we are too busy working. We don't have the money to send our children to private schools. In government schools, the teachers get their salaries, come for a few days each week and don't teach the children properly.' I asked if he would rather have his children live in the village or the city. He exploded, 'They can't survive in the village, what will they do in the city? There is not enough money to educate them in private schools. We want them to study a little so that they don't become slaves, because we are slaves.'

It was the same story all over again. 'There are no engineering colleges, no higher universities. Our Lalitpur is more backward than everywhere else. Here you can't become anything,' the man trailed off regretfully. Bereft of anything else to say (what can you say when a man believes he can no longer amount to anything), I asked him how the rains were. They were okay that year, but there was no round-the-year farming in Lalitpur. 'When it rains, we farm; when the rains stop we look for some rich farmer so we can work as *mazdoors*, or we look for some big *thekedaar*.'

Silence reigned as he stared into the distance comprehending the awfulness of his circumstances, for one of the worst things about speaking of your life is being forced to contend with the reality of it all. He pointed to an old short man who had meandered into the group as we spoke. He stood ramrod straight with hands clasped behind, he looked like he might have once been strong. 'Take him, for example. He works as a guard in the brick factory. He gets 60 rupees a day and he has to make his own food, bring his wheat and dal and vegetables and cook it on the premises.'

"And it's a 24-hours duty Babuji,' the old man piped up sadly.

'The whole day?' I asked incredulously.

The old man nodded, 'The whole day.'

The younger man spoke, 'So imagine that. He gets 1800 rupees a month, and he has to cook his own food here, and send money back home. If it's 60 rupees a day, then it's 20 rupees for eight hours.' 'Two rupees fifty paise an hour,' I thought, 'for work.' It broke my heart to look at the old man: something about the terrible nature of old people having to work for a living always cut me to the quick. But what was the point of all the feeling if it didn't engender any action?

'*Yahaan sab thekedaar ke gulaam hain*,' (Here, everyone is a slave to contractors) he gazed into the distance. The old man politely took two steps backward. 'They've bought all the *mazdoors* by handing out loans. Someone needs to bury their mother, or marry their daughter, or bribe someone to get a job for their son…the *thekedaars* hand out loans. And how much? Small amounts—10,000 rupees, 15,000 rupees. The *mazdoors* spend the rest of their lives paying off the loan. Over here, only 10 per cent of the people have money, 10 per cent of the people own everything in Lalitpur. The remaining 90 per cent are troubled.'

We stood in silence. He scuffed the gravelly ground with his feet, 'The land here is rocky. Only 25 per cent of the land is arable, the rest is not. We sow *sarson* and chana when it rains. It's all we can do.' I foolishly asked him if he would like to say anything to the then chief minister of Uttar Pradesh—Mayawati. He shook his head, 'What can we say to Mayawati? We don't belong to her caste. We are Yadvans.' I asked if he would like to speak to the then Prime Minister Manmohan Singh. He snorted, 'What is the point in speaking to Manmohan Singh? He is the prime minister of the country. What can he do for us? It makes more sense to speak to Mayawati, at least she can do something.' We both laughed.

'This year, they wanted to declare Lalitpur a drought-affected district. Mayawati inspected the district. That day, a light shower had fallen and coated everything in dampness. When she arrived, the slightest of drizzles started. "Look how wet this place is! How can we declare this place drought-affected?" and then, Mayawati left. When we complained to the politicians who came with her, they said, "Be thankful she came here and brought the rain. Without her, you wouldn't even have got this."'

It was time for me to leave too. He offered me water, we walked to his house. He showed me some adivasi huts: old bedspreads and tattered plastic sheets strung across thickets of brambles twisted together into an intricate maze that offered scant protection from the cold whipping night breezes. 'That's where they live, in winter, in summer, in the rain—the whole year round,' he said. The man's house was clean and sparse. It was made of bricks from the cement factory. It was only a single room, two suitcases were on the cemented loft, a few plates, mugs and utensils were gathered in one corner. Bedding for the night reposed in another.

There was no furniture. It had taken him three years to build his house and it cost him 80,000 rupees. The roof remained to be cemented; he hoped to finish it when the rains halted. The man's tumbler was clean, his water refreshing and cool.

I got onto Nautanki thinking about the mortification of the

boy as he got told off by an elder in front of a rank stranger—all because he hadn't answered one of my thickly accented questions. The sheer mute terror of being a child!

And then the child grew into a man and discovered the endless terror of his days, the constant doubts, the slow-building hate, or the gathering powerlessness. It was too much to think about. The sun beat down with relentless violent laughter. The lengthy unscheduled stop had thrown me out of gear; I was no longer loose and lithe, I was coiled tight. I slaved on Nautanki until I found a stream where kids played and teenage boys fished with bare line. I stopped in high relief. I washed a pair of clothes for the next day's ride. I hung them to dry on some steaming rocks and went across the highway to a chai shop. People had been watching the Innova. They asked if I belonged to the same group. When they heard I was on a long cycle yatra, they told me to watch out for my testicles swelling up. They gave me all manner of preventive remedies that included coating my balls with turmeric and tying a damp muslin cloth around them before getting on the cycle. The ideas came thick and fast. I laughed at it all.

Two teenage boys clattered in on a motorcycle. They were headed to Pappu's dhaba. They had borrowed his motorcycle three days earlier and were returning it. They couldn't stop raving about what a magnificent man he was. I felt like we were old friends because I knew Pappu as well. The crew was holed up in the car. It was too hot to follow me around, there was nothing new anyway. I enjoyed the solitude and went back. Naveen was sleeping in the driver's seat. Prashanth and Achyu were asleep in the middle. Arjun shot white and black wagtails pecking at the stream from the car's shaded comfort. Three men came by on a motorcycle with their catch of fish hanging from a string threaded through the gaping mouths. The silvery scales rippled in the soporific heat. They had exploded a bomb in the stream to snare their catch—four large fish. A hundred rupees a kg was the going rate, the bomb had only cost fifty. I asked if they were going to plough their profits into another bomb. The rider of the motorcycle shook his head and drawled, '*Champagne peeyenge.*' The spirit of enterprise ran shallow; it was too hot to work too.

Ram Sevak

I slipped into the final 500 km. We came upon the fantastic corpse of a car; I slowed to take a look. A few metres away was an inviting chai shop, we stopped. Achyu and Naveen placed bets as to whether the moulded hump of metal and steel had once been a Xylo or a Sumo. The roof of the car was smashed through, the bonnet had caved in and the bumper was bunged up like a swollen eye after a fight.

The car looked like it had been compressed by a garbage processing truck. I sent up a silent prayer to God knows who for its final occupants. The man who served us was bare-chested with a little nose of hair protruding from his occiput. The rest of his head was bald, his face bore a scraggly salt-and-pepper beard. He asked about Nautanki. I told him. He didn't seem the least surprised and smiled, 'Last year, I went on a similar trip. From Gomukh to Kanyakumari.'

I quailed at the thought. 'On a cycle?'

'On foot,' he replied with a grin.

'On foot!' I yelled. 'How long did it take?' I was agog. Here was a story I hadn't heard after all.

'Three days and five months,' Ram Sevak replied. I plugged him with questions, he was calm and cool. He had taken a bus to Gomukh: I didn't know where it was. He explained, 'To

Gangotri where the Ganga starts'. Having collected her waters, he had walked all the way to Kanyakumari. I tried to imagine it, I made the calculations. He walked for 30 km a day, he said, sometimes 35. By chance, if he didn't find a place to sleep, he stretched it to 50. Some days, he walked till midnight. Where did he sleep? 'Wherever I wanted to, any open field was enough.' He ate whatever he got—rice, roti, vegetables. When that was unavailable, he ate fruits. He had walked through all kinds of terrain, all sorts of land. He had been through Chhattisgarh where the Naxalites lived, he said, but he hadn't had a single problem there, hadn't met a person who wanted to do him harm—except 100 km from Chennai where his phone was stolen in a temple.

Shades of the Rameshwaram temple flew back. It was a cheap phone, he said, pulling out a phone from under his table to explain better. 'I went and told the police about it the next morning. They asked me to wait until afternoon. I told them, "even if you give me 500 rupees, I can't stay", because every day that I idled, my expenses would mount. Look, every day a minimum of 100 rupees will definitely be spent. You can't help that.' He had spent 13,000 rupees on the entire trip. In Visakhapatnam, the police had taken him into preventive custody because the chief minister was having a rally. When the rally finished, he'd been released. He had a book chronicling all the places he had stayed at, all the people he had met. I asked if it was around. He delved into a drawer and came out with a little pocket book.

I pored over his handwriting; inexplicably, it changed from entry to entry. There were addresses and phone numbers. It was exactly like the opening pages of Shikaari's 1982 rexine-backed diary that detailed his trip—a diary I would later lose. Shikaari had advised me to do the same as Ram Sevak had done. It would make a good record of the trip, he'd said. I hadn't bothered, I had collected my evidences on scraps of paper and bills. Who knew where they were, had they curled up forever in the rain like forgotten poems? But what did it matter—at lunch I had heard Achyu tell Prashanth in awe, 'We've just gone over 1 terabyte of footage.'

'I've been through places I had never imagined before,' Ram Sevak continued, 'How else would I get to see the places I have walked through? I'm an uneducated person, a poor man.' I nodded. I felt the same way. I could never have dreamt up the beauty of the places I had cycled through. I was ashamed thinking I was 30 years old and unaware of how wild and enchanting my country was. I was only streaking through it on a black highway. How much more beautiful were the insides? 'In Chennai, there was no one who could tell me the way. I couldn't speak their language and they couldn't speak Hindi,' he laughed.

He had taken a train back after walking the length of the country with Ganga's waters, strictly adhering to all the rules laid down for the pilgrimage. He couldn't eat garlic, oil and onions; he had to bathe after he ate, went to the latrine and when he woke up from sleep—only then, he could carry the holy water. I told him his journey must have been doubly difficult. 'Why difficult?' he waved me aside, 'I just chanted God's name and the time passed.'

'I had gone in search of God,' Ram Sevak said into the distance. A walker came to drink some water.

'Did you find him?'

'*Arrey kahaan?*' Ram Sevak answered. 'But I found peace,' he said with an abashed smile. He turned to the man ladling water into his mouth and said sternly, 'Hello!' When the man turned, Ram Sevak dropped his voice and said kindly, '*Upar se peele bhai.*'

I ventured maybe peace was God. He nodded and said softly into the distance, 'Only one who is formless and without thought can find God.' He turned back to me and said, 'Brother, everything in this country is fine...except the police. They trouble people too much. They kept asking me questions throughout my journey. In Chhattisgarh, they kept ordering me, "sit here, stand there". I had a lot of difficulty because no one is supposed to touch me. Those are Gangaji's rules, and the police kept pushing me around. They would keep telling me, "Don't walk here, don't walk there, there is danger everywhere." I told them if there was danger, I would face it. I have no enemies. Why would anybody want to do anything to me? But they wouldn't listen. I had even taken a letter from my local police station and the Zilla Adhikaari!' I asked to see the priceless document.

He opened another drawer and gave me some laminated letters studded with his photograph, several rubber stamps and sprawling signatures. I looked at the face that stared back at me. It was a different Ram Sevak. His perambulating pilgrimage had changed his face irrevocably. He looked older now, more handsome, calmer, wiser, more religious too. I read the letter and told him how every authority I'd met asked the same question, 'Where is the letter?' He laughed and nodded his head in recognition. He hadn't seen a single wild animal the entire trip. I was still turning the pages of his diary. He hastened me on, flipping pages, until finally I found the page where it was written—5/10/09 Kanyakumari—*aur yahaan meri yatra samaapt hui* (And this is where my journey ends). I loved the finality of the entry. I burst out laughing, imagining Ram Sevak perched cross-legged on Vivekananda's Point gazing out onto the Arabian Ocean, putting down that line.

Shikaari's story about the cyclists he kept bumping into

(Basavva himself), had made me believe I would meet a horde of cyclists along the way. I had imagined a bunch of us, arrowing straight into Delhi from far-flung corners of the country, all coming to see the Commonwealth Games, converging like the rays of a star returning to her core, our paths criss-crossing so we could swap travel stories, but I hadn't seen a single long distance cyclist. I had finally found another traveller—a peregrinator no less, like The Wandering Monk had been for much of his time, and his journey was so much bigger than Shikaari's or mine. The whole afternoon I'd been struggling to contain a mildly rising joy at slipping into the last 500 km, almost exulting at the immensity of it until I met a man who stilled my pride with the enormous scale of his own adventures. I exulted instead over the humility I was learning. Even before I had started, I had vaguely known that the one thing I would learn on the cycle ride would be humility. Now it was all coming together in ways more intricate than I could have conceived.

Behind the branch-and-trunk chai shop stood a defunct school. It had a little man-made lake out in the front. It was a tremendous place to pitch a tent. I asked Ram Sevak if we could sleep there. His face fell, he half apologized for not having the keys. They were with an officer who lived in Basai 4 km away. He would have opened it if he had the keys, but what could he do? I enquired about temples. There was a Shiva temple 2 km inside Basai where travellers could sleep the night. I said goodbye. I passed the beat-up car thinking how strange it was that this was what had caused me pass like a shadow across Ram Sevak's walking path.

Beneath a bridge, the Dukwa reservoir thinned to land before ballooning on either side into vast bruises of water. It was the last possible night I could camp out. Jhansi to Delhi was a motley run of towns and cities, I wasn't hoping for vast tracts of open land. I was excited for Naveen. He could finally show off his survival skills like he had been itching to do. He could kindle his beloved fire all night, I thought and grinned. He was already scouting for a gently sloping patch of land that would make the perfect camping spot. He pointed out the dry brush lying around and loudly said it was good wood to build a fire.

Achyu laughed and told him he was accompanying the equipment to the nearest lodge. Naveen's face fell. He threw a tantrum. He sidled over to me with a host of suggestions. He would drop the crew and return to sleep with me, we could pick them up in the morning; but Achyu was firm. I shrugged my shoulders. It wasn't my rig to give orders. Naveen sulked but soon busied himself with the plastic tarpaulin sheet, the bamboo sticks, the nails and the hooks that the crew had bought in Nagpur for a night such as this. Naveen gathered armloads of kindling for an all-night fire. I bathed, imagining myself sitting before the flames licking the black night. The crew left to find a lodge.

I sat on the rocks abutting the reservoir's edge. They were warm to the touch. It was good to be alone without the thoughts others wrought. I watched the sky go technicolour. When it went black, I lay down on the uneven rocks testing several different attitudes before I found the position of maximum comfort. I watched the stars drop into the sky. The darkness faded as the night got moony with stars. I felt an immense pride. I hadn't managed a 100 km but it had been good strong cycling and I was finally sleeping out in the open like I'd always dreamt. I stretched on the warm rock feeling a quiet pride in my body and what it was capable of doing. It had been a long time since I had known that serene pleasure. I had felt it through medical college where I made it to every sports team there was, not out of any overabundance of talent but because everyone else was too busy studying; I was only too happy to make up the numbers. When I had started working, all the avenues of playing were lost; alcohol and cigarettes had become part of my staple diet, I had let the body run to ruin. I was beginning to feel the joys of proud flesh again.

When Achyu came back, I was sound asleep. I woke up, wolfed down the food and asked for more. He apologized, it was all he had brought. The moon made a fire unnecessary. Naveen's firewood lay unlit. I fell asleep immediately thinking about the 145-km ride into Gwalior the next day.

27 September 2010

The White Sands of Uttar Pradesh

It was to be a day of no conversations. I wanted to reach Gwalior as early as possible—that meant a good eight hours in the saddle. After waiting for long enough to capture the sun showing her snout above the horizon, we were away. The highway ran through verdant army land. Nautanki's ball bearings made familiar groans. I zoomed through Babina, surprised to see a cycle shop open for business. I gave Nautanki a quick overall that included an oil bath and fresh blow for her tyres. Next door, hundreds of samosas were being made to start a new day. Naveen was hungry. I left the crew to wait for the first batch.

There were numerous cyclists on the road on their way to school or work. I looked for a boy cyclist behind whom I could draft to save energy. I remembered the days when I cycled to school, when after years of entreating, I was finally allowed to do it: how I had thrilled at that simple joy—the sheer independence of it. I would take incredible risks as I cycled furiously to school and back every day, repeatedly trying to shave seconds of my own record for the 4-km stretch from Siddapura to Museum Road. Bijauli passed in a flash. Past Jhansi, I stopped for a break. It had been a good session—decent roads, shady trees, the sun hadn't yet turned bellicose.

Coming out of Jhansi, I cycled slowly, trying to build another steady rhythm when I heard a loud explosion. Nautanki sank beneath me. Her rear wheel started jumping periodically. I walked her. I remembered Sibi and our unseen leopards. Luckily, not a kilometre away was a puncture shop. Ghan Shyam sold tea as well. He set a fresh round of tea to boil and sat down on his haunches to tend to Nautanki. I tried not to but felt rueful. I had been fantasizing about Nautanki making Delhi without a puncture. What a story it would be! I'd been imagining it. 'I cycled from Bengaluru to Delhi and my cycle didn't get punctured once.' I had secretly nursed the ambition of emulating Shikaari but the dream had deflated. I consoled myself and Nautanki too. It wasn't really a puncture after all, I bluffed. The cycle-repair man at Babina had put too much air in with that pressurized nozzle of his. I told Nautanki she was an incredible girl, she had been spectacular thus far, and we were getting her a brand new tube as a prize.

I didn't want to go too fast with the new tube, I wanted to test it out. And even if I did want to go faster, I couldn't have because the stretch from Jhansi to Datia was covered with the white sands of Uttar Pradesh. The heat belted down on the treeless highway, the mind protested. I vowed to stay stoic. I trudged along at a steady pace. Each time I came upon a mild slope I'd stand on the pedals trying to mimic Alberto Contador's inimitable ceaseless flowing cycling cadence tuned to perfection. Despite the mind flagging, the body was holding up well. If the body started protesting too, the mind would go to pot. I attacked slopes silently, rolling Nautanki between my fingers, swaying like an upside down pendulum on a crossbar. We were like two bodies slow-dancing with each other till eternity came and went too. I was getting tired. I ignored the solace of receding milestones. I pretended it was the fourth leg of training and I was cycling to suffer, when in reality I was only cycling to the next chai break. I no longer felt light but was determined to enjoy the effort of it all. I dreamt of lying in a bed in Gwalior.

I had a chai at Datia. The roads spruced up, so did my mood. I no longer dreamt of the Rani of Jhansi. I simply dreamt about the love I had known and the love I would make, and only the good parts too. They were the only bits that made sense, the only thing I was prepared to risk all for. Everything else could go hang. An hour and 25 km later, we stopped for lunch at Dabra. My beard was sanded over, my eyelids were covered with road dust, the sweat dried to salt as I stretched. My legs quivered like finely tempered steel, as if they were on the verge of tears and would break down any moment. But Gwalior was only 46 km away.

We were offered a little alcove in the restaurant facing the highway. A pedestal fan was introduced to the party. The curtain fluttered in the fan breeze. I drew it aside to look at the highway. The alcove was awash with flies that hassled and buzzed. The dhaba was manned by a small platoon of young boys. A small boy ducked under our feet to clean up. He resurfaced with a five-rupee note and handed it to me saying, '*Aapka jeb se tapak gaya*' (It fell from your pocket). I gave it back to him and said, '*Tu rakh le. Tere haath aane ko tapka tha*' (You keep it. It fell so that you could get it). He laughed and gave back the creased note. I insisted, his face burst into a beaming smile. He couldn't believe his good fortune.

Dholu was the waiter I had tipped, or at any rate, he was the cleaner. He was 14. His default expression was a broad smile. He kept breaking into large grins. He was the youngest of five brothers, all of whom worked. I asked what he wanted to become when he grew up; he said he wanted to be a big man. I asked what he meant. 'I want to have lots of money, and have a car, and a job. That's how you become a "big man",' he reasoned. He was going to Delhi when he was 16 or 17. His future was decided. He trusted in it implicitly, the way children do. He would do whatever job he got when he went to Delhi, he said, it was the only way to become a 'big man'. I asked why he so badly wanted to become a 'big man'. 'Only when you become a big man, you can get married,' was his logic. I burst out laughing.

All I had done in my spare teenage hours was dream about getting married and living alone with some girl. I told Dholu that he didn't really want to be a big man, he just wanted to get married. He laughed in denial and got shy. His favourite actor was Salman Khan; Juhi Chawla was his favourite actress. I cracked up. I told him Juhi Chawla was too old now, thinking of the many boyhood hours spent in the happy contemplation of the paradisical nature of my marriage to Mrs Juhi Chawla-Franks. I asked what he thought of the present crop of actresses. '*Sab achche lagte hain Uncleji*' (I like them all, Uncleji). I thought the same way about girls too. I could have been Dholu in a different set of circumstances. He had large crusting scabs on his lips and cheek. They reminded me of a diseased nipple; I thought they were getting infected. He said they were the remnants of a toss he had taken on his cycle.

He had been pulled out of school a month ago, 'It feels good to study Uncleji, but I can't try. It takes 200 rupees to get admitted, 200 rupees during exam time. So mummy and pappa told me, "Don't worry about school now, first you work, after sometime we'll put you back into school. Then you can study as much as you want".' Someone shouted at Dholu: couldn't he see a new table had been occupied? He disappeared. We shifted into the main dining area of the dhaba. Dholu bent beneath a table and swept the spent whisky bottles from between the customers' legs. The bottles grated on the floor. With a broom bigger than him, he swept up the carcass of the previous meal—bottles caps, plastic cups, beedis, lemon rinds, bones picked clean, damp cigarette butts, matchsticks. He shepherded the refuse through the aisles. Balancing a broken dust pan on his foot, he swept the mass together, picking up the bits that had fallen out with his hands. He was new to the job and swept clean. People streamed in while Arjun filmed Dholu working. Some drunks clowned for the camera; another warned, 'Be careful, these press people will shoot children working and then make a big fuss.'

When we were done eating, we fooled around with the boy-waiters. Dholu zipped around on his cycle. I took a shot at it. It was so badly kept I struggled to turn the wheels. Rust, dirt and age had slowed all the moving parts. I couldn't fathom how Dholu hit the speed he did. When I came back to finally give up, he was sitting on a parked motorcycle turning the throttle, pretending he was riding to who knows what adventures. I lazed on the charpoy and watched the boy-waiters play.

I headed out thinking everything was a matter of luck. I thanked whoever for the good fortune of belonging to the family I owned. It was only because I'd been born Anglo-Indian that I'd become a doctor in the first place. One medical seat reserved for Anglo-Indians for the state—and it had fallen to my happy lot! And what tremendous luck to have been born in Karnataka too—other states didn't have the same reservation.

And soon after becoming a doctor, I had quietly stepped out of medicine because merely being a doctor could not contain the vastness of my desires. I reckoned it would take me two and half hours to hit Gwalior.

Nautanki entered the BSF Station at Tekanpur. I was back to the beauty of trees casting long shadows across the highway. Like all army areas, it was faultlessly clean. Hordes of jawans and recruits cycled slowly in the drowsy end-September afternoon heat. I passed them all with their crew cuts and brown woolen socks matching their khaki shorts and green canvas shoes.

It made me think of my father who had been forced out of school to join the army at the tender age of 16 so he could supplement the family income. And just like Dholu, he had loved nothing better than to study. When I had bought Nautanki, my father had told me stories about his cycle—how soon after my mother and him were married, every month-end, he would cycle to a pawnshop in Majestic to pawn it; some months, he'd pawn his wedding ring too. Then, he'd take a bus home and wait for the next month's salary to redeem the only articles of value he possessed. He never went to the pawnshops close to the army quarters because he didn't want anyone to know he had difficulties. It was impossible not to think of my father as I cycled through Tekanpur.

Everything about the place brought back memories of the Madras Engineering Group's vast land holdings in Bangalore—me playing on the obstacle course while my father shopped at the canteen, me saluting all the guards and their crested turbans, me sitting on a stone bench watching some obscure hockey match between army cadets.

An entire peloton of cyclists in green tights and white T-shirts complete with bib numbers approached from the opposite direction. They cycled much faster than all the others I passed. How I wished I could join them. What were my father's thoughts as he cycled through the shaded cool of his army camps? Did he whistle and sing or did he curse and dream, did he have races with himself, did he feel absolutely free from all concerns about the future or family, or did he remember the errors he made and the love he had lost?

The highway went to pieces and so did my mind. I couldn't find the mental fortitude to pedal quicker. Either my mind wouldn't speak or the body wouldn't listen. I began to tire, my spirits flagged. I was no longer concerned about making Gwalior in a fixed time. I was no longer interested in taking breaks at regular intervals. It didn't matter what time I reached. Even if it was 10 in the night, I still had to make Gwalior that day. Then I could rest. I abandoned the idea of taking it 100 km at a time. I took it 10 km at a time instead; finally, I took it one kilometre at a time. All I could say was 'pedal, pedal, pedal' as we took the journey, one revolution at a time. Maybe the soreness and stiffness and tightness that Shree had cautioned me about had finally set in. But that wasn't it. My body felt all right, I knew it would hold up. It was the mind I was struggling to master. Shikaari had written that the stretch from Nagpur to Gwalior was 'challenging'. It was my sixth consecutive day in the hills, upslope and downwards—maybe I was paying the price. Or maybe this was the part where I gave up because that was the sort of person I was. I didn't see the point in striving after a while. I couldn't see the point of perfection, the exuberance of excellence, the virtue of hard work. It was the story of my life—a happy non-belief.

The highway got clogged; it was always that way descending upon a city. Buses with people atop the roofs passed, motorcycles sped, cars glided, tractors and trucks humped noisily across the road. I stopped to drink some chai at a dhaba. Gwalior was 30 km away. The afternoon stretch had been slow-going. It was when I usually made up the pace. Achyu asked me questions but I couldn't speak. All I wanted to do was jerk off and sleep.

Naren

Two men were in the dhaba; one lay prostrate propped up on his elbows, the other reclined comfortably across two charpoys. We started a conversation. The road from Gwalior to Agra was fantastic they said, there were no ups and downs, except a few at Dholpur. I asked if they knew about the Commonwealth Games. The man propped on his elbows did—only a few days earlier, the Commonwealth Games Torch had passed by on its way to Delhi with much fanfare and he had seen it. I thought about the torch when it had come to Bengaluru.

It had been an evening training session that day. The police had stopped traffic on Double Road. I had shifted to the footpath, walked past the traffic revving to go and had heaved Nautanki back on the road. A loudspeaker had accompanied the banging of drums. I had cycled in the procession of a colourful float mounted with the sporting stalwarts of Bengaluru, government officials and minor celebrities. It had been a flat-out 90-minute cycle ride and the only thought I had possessed as the float disappeared below me on the Double Road flyover was, 'We'll see the torch when we get to Delhi, for now we'll just cycle.'

'*Kila dekhna*,' (See the fort) the reclining man said. 'That's where the Rani of Jhansi jumped from. Make sure you see it. It's a big thing in Madhya Pradesh.'

'What will happen tomorrow?' I asked. The Ayodha verdict was expected the next day. The propped man replied, 'Riots will happen.' He thought for a while and corrected himself, 'Riots will have to happen.'

He smiled, I laughed. The reclining man chimed in, 'Brother, this, I don't understand. If there was a temple there, then why do you want to build a mosque; and if there was a mosque there, why do you want to build a temple? What has been razed to the ground has been razed. Why rebuild it again?' I nodded. I told him what another man had told me, 'Instead of rebuilding a temple or a mosque, why don't they make something useful there…like an orphanage or a college—something that everyone can use.' The reclining man nodded and said, 'That is correct. They should build a hospital for poor people there, or make houses for the homeless, or better still, a school where people can go study and become something. See how many people have been affected by what has happened. Think of the money that has been wasted, the property that has been destroyed.'

Well, I remembered 6 December 1992 when the Babri Masjid was partially demolished and the riots that came in the aftermath. My father would rent *Newsline* videos on weekends and we would watch people and things go up in flames. It was the first time I had become aware of the world outside Bengaluru.

The propped man spoke softly into the distance, 'If you take away the places of god, where will man go? What will become of man? What will remain of him?'

The reclining man clicked his tongue in impatience, 'God is everywhere, you don't need to go to a place to find him.'

The propped man stood his ground and reasoned, 'It is important to allow some sites to remain holy. It is important to not allow another faith to reclaim history.'

The reclining man said, 'You know it, I know it and that's what's important. If the mosque stays, you think I'll stop believing Ram was born there? Why should we bother about who believes what as long as *we* believe?'

The propped man said quietly, 'It's important to make other people recognize it too.'

The reclining man said, 'This country is 90 per cent Hindus, only 10 per cent are Muslim. What do you want them to recognize? What are you scared of?'

'They should agree to it too.'

'What is there, they should let that remain. At least that's the way I feel,' the reclining man finished.

The propped man said simply, 'If Ram was born there, there should be a temple there.'

A young boy sat down on a charpoy. He was all eyes for the camera. The reclining man tried to convince the propped man, 'Brother, God is in every human's heart.' He turned to me for encouragement; I nodded in non-belief. A bald-headed man with a thick moustache, bare-chested, his hips draped in a patterned lungi, stormed up to us. He was the cook at the dhaba, his eyes shone with anger and hatred. He stood there and spat his words out, 'Now we only work and fill our pockets. The whole world has become this way. We work from dawn to dusk, collect our money, and go home to sleep. When we don't have time for our family and friends, where will we find the time for God? That's why God is saying, "You don't have time for me, I don't have time for you. Go get fucked. Get out, it's over".' He could have led a mob that killed the way he spoke. A silence fell over the dhaba.

The young boy settled himself in a chair close to me, 'You're cycling across our country, how long did it take you?' he cut into the conversation.

'20 days.'

'You had to go by a cycle only; you couldn't go any other way?'

I nodded.

'Okay, so you're cycling through our country, how is it?'

I told him I hadn't imagined it would be so beautiful.

At this, the young boy smiled and said, 'We are all one country, just different faiths, no?'

I told him different languages and different food too.

'There are 29 different states in the country, right?' he said confidently.

I told him I had cycled through six.

'Six?' his bright eyes opened in surprise. The sun cast a diagonal shadow across his face.

'How?' he asked, astonished.

I told him I had cycled 1,700 km from Bengaluru. He wrestled with the idea—his eyes narrowed, his forehead crinkled. I assumed he didn't know where it was.

'And how much more do you plan to cycle?'

'Another 350 km.'

'And then what will you do?'

'I'll watch the Commonwealth Games.'

'And after that what will you do? Will you cycle back?' he pressed. I told him I hadn't decided. I asked if he would accompany me if I did.

'I won't come,' he shot back.

'Why?' I asked. He shook his head. 'You wanted to know how beautiful the country is? Come see it with your own eyes,' I challenged.

'We are born here, we will die here,' he said, matter-of-factly before his face broke into a small smile. Everyone in the dhaba laughed. The scary thing was that he said it like he meant it. I softened a little and asked why he said it.

'I'm saying it because that's the way it is,' he said with a half-mocking smile.

'Why?'

'Because I don't have a personality like yours for me to advance in life.'

I told him it wasn't about personality, just a desire to do. He shook his head dismissively. I insisted.

'There's no money, we are poor people,' he offered.

'What do you do?'

'*Mazdoori.*'

I had come to hate the word. He made 50 rupees a day. He was 15 years old and had been working for two months.

'And what did you do before that?' I asked.

'I studied.'

'Now?'

'I've stopped.'

'Why?'

'Because there's no money in the house,' he said, leaning forward and raising his eyebrows in question, 'Who will give me the money to study?'

'But aren't government schools free?'

'They are, but they ask for money to put your name on the rolls.'

'How much?'

'600 rupees.'

'How many brothers and sisters do you have?'

'Two brothers and two sisters. My sisters are married.'

'What do your brothers do?'

'*Mazdoori.*'

The boy's name was Naren. I asked him what he wanted to do in life.

'I wanted to do many things,' his eyes rolled gently backwards.

'Wanted to?' I drew out the past tense slowly. He nodded his head.

'What did you want to do?'

'There was a lot that I wanted to do,' he hesitated, 'but the times are such that now I can't do anything.'

'What did you want to do?'

Silence.

Naren stared at me, his mouth half-open, lips twisted from a cold knowledge, as the rest of his face flickered with some long forgotten emotion. His eyes were bright and his mind was exceptionally quick, it was as plain as the heat from the sun.

Someone prompted, 'Tell him what you wanted to do.' Naren stalled. The bald cook bellowed from the open kitchen, 'Say what you wanted to do.'

Naren started, he was hesitant like he was confessing to a crime, 'I wanted to... study...and become a big...doctor. But there's no money and so I am not worthy enough to study,' he finished in a rush and his smile returned.

'You won't go to the city to work?'

Naren shook his head nonchalantly. He was too intelligent to still believe in childish dreams like Dholu.

'What will you do?'

'I will drive a truck,' he rocked in his chair, 'I'm learning, or at least I'm trying to.'

'Who's teaching you?'

'I have an ustad, he teaches me.'

'How long do you think before you learn?'

'I think it will take me two months,' he said confidently. Then he added humbly, 'At least in my opinion, I think it will take two months.' I didn't doubt him.

'What do your parents do?'

'*Mazdoori*.'

Someone called for Naren. He left. I was numb with sadness. I sat there as the tears began to roll. I clenched my jaw and bit my nails trying to blink back the impotent tears. It was shameful to see enthusiasm and intelligence laid to waste so easily. I wanted to sob but the camera was on me. Naren was only a boy, but he had been forced into growing up before his time. He acted like a man and talked like one too. Achyu asked me what the moral of the story was. I told him stories like this had no moral.

Achyu was spitting anger, 'Look at him man,' he said jerking his head towards Naren who was climbing into the cleaner's seat of a big yellow dumpster truck. 'I wouldn't be surprised if 50 years from now he'll be sitting here, in this same dhaba just like the two men over there.' The door slammed as Naren watched the rear end of the dumpster truck backing out. When he was sure it was safe, he waved at us as the sun washed over his smile-drenched face. The garbage-collecting truck roared and Naren was lost to us forever. 'In 2060, he'll still be sitting in this same dhaba,' Achyu said disbelievingly. 'What a fucked up country man!'

I told Achyu I'd begun to think that India had so many problems, I didn't know anymore who could solve them, or whether they could even be solved. Achyu fumed, 'How do you solve something like poverty? How do you solve a person not having enough to eat?'

'How do you solve obsession with money?' and this was where I believed the solution lay.

'That's a worldwide problem, Dominic,' Achyu countered.

But I believed if we could rid the world of its love for money and the things it could buy, we would be better off. There was nothing left to do but get happy again (or at least attempt to). I told the crew with a laugh that Naren had taken all the joy out of 1700 km. The sun had started her free fall and on the rolling hills that rung Gwalior in on her southern fringes, I blew myself out thinking the sun had already set on poor Naren's life. I thundered down on Nautanki's pedals trying to cycle off the anger and hate. He was 15 and had lost the capacity to dream. He was cast in stone and spoke, in Achyu words, 'like a child who's seen the difficult side of life'. I remembered myself at 15—not a care in the world, my only aim being to go stumbling in laughter from class to laboratory, and pass my exams with marks good enough.

I had been 15 when I had sat in the sweaty Sports Room looking goggle-eyed at Shikaari narrating snippets of his 1982 cycling expedition as his newspaper clippings passed hands. I had calmly filed away the story for future use. 'I will do it when I am older,' I had thought, 'when I will earn my keep and fend for myself.' At that tender age, I had forever been bursting with dreams, always thinking about and planning the life that had lain ahead.

The sun was hiding behind the hills, I cycled with furious abandon. It was what I had always done whenever life got too disgusting and dry, too deranged and dirty, too dreary to dream, too difficult to comprehend. I'd get on a cycle and bust my balls until I could cycle no longer, and by then, the anger would have dissipated or the insides would be more steeled. I thought about Naren voluntarily committing academic suicide, like Dholu—like thousands, lakhs, crores of young boys and girls all across India. Who knew the real number? All of them were giving up an education for the bare necessities of the stomach; well, I knew what an education did.

It taught one the capacity to dream and the means by which to attempt it. What more did a human being need except the ability to defeat the drudge of existence with an exuberant imagination? I took the winding turns at speed, barely touching on the brakes and when I came upon a slope, I attacked it with vengeance, and this time I didn't stop until I reached the top. And if all these kids were indeed committing academic suicide, then wasn't the state culpable too? Was it not guilty of aiding and abetting them? Wasn't the state guilty of academic homicide as well—possibly the worst sort of murder there is—to murder the capacity to dream, to condemn someone to a lifetime of mental paralysis, a sapping of the spirit, a deep emotional void that would only fester and grow more bitter with the passage of time.

Nautanki swooped through the hills as the sun came back into view. It hadn't yet dipped beneath the horizon. A man dressed in white floated by with a rifle slung around his neck. A cow led its owner by the tail as it scampered across the highway. We stopped to ask a man for directions. He was deaf—he pointed to his ear in which nestled a hearing aid and laughed. We shouted into the browning day, he shouted back. He pretended to turn up the volume, we laughed. Finally, he told us how to get to Gwalior, but not a single vehicle went the way he pointed. We ignored the deaf man's directions.

Now that the initial swell of emotion had worn off, I began to think honestly again. In the rutted roads that bypassed villages without street lights, I felt shame. I had thought about asking Naren if I could spend the night at his house. If I was really the student and the scientist I believed myself to be, I would have wrangled a bed where Naren slept, to find out what his life was like, speak to his *mazdoor* brothers about what lurked in their heads, find out what attempts his *mazdoor* parents had made to keep the ship afloat until circumstances hardened their desires and forced their intelligent son's hand to the harsh wheel of work.

But I hadn't said a word because I wanted to reach Gwalior that night to sleep in a warm comfortable bed. I didn't want another rough night of sleeping in the open, I didn't want to waste my rest day filming and cycling. I speeded up, I cycled to exhaustion, I cycled to failure—my own failure at the paucity of my emotions. It was enough for me that I felt bad about someone else's fate. That was where my involvement ended. I was as selfish as everyone else. I didn't have the energy to care anymore.

Gwalior was lit up by the slow-moving lights of a massive traffic jam. It seemed a rare occurrence because newspaper photographers and television cameramen climbed the roofs of cars and trucks to document it. Policemen frantically waved vehicles this way and that, mixing everything up further. Everyone was itching to go and struggling to squeeze past. The horns went like mad. You could detect the murderous threats and the anguished wails. I pulled Nautanki onto the footpath while Achyu made enquiries about a place to room for the night. I climbed the walls of the compound of a government building to watch the bedlam and mounting confusion as I slowly pulled on a cigarette. The cacophony of the automobiles was ear-splitting. Through the many-tenored wail of the horns, a song wafted through. I cocked my ears. The song grew as the boisterous traffic jam blended into background noise. I closed my eyes to listen. Someone was singing rhymes or prayers, it sounded like it came from a tape recorder broadcasted through a megaphone. It sounded like the Voice of Pure Reason in the mishmash of all the impatient noise. The toughest leg of the tour had been eclipsed.

28 September 2010

The Voice of Reason?

I washed my dirty clothes while the crew shot the martial monuments of Gwalior. The sun came in spears; the aluminium bars fencing in the terrace of Hotel Grace were hot to the touch. In half an hour, my clothes were dry. I mailed the ones I love, rereading a one-line mail that Shilpa—an old doctor friend—had sent back in reply to an earlier mail of mine confessing I was having difficulty making any sense of the trip, as I hurtled headlong from one emotion to the next, quietly rediscovering the joys of the body and unearthing (in the most minimalistic way possible) the latent beauty and harsh reality of my country. It simply said—'Don't even bother trying to make sense out of this trip now Dom, it will take you years to understand it.'

It was good advice and I was content to put off hard work for a few years. We drove back over the little hills to meet Naren. We timed our drive to coincide with our stop there the previous day. The men on the charpoys weren't around, neither was Naren. Only the raving bald cook was familiar. He still looked sullen, but he was polite in response to all our questions. He knew Naren lived in a village 3 km away but he didn't know where. Naren came and went to the dhaba without a fixed timetable. The cook didn't know where he worked either and couldn't say for sure if he would definitely come back that evening. We settled down to wait with an endless row of chai. After an hour, we left. The enormity of the country had swallowed Naren forever. He had become anonymous.

We went back. The Voice of Pure Reason we had heard the night before droned upwards into the night. I asked the hotel security guard about it.

'You didn't hear it last night?'

He was incredulous, 'You must have heard it last night when you were coming in.'

I told him I had heard it but was too tired to be curious. 'It has been going on for 14 years,' he said. I asked him to imagine the life of the man whose job it was to change the cassettes on the tape recorder each time the tape ran out. The guard scoffed at me and said it wasn't a tape recorder. It was a live act, with men switching places on a microphone at regular intervals, perpetuating the drone till eternity, and it was right down the street from where we were staying. I asked again to be doubly-sure—I didn't want a rerun of the Shani Dev Mandir episode. I ran upstairs and told Achyu about the phenomenon. A flurry of activity ensued as we readied for a shoot.

The temple stood out like a beacon. It was nine at night and people were still streaming in. Middle-aged men came by in shorts, college boys prayed fervently in T-shirts, women covered their heads with their dupattas and pallus and rocked slowly with closed eyes. The man who sang was old and bearded but his voice was strong, he churned out the chants without paying attention to anybody. When he was done, he bowed to the book that lay before him; after a few more gestures of respect, he stood up. Waiting in the wings was another, ready to take his place. We met the man who had finished singing. 'They are all verses from the Ramayana,' he said.

A few people gathered around the camera. The Voice of Reason had been on from 8 April 1997. No one knew why it had been instituted, no one cared to know either. I insisted there must have been something or someone that had sparked it. They showered me with sympathetic smiles, they couldn't believe my non-belief. They were content that it went all day and night. One boy said it was started to serve society, he didn't know who had started it either. His face kept retreating into a beatific smile. The temple was the Mansapoorna Hanuman Mandir. It was called 'mansapoorna' because whatever wish one asked for was granted. He came 'per day', he said. He looked tremendously peaceful. I watched the faithful in trance. Achyu wanted to shoot some more; I left after one last look wondering what demon possessed men and women to believe so stoutly in God.

Outside the temple, I smoked a cigarette. A thin wiry man approached and asked me (in confidential tones) not to blindly believe whatever I'd been told. He showed me some identification papers by way of introducing himself. He had been an official in the temple, he said—a secretary. He pointed out the row of religious mendicants lined on either side of the temple's entrance. Devotees dropped coins in the bowls of the hands of the beggars as they left. 'You think these men are harmless, that they are men of god. But I can tell you, one of them is a murderer, and there's another,' he turned to look at another row of long-haired, long-bearded beggars, 'who is a rapist.'

I asked if he would like to come on camera. He thought for a while and shook his head. He didn't want to, he said—it was the same reason he had quit his job in the temple—he didn't want to anymore. I asked why he was still around the temple if he had left it of his own accord. 'I worked here for many years and I have a few friends here. I come to speak to them, they give me food.' We were interrupted by a loud slanging match. I heard imprecations so foul, I couldn't help but be impressed by the coarseness of the content and the vigour with which they were delivered.

One of the beggars was chasing another begging sadhu down the street. With his left hand, he had gathered the swirling folds of his lungi, in his right hand, he brandished his begging bowl over his head, swinging it in wild arcs at his victim, threatening to let it fly. They ran into the enveloping darkness where the street slid away from the brightly lit temple. The sadhu being chased had skirted his loins with his lungi—he ran furiously, dodging walkers and onlookers, pumping his fists in which he held a *trishul* and a bundle of clothes.

I started to laugh because it was such a comical sight. It was a shame the camera wasn't around. I asked the man what the source of the disagreement was. The sadhu being chased had just come back from a sojourn in Haridwar and had occupied another sadhu's begging station. There was severe competition to get to the top of the line, he explained, because that was where the most money was—the generosity of the faithful apparently diminished at any alarming rate as they moved further away from the temple.

Achyu wanted to record Nautanki's sounds. I left him to his work. I was lying in bed when he threw open the doors panting. His torso was wet with sweat, his breath came in short gasps. I thought the steep uneven stairs of Hotel Grace had laid him to waste. He put the camera down on the mattress and dived for my feet.

'Fucker,' he exclaimed, 'let me touch your feet man!' Then he told me the story—he had cycled up a flyover with Arjun sitting behind, so they could record Nautanki's audio. 'I don't know how you managed to do it so far,' he finished in a gasp of breath.

I told him it was bound to be tough, straight up a slope with a pillion in tow, bending down low with a recorder at his heels, documenting the sound of Nautanki's wheels, all without a warm-up. He simply shook his head and gulped a deep lungful of air, unwilling to listen to reason. I went to sleep, smiling mischievously, as Nautanki grazed outside Hotel Grace in the moonlight, thinking maybe my feet were God after all.

29 September 2010

Ram Sanehi

The plan was to catch Taj Mahal at sundown. The hotel security guard had finished his duty. It was good to cycle with a partner, I didn't mind the slow pace. The guard pointed out sights and told stories. He showed me the fort where Jhansi ki Rani had leapt to her death. She was a *moti* he said, built like a man, and she wrestled men for fun along with many other sweaty male pursuits. I made a mental note to obliterate the Rani of Jhansi from all future fantasies I had dreamed for Nautanki and me. It was the statues that had gotten me all confused—she seemed, as my father might have remarked, 'a lady with a good frame'.

I set a quicker pace when we waved the guard goodbye. Morena was 25 km ahead. When Achyu worked at an English news channel, he had shot with Ram Sanehi. The sky was pale blue and cloudless. Towards the end of the stretch, I began to tire but Morena had been breached. I smoked a cigarette and drank chai while stretching as Achyu went in search of Abhyuday Ashram. His dyslexia didn't allow him to remember directions.

Ram Sanehi's ashram was nestled in a small side road in a residential locality. He sat with his associates in a circle of plastic chairs under an asbestos shelter beneath the shade of a tree. I shook everyone's hand. Achyu introduced himself and tried to jog Ram Sanehi's memory of the shoot from three years ago. It was a futile effort; nonetheless, we were welcomed.

Ram Sanehi's associates told me of his impending departure to Mumbai. He was going to be felicitated for the work he'd been doing for the past 70 years which was nurturing the children of prostitutes from the Bhediya community. The ceremony was to be attended by one of the Ambani brothers. Ram Sanehi didn't know which one, he'd been told it was the older of the two brothers. Someone prompted, 'Mukesh Ambani'. Sanehi nodded softly.

They showed me the invitation to the event. Ram Sanehi said, 'Even...that...what's his name...Jeetendra is going to be present'. He turned to his associates, 'Who is he?' One of them replied, 'The actor'. Sanehi nodded and looked away into the distance. He was calm and completely at ease, oblivious to the cameras or our conversation.

One of the associates said matter-of-factly, 'The work that he is doing, no one in Delhi is doing and no one in Madhya Pradesh is doing; and they can't do it either.' Ram Sanehi gave a short laugh.

'He's had so many run-ins with the authorities...no one knows how difficult it is.' Sanehi smiled.

'It just seems that way, but it's not,' he replied without looking. I asked what sort of run-ins. The Zilla Collector would call Ram with information that a raid on a brothel had been conducted and the girls had been impounded in a particular police station. Ram would descend on the police station to haggle with the cops, file cases on behalf of the arrested girls and sign bail forms if necessary to get them released.

'Everything keeps happening,' the associate concluded as if it was an affair that would never end. Ram laughed again and said without looking at anyone, 'Everyone is doing their work—that's all. We do our work, the police do their work,' he paused and laughed again, 'and the media does their work.'

He searched for Achyu, 'Things go on.'

We were ushered into the ashram's office. An entire wall of the single large room had been wallpapered with photographs detailing the passage of time. In it was Ram Sanehi, the work he had done, the famous people he had shared a stage with, the awards he had won. There were 215 children living and studying in the Abhyuday Ashram. 'Don't take me,' Ram Sanehi insisted to Arjun, 'go take the children.'

Achyu said it would all be done, we just wanted to speak to him a little. I was hoping the interview wouldn't last long. The morning heat had been stifling and it was 10 a.m. already. Sanehi wanted to sit outside. I liked him immediately. Tea was served. Prashanth declined. One of Ram Sanehi's friends asked, 'You don't drink tea or you're not drinking? They are two different things.' While Arjun set up the frames, I wondered what I was going to ask Ram Sanehi about. He started to speak. I couldn't understand a word of what he said. His Hindi was so chaste and pure, I couldn't decipher the vaguest import of his talk with my meagre stock of words. He used words like *naitik shiksha* (shiksha was education but what was naitik?) and *upasthith*. My mind began to unreel.

Sanehi carried on unhindered—*charitra*, *samvedana*, *sanstha*—the words came and went, they buzzed about my head and confused me further. I hadn't the faintest clue what Sanehi was talking about. I began to despair wondering if he'd latch on. I felt like an idiot interviewing an eminent specialist; an idiot who not only did not have the faintest inkling about either the specialist or his work, but also one saddled with the curious conundrum of conducting an interview in a language he didn't understand. I didn't know what I felt more like—a fool or a fraud.

Fool enough to think I could discover the people of my country with my atrocious Hindi; or fraud enough to masquerade as a media man, and worse still, rob Ram Sanehi of his time. I felt sick and disgusted. I didn't care any longer, I wanted it to end. I was too tired, too bored, I had been on the road for too long. I was overcome by a sudden desire to sleep. Ram Sanehi's talk became garbled. He gurgled like a brook. I stared at his face hoping he would think it was a deep and rare interest I was radiating, but I was struggling desperately to contain my yawns.

Ram Sanehi stared back at me, all the while talking, pausing in between phrases, jerking his head to make sure I was following his drift. I began to nod once in a while, I shook my head when what he said sounded like a truism, interrupting his steady stream of thoughts and ideas with a regular whimpering of 'hoohs'. The wave of sleep passed but the complex Hindi carried on. I contented myself with examining the physiognomy of Ram Sanehi's face. I heard him say, with such a fantastic lilt it seemed he was reciting a poem, 'The happiness that exists in our own joys does not compare to the happiness that comes from obliterating someone else's sadness.'

All of a sudden his language became simpler and I began to understand.

'A butcher has more sympathy for the animals he slaughters than men have for these women. There are two types of prostitution—the singing and dancing type, and the type that involves soliciting. And in this way, a woman becomes a machine. The pimp—he develops a fixation that he has to collect a certain amount every day. So, the pimp says, "You need to make 1500 rupees a day."'

'What does that mean?'

He answered, 'That the woman has to perform over 50 times. How does she remain a woman anymore? She's nothing more than a machine. And people say that a prostitute has sexual desire,' he spat. 'How can she have any desire? She's a sexual *mazdoor*. And the men who visit them, they get drunk, they beat them up. I am from the Bhediya community where prostitution is a community profession.'

I expressed my surprise. He glossed over the historical antecedents in words I couldn't understand, explaining how the scourge had come to afflict his community.

'When a girl turns 13 or 14 years old, her own fathers and brothers make her a prostitute, and that is the life she lives until she dies, or until she loses her appeal. What is the fault of that poor girl? Only that she was born into that particular family? The lawmakers don't know the seriousness of the situation.'

I thought I could salvage some credibility; like a fool, I piped up, 'But prostitution is illegal in our country.'

Ram Sanehi stared at me and started, 'According to the Immoral Traffic Act,' (they were the first English words he had spoken since I had come in) and then he began to quote the law in Hindi, explaining various by-laws and subsections. Once again, I couldn't understand.

'How is there a law to convict women for soliciting and there is no law against the men? If this is the case, then either the lawmakers don't know how to frame laws, or they must be men of bad character to create so many loopholes in the law for men. And the NGOs! I know famous activists working in these NGOs who are scared to go into red light areas.' He laughed, 'They sit in five-star hotels and spend foreign money on conferences. The solution won't be found in five-star hotels. And how do NGOs work these days?' he asked. 'They're only interested in finding out where the funds are coming from. Till today, I have not taken a single rupee from a foreign institution. They come to me and say, "Ram Sanehi, come, take money from us". They offer money not in lakhs but in crores. But I don't take it. You know why?'

I shook my head blankly.

"Because I'll have to give them a 30 per cent kickback. If I do that, how am I serving society? Then I have become a businessman. I may as well become a dacoit from Morena and loot banks and shops. Prostitution is a bazaar for AIDS. When I saw my own sisters and mothers and daughters being converted into prostitutes, I started doing this work.'

He was 82, and had been working for 68 years.

'I didn't do this for any personal recognition, the awards came by themselves. There's a danger with awards too. It gives people an unnatural opinion of themselves,' he averred. 'Nowadays, what is the word for it,' he said grasping at the air like he was blind man trying to catch a bird, 'Entertainment! That's making the problem worse.'

The ashram had been started in 1982, more than 5000 children had passed through it at some point. Some of them had even become graduates, Ram informed us proudly. I asked him what made him happy.

'When one of the children from the ashram wins a medal in the district level sports, or they pass some entrance examination, I feel happy,' he smiled, 'but what makes me most happy is the thought that people get married and they have two or four children, but here I am—unmarried, with not one or two, but two hundred and fifty children of my own all the time.'

I asked him where his money came from.

'The Madhya Pradesh Government.'

I nodded, relieved.

He mused with a trace of irritation, 'The problem with the government is that the funds don't come on time. The money comes in two installments. If I apply today, then I'll only get the money three or four months later.'

What did he do then? 'I run up credit. I have that much standing. There have been times when I've taken eight, nine lakhs on credit,' he smiled, 'the ashram has to continue. Things go on.' There was silence as he looked away and whistled softly into the distance, 'Only God knows what will happen.'

He looked at me and said, 'Where have I met you before?'

I told him it wasn't me he'd met, but Achyu.

He called for a teacher and told her to take us around the school. The examination was in progress, she said.

'It's okay. Take them anyway, let the examination go on. After that, take them to the computer room.'

We were led up a flight of stairs into a long corridor. Children sat cross-legged on the floor, bent over their answer papers as they mulled the questions. In the computer room, teenage girls sat before flickering screens. Cobwebs trailed the corners. I watched their intent faces and thought how they must revere Ram Sanehi. We visited a few classrooms where the kids chanted in unison for us—that was when a different side of Ram Sanehi took wings. In the interview, he had been serious, breaking into the occasional smile. Now he stood there with his eyes closed, listening as the smiles flew across his face in quick succession. All the little birds of joy were going home to rest. His lips twitched as he tried to contain the smiles that came in waves. He opened his eyes, looked around and smiled some more. And when the children were done reciting, they smiled as much as him. He asked the teacher what they had been studying.

'Meanings,' she said.

'Meanings,' Ram Sanehi mused. 'They must be tired then,' and he strode towards the next classroom.

Back in the office, we met his widowed daughter-in-law. Her husband was Ram Sanehi's nephew, she clarified. She had worked in the ashram since she was 18. She remembered Achyu, even remembered the names of students he'd insisted on shooting. She showed us old magazines where Ram Sanehi had graced the cover. One story headlined him as 'Brothel Buster'. 'Everyone calls him Chacha,' she said.

'In the ashram, there's no lack of anything. In some other homes you see the children getting sick, not getting good food, but over here, there's nothing like that. If someone is sick they are taken to the hospital immediately. Only last month a girl got sick, and the hospital fees was 20,000 rupees. But Chacha doesn't care. The children shouldn't lack anything—that's all he cares about. Whatever he has in him, he pours into his work. He throws everything in. Even now, we're running on credit, but he doesn't think about tomorrow. "Today no one must suffer." Not everyone can think like him, not everyone can be like him,' she finished, half-rueing, half-proud.

'He's the first person I've seen who has spent his whole life serving people. I can show you his biodata if you want.'

'You say it,' I told her.

'It's too long,' and she burst out laughing. She had never been on one of Sanehi's raids but she had heard the stories.

'The police has started helping him a lot,' she said.

'But in times gone by he'd been beaten up and threatened. Even now, once in a while, people try to barrack him by saying he is kidnapping their girls. But Chacha is fearless. "What can they do?" he asks, "All they can do is kill me". Even now, I feel very scared,' she confessed. 'He may be brave, but not everyone has his courage. I don't know what will happen once he's gone.'

I opened the magazine stories; my eyes popped when I read that Ram had stayed celibate all his life. He believed the root cause of all evil was sex. The man seemed like a combination of Buddha, Christ and Guevara. We ate our lunch sans Sanehi.

The afternoon was on fire. I was 85 km from Agra—four and a half hours was what I imagined I'd need. I wanted to finish the shoot at the Taj that evening itself. Rejuvenated after meeting Ram Sanehi, I set a strong pace. In the sweltering heat, we clanked through the Chambal ravines without a dacoit in sight. I looked with envy at the rutted tyre tracks branching from the highway before slithering into the ravines. I wanted to take one of the tracks and see how far Nautanki would go. All around were thousands of hillocks getting denser and steeper as they coalesced into one another all the way to the horizon. It was a fantastic place to play hide-and-seek in. I thought of Shikaari specifically remembering the Chambal and telling me I would see it too, only then would I realize how easy it was for someone to get lost there. There must have been people who had roamed those hills for years, he'd said, trying to make their way out. We crossed the Chambal river, snaking across the highway. It was a motionless body of water that glittered in the sun as she marked out the division between Madhya Pradesh and Uttar Pradesh. Remembering Dholpur was 'up and down', I steadied myself for the climbs thinking about Ram Sanehi and his immense resolve.

When the climbs came, I tried to make sure I didn't sit until I crested them. I failed. I began to tire, headwinds hit me. I resolved to not speak to anyone for the remainder of the journey. I could no longer establish communication with the body or the mind. It was pointless trying to be strong. I was finished. I knew I would cycle to Delhi, but I didn't care anymore. All I wanted was to be in Delhi, find a friend's house to shack up in, and hole up in a soft bed to sleep. I wasn't enjoying the ride any longer. I merely went through the revolutions, waiting for Delhi to crawl closer. The next time

I went on a cycle ride, I wouldn't go beyond 70 km a day, I promised myself. It was ridiculous to blow myself out in the boiling maw of the afternoon just to finish 100 km. The next time I wouldn't even head out without a companion, and I would travel light with only two pairs of clothes.

I stopped for chai past Dholpur, there was none. I contented myself with a cool drink instead. Even before the bottle was opened, I was dripping sweat. The shopman had a cycle pump. My legs quaked like in the aftermath of a fight. I couldn't coordinate my fingers enough to properly screw the pump into the tyre-nozzle. After watching me struggle a few times, Naveen spat, '*Ay thu!*' and did it for me.

Leading out the Milkman from Agra

I was desperate for an easy ride. Soft breezes stirred again. We crept up on two cyclists hovering gently in the mildly diminishing afternoon heat and floated in their shadows. They were too slow; we were tiring ourselves by keeping pace. I overtook, hoping one would jump. The younger of the two cyclists accelerated. I looked to see if he was trying to keep us within range. He was, but the old man began to fade away. I gradually increased my rhythm sneaking glances behind when I didn't hear wheels. The old man caught up. The young man jumped past me, I jumped with him.

He cranked on the pedals, I matched him stroke for stroke. I didn't think the old man would be able to keep the pace, but he slotted in between us until he tired. I didn't bother about the old man; I chased the young man intent only on sticking behind his rear wheel. When I first discovered drafting on the Internet and read about the incredible amount of energy cyclists save by hiding in the shadows of another, I told myself that once I hit the highway I would draft behind every vehicle I got. If the cyclists were too slow, I'd pick motorcycles and cars. But there hadn't been a cyclist who had made me exceed myself, and my road trips were so rare, I'd forgotten that highways were mostly empty and enchanting.

I was finally drafting. I forgot about the tiredness of resolve. It was so much easier to cycle with a companion, and if they were of a similar fitness level, they could compete against one another, working in tandem to test the other, while lightening the load as the kilometres slipped by beneath their ceaselessly revolving feet. From out of nowhere, the old man jumped and picked the perfect place to do it too—an incline. He shot past and began to pull away. The young man and I took deep gulps of air and bent to the task of catching him. Slowly, we reeled the old man in but he didn't slacken. He kept pounding out the rhythm, we followed in his wake.

The young man sat behind the old man, I slotted in behind him, and thus we flew for a kilometre or two, like a little three-bogey-cycle train chained together by a shaft of suctioning air. I prayed they were cycling all the way to Agra—with companions like this, Nautanki would make it without blinking. Visions of the three of us belting out the kilometres floated before me, each of us taking turns to lead, one leaping forward as the other flagged, our pace never slowing until we rolled upto the gates of the Taj Mahal in a simmering vapour of sweat.

We were all thundering down, the old man the hardest; each time he swerved to avoid a minor pothole or a little pebble, or in response to some undeniable whim, we moved a split second later like a shadow out of sync, like partners in a precise dance. The old man wandered away down a non-descript tributary of the highway. I was heartbroken; half a kilometre on, the young man waved goodbye too. The drafting was done and it hurt like a mad whirling love affair that had gotten over too quickly—and I'd begun to believe what was unfurling was to be the grandest ride of all.

There was nothing to do but cycle on. The cyclists had given me a fillip. The signboards said Agra was 25 km away. I stopped for chai. I asked the chai stall man if chai was available. I went to a nearby borewell and gave my arms a good scrubbing. When I returned, the owner was still sitting outside his stall. I asked for my chai. He jumped to make it. I lost my temper and berated the man for 'wasting five minutes of my time'. I went back to the borewell and in my anger drove the pump handle so hard the entire structure began to shake. I put my head under the thick stream of water to cool off. I was in a ridiculous rage.

Achyu finished shooting his set of questions and then said, 'Dom, what's wrong with you man? Don't become this way. Why are you spoiling it at the very end?' It was true, it was the first time the whole trip I had felt physical rage, all because I was tired and the possibility of making the Taj before sunset seemed unlikely. I had become petty and churlish. I sat there irritated at giving in so easily. The trip was supposed to have taught me not to fly into silly tempers over trivial things, and I thought I had learnt it along the way. Evidently, it was easy to slip into bad habits. Three hours of cycling in the sun had made me go soft with self-righteousness. I took off my cap wondering how Ram Sanehi had soldiered on for 70 years. What fibre must he be made of?

I looked at the cap beside me. I had made the mistake of throwing it into the laundry in Hyderabad—since then it had remained unwashed. It bore the brunt of the trip—livid streaks of road grease, dull patches of dust, brown in pockets and crusted over with sweat and dry salt. Achyu was right; it made no sense reverting to the ways of the city. The chai came. I promised myself for the rest of the journey that whatever happened, nothing would affect me—I wouldn't be phased.

Opinion about the exact distance to the Taj Mahal varied between 15 and 35. I'd put in a steady ride and leave the rest to the passage of the sun. In the distance, I saw a cyclist tramping on the pedals; he looked like he might be pulling away. I hunched into Nautanki to accelerate to him. When I approached the mad cyclist, I slowed my pace to match his. Then I watched him, for the most important thing about drafting is to trust the cyclist ahead. The more I trusted him, the closer I could get. His head bobbed when he stood on the pedals. Every once in a while on a slope, he'd duck his entire shoulder into a pedal stroke—I thought he moved himself too much and his cycle too little. But it was good speed he was going at, who was I to complain? Achyu later told me that when the milkman stood on the pedals, his cycle stayed ramrod straight. I drew closer. I watched his legs' rhythm to see if he suddenly stopped pedalling to take a break, but he had set for himself the task of cycling relentlessly.

I watched the fingers on the brakes to see if they were trigger-happy, but he hardly used them, preferring instead to negotiate the traffic on the road with precise assessments of distance and time, speed and space. Only then did I pay attention to the aluminium milk can strapped with rope to the reinforced carrier of his cycle. I read the embossed letters on the tank—40 litres. I raised my eyebrows and settled down to the concentration that close drafting demands. Nautanki was a hissing distance away from the milkman's back wheel. I kept pace easily as I sat in his slipstream, content to let him do all the work as he reeled me into Agra like a fish on a line. I saw his shoulders rock and felt his speed flag on small inclines, but he always bent to the task again. I sat back to do nothing but stay within a foot of his rear wheel. Each time we went past a cyclist, he redoubled his efforts as if some inner voice was spurring him to out-cycle everyone on the road; the more cyclists bunched together, the more vigour he expended.

The sun was dipping, it set up a surreal glow on the horizon. The road was getting wrapped in shadows and cool breezes. The stage was set—I had nothing on my mind except the milkman; I knew I was helping him too—15 per cent energy saved for him, 35 per cent for me. I recovered my energy while keeping the pace. It was easy though the cycling was fast, like a vigorous warm-up before the thrill of a game began. When I saw the milkman taking deep lungfuls of air and slowing his pace a fraction, I stepped out of the shadows, shot ahead and drew back in front of him. I turned; the milkman was standing on his pedals staring stonily at my back wheel. I thundered on the pedals hoping he wouldn't want to race. And he didn't—he simply sat in behind me and drafted quietly. Wasn't this the same 'spontaneous intelligence' that Gopichand said sport fostered? The milkman didn't need to go to the Internet and read articles on cycling to learn about drafting. He had learnt it on the road, through the innumerable kilometres he'd cycled everyday over the years, ferrying his milk cans to Agra and back.

There were hundreds of milkmen lugging their cans into the city to make the famous Agra *petha*. We passed all who rode on cycles; milkmen on motorcycles (some with three cans strapped to the seat) passed us. The Innova sped up. It was high-speed cycling and the car ran close to get the best shots. The milkman turned to see what was happening. Prashanth egged him on in the interests of the documentary, '*Arrey...bhagao, bhagao*.' I hoped the cyclist wouldn't take the bait but he did.

It was like a race. The milkman was young, a boy barely out

of his teens; he ran up alongside. I pounded out the rhythms, matching his every stroke, eyes trained on the gathering traffic on the road; the milkman stood on the pedals in response. Achyu whoopeed in the background as we sped. There was no way I would make Agra at that pace; I slipped back behind the milkman. If he wanted to bust his balls, I was content to watch his rear wheel. The setting sun jumped off the milk can. It had stooped to eye level; every once in a while it popped out from behind the curtain of eucalyptus trees—even the sun was peeping to watch the spectacle. The milkman began to flag again. I cycled up and asked his name. 'Vinod Kumar!' he replied with a flourish. I loved the way he said it. His shirt started getting buttoned at the navel; he wore a black T-shirt beneath. He looked cycling fit. I asked him what his age was. '18 years.' I asked if he was going to Agra. He nodded. Was the can filled with milk? He cocked his head and raised his eyebrows. At the speed we were going at, speech had become a luxury. '*Waah!*' I said in admiration and shot ahead again, amazed at the strength Vinod Kumar possessed.

The time had come to play lead-out man for the milkman into Agra. I laid down the pain, cycling as if it were a training session. Vinod was cycling like a madman because he was late delivering the milk. In my head, I told him I'd get him to Agra as quickly as I could. I tested him out. I marvelled at the strength Vinod's young body possessed—cycling 50 km every day, ferrying a 40-litre aluminium can filled to the brim one way. 'The can must weigh another 10 kg,' I mused. I beat out the rhythm as the highway unreeled with the shacks, the trees, the houses, the jangling horse carts, the cycles, the slow-moving motorcycles, the tractors chugging, the transport autos slowing to disgorge or swallow passengers—we passed by them in a flash.

There wasn't another cyclist that passed us in the gathering traffic of people returning home at eventide. Thus, we flew into Agra, like a double-headed arrow, me all the while thinking they should take Vinod and see if he couldn't be churned into a top-notch cyclist. The longer we held pace, the more I tried to test him out; we jumped red lights and increased people's honking as we dodged past trying not to slow. The car was having difficulty keeping pace as the road got clogged as Agra came closer; it was such an exhilarating session of cycling that even Naveen had caught the bug and drove just as well to keep up. We must have revelled like this for 20 minutes; I was feeling young and reckless again. It was the most thrilling self-assessment of my abilities on a cycle.

We entered Agra; the focused zeal of the ride made us take winding turns at speed. Nautanki lassoed the left of a roundabout; the milkman decided to take the shortcut and swooped right. Naveen was so intent on watching the milkman, he went right almost as if he was drafting behind the milkman; and we heard the warning yells and the shouts of the crew to take a 'left, left, left, left' because he was headed straight into oncoming traffic. At an intersection, the milkman said he was turning left. A shake of hands was our farewell. I spun all the way to the next chai shop thrilled at what had been indisputably my best bit of cycling since I'd started training nearly two months ago.

In the strange crepuscular colours of twilight, I smoked and had chai thanking Shikaari for having allowed me to recover my body enough to let a road unfurl in tandem with a good cyclist. The phone rang—it was DJ, an old colleague with the right connections. I had called him in Gwalior to ask if he could rustle up a pass for the Opening Ceremony. He gave me the number and name of a person to call once I reached Delhi—there would be a pass waiting for me. It was a tremendous reward for doing a decent job of getting Vinod into Agra on time. I sat there smoking and smiling—legs shaking, muscles quivering, sweat drip-dropping into the mud, thinking that everything was tied together after all.

Fly

Agra to Delhi

30 September 2010

The City of Mad Cyclists

I had previously seen the Taj Mahal and been bored by its magnificent opulence. I wanted to get the customary shoot over with quickly. We walked the road leading from our hotel to the Taj. Horse-drawn carriages festooned with fresh marigolds and rusted tinkling bells rolled by with their load of tourists. We were wondering how we would get the equipment in—videography was expressly forbidden. The plan was to stagger the entrants; Prashanth was assigned the most difficult job of smuggling the audio equipment in, he would enter after Achyu and Arjun passed of their cameras as still cameras. Poor Naveen had to stay back in case Prashanth was unsuccessful. Naveen was dying to see the Taj Mahal; it was the only thing he had evinced a keen interest in doing if you discounted eating fresh *nati koli*, pitching a tent and building a fire to sleep out into the open. He walked away cutting dry jokes. He had gotten used to getting the short end of the straw.

We'd been told the best time to visit the Taj was as soon as it opened; apparently, no Indians were around then. Our advisor was right. The only Indians around were the tourist guides starting work for the day; they accosted foreigners, taking their places at the back of lengthening queues. As soon as we entered, we were arrested by the sight of a dog standing on its hind legs like it were a ballet dancer, expelling little pellets of shit on the cemented walkways of the arcaded garden pathways. Typically, the foreigners' cameras clicked the dog more than they did the Taj. I walked to the monument doing a few dynamic stretches along the way.

Lovers posed before the monument, tourists prostrated themselves beneath marble benches to capture the reflection of the Taj in the still waters of sleeping fountains. Prashanth had been prohibited; Achyu left to relieve Naveen. I watched the swirling waters of the Yamuna with garlands knotted around the barbed wires fencing the Taj. I thought about Shikaari when he had visited. It was his first time too. During his trip, he had met some gymnasts on cycles. One of the gymnast's father worked as a watchman in the Taj. Shikaari gave the watchman a call on reaching Agra and had enjoyed the rare privilege of watching the Taj by moonlight; and best of all—it was in the light of a full moon. He had shivered as he remembered how beautiful it had been, 'It's something to see the Taj in the moonlight,' he had said.

The plan was to clock 140 km that day and leave for Greater Noida, 60 km away. The next morning, I could stop over at House of Kapaali—a bed and breakfast my friend Suhani owned—for a sumptuous breakfast after which I'd spin casually through the final 40 km to Delhi. I told Achyu I was finished with talking to people. I wanted the simple unadulterated joy of cycling the last 200 km. The city wasn't bustling but hordes of cyclists dotted the roads. I searched for a cyclist I wanted to match wits with.

Soon, we hit the four-laned Agra-Delhi highway lined with offices and buildings too short to shield the sun. It was divided by a median; the sun whipped the road into a blinding lather. I focused on my shadow bobbing at the front wheel as I tried to perfect its dance. I kept the pace, waiting. The road leading out of Agra was filled with cyclists on their way to work in the many offices, industries and factories fringing the outskirts.

A pack of donkeys crossed the road, I mulishly refused to slow my speed. I would have collided with the first one of the pack if it hadn't turned its face away in fright. Camels loped by, their necks bobbing like buoys on a calm sea. The offices disappeared and were replaced by tall eucalyptus trees. Green and yellow autos plied the highway—the same colour of the autos in Delhi. Whoopiee! A guardian angel arrived when I was beginning to tire. A youth in his twenties in a lime-green shirt, his red hot-case strapped obliquely across his torso, went by in a flurry of wheels. I caught up and drafted behind.

Seconds earlier, I had been urging myself on for a few more kilometres; now I was barreling down the highway without a care in the world. The lime-green shirted youth kept shoving the hot-case onto his back each time it slipped under his armpit. I hoped his office was halfway to Delhi. A few more kilometres passed before he turned off, immediately, the cycling got more difficult. The morning session had opened up my body like a flower. Breakfast was bananas and apples. I stretched over chai thinking how for most people, Agra was the city that housed the Taj; but for me, irrevocably for evermore—Agra would always be the city of mad cyclists.

I tried to set good rhythms. Delhi was 170 km away, Nautanki ducked under a sign saying Mariam's Tomb. I thought to myself—who Mariam? Don't know, didn't matter—160 left to go. We passed a bunch of Shiv Kavadiyas on their cycles, their red flags fluttering in the breeze. Naveen shouted for me to stop. I waved my hand in refusal. I wasn't even stopping for God that day.

The traffic thinned, the cyclists got scarce, the greenery became more intense. It was slow-going, I counted down the kilometres. A trailer loomed. It was packed with cement bags on top of which passengers swayed. I latched on. The ones closest to me were a family—a father with his daughter perched between his legs, a mother who cradled a baby on her lap. The suspension of the old contraption was so bad the vehicle didn't roll; in fact, it bounced along the smooth highway. I settled to enjoy the free ride. The little girl stared at me, her eyes were brown whirlpools, I was convinced I could get lost in them forever. She sat motionless, slowly eating her Parle-G biscuits. When she was bored with me, she examined the trees streaming by. Her father occasionally whispered in her ear. I wanted to stare at the little girl without regret, but instead watched the road for loose pebbles and potholes.

It suddenly dawned on me that the mother was breastfeeding her baby. I looked away wondering at the strength of the baby's jaws for it to stay rooted to its mother's breasts while we bounced along the highway. It was like being on a boat gently thudding against the waves. I ran through the possibilities of me slipping under the wheels of the tractor in case Nautanki and I lost balance when we hit a pothole at speed. It was a physical impossibility; I'd have to be a stuntman to contrive to do that. The trailer slowed, I hoped it would stop. I wanted to buy the girl another packet of Parle-G. But it turned down a side road and I went on. An empty passenger auto came along. With a burst of acceleration I managed to latch on, but the auto flew so quick I was too scared to hold firm—it was too dangerous.

The Final 100-Km Ride

The moment I slipped into my final 100 km, I stopped for lunch. Achyu asked what I thought about clocking another 100. I'd been nursing similar thoughts, but Delhi wasn't on my mind. The goal was Greater Noida—I estimated it was 80 km away. It would be imperative to take the help of all the guardian vehicles that came our way. I started again, eager to make good time. An elephant ambled; we got our customary pachyderm shot.

The ghosts of Sunny Deol Mandir were laid to rest.

A passenger auto went by. Two ladies sat at the back, their legs dangling on the footrest. The auto stopped to pick up more people. I turned Nautanki loose. The most difficult thing about riding pillion on a motorized vehicle while cycling is gauging the precise moment to make the catch. While holding the pace, you have to take one hand from the handlebars while keeping the cycle steady and watching the road for unevenness, the sides of the vehicle for safety, and choose the right moment to reach out and make the grab. None of this was made easier by the woman at the back. She sat close to the edge, one arm holding the bar above her head. Her breast dangled perilously close to the bar I intended to latch on to, I had to make sure my hand didn't brush her body. But I managed so well, the lady remained unperturbed and carried on her conversation with her companion.

Now I really flew, the auto barreling at speed. I watched the loose gravel, the small stones, the pebbles, the fledgling potholes, the scars and bruises of the road, the sting of the leaves, the cyclists we passed, the people walking by, the motorcycles coming the wrong way; watched it all intently because even the slightest contact at that speed would have sent Nautanki crashing. I had to let go once in a while to not get hit by the swinging leaves at the side of the road. I knew from experience that at the speeds we were travelling, a stalk of leaves held the whiplash of a branch. Each time we promised to come too close to a pedestrian, I stetched my arm out—in this way I could let Nautanki slip closer to the auto, almost allowing my front wheel to roll freely under the auto's backside. I felt my biceps being stretched out, I kissed my arm; all that lifting weights during training was coming in handy. My arm was working as much as my legs. It was high-speed concentrated motion with no cycling involved and it was exhilarating.

I let go to avoid a bush that threatened to envelope me. I was desperate to climb back onto the passenger auto because we were making such good time, but as hard as I cycled, I couldn't close the distance. I clapped my hands and cursed for not striving harder at my suicides. In training, I had never been able to complete the full complement of 10 suicides I had set myself as a goal. The most I had ever done was seven, that too only once. I was paying the price for my lethargy.

I tried keeping a good pace in between latching on to vehicles but it wasn't as easy as I thought it would be. Arjun shifted to the back of the Innova to make sure we had our full complement of shots. Achyu contemplated paying one of the autos to haul me all the way to Delhi. We were all bored stiff by now. I tried to grab two more autos but they were going too fast. Naveen got in on the act; he slowed the autos for me by innocently straying in front of them.

Hodal passed. There were no signs of any violence. *Ek sau chawaalis* was in place and the biggest clumps of people on the road were the policemen banded together, all looking bored. They had mentally prepared themselves for nothing. The kilometres rolled by in a hurry. The sheer excitement of reaching Greater Noida by nightfall was too much to behold. It was too much to ask for! In between the times I wasn't holding on, I cycled at speed, urging Nautanki and myself through the building fatigue. It was like an early training session all over again. Palwal was eclipsed by late afternoon, and thus, Nautanki reeled Delhi in, either on the strength of my efforts or on the flying wings of an engine and a motor.

The strangest thing happened. I jumped onto an auto painted sky blue. The driver looked at me through the rear-view mirror, I looked at him to see how he would take it. His face didn't flinch, his eyes turned to the road. We stole glances at each other. Ahead was a cyclist going too slow for comfort. I missed him by a whisker because the auto ran close. I didn't imagine anything was wrong. The auto wasn't going fast enough to be anywhere but the edge of the road. Again, the driver and I traded glances. We passed a man on a motorcycle; I had to unspool my arm to stretching distance to avoid a collision. I suspected the driver was trying to run me off the road. We duelled with our eyes, me still holding on; I wanted to confirm my suspicions. A cycle-cart came up and I braked to avoid getting squeezed between the flanges of the cart and the auto. I let go to keep balance.

Nautanki's front wheel clipped the cart and we wobbled. I set off after the auto driver but decided against it. I'd been reading about cyclists in foreign countries complaining about bellicose truck drivers. One blogger's advice was sane—do not lose your temper, note the number of the offending vehicle and call the police with the information. It was the first time in over 2000 km I'd come across a driver who jostled with cyclists for fun; I thanked my good fortune for living in India. The sun was looking like a red coin that had just been minted in a foundry.

I stopped for juice in the swirling industrial grime of Ballabhgarh, I could taste the fine dust that heralds the arrival into Delhi. The map had a bypass branching towards Greater Noida, it didn't look more than 20 km long. It was arrow straight and the index labelled it as 'other road'. We asked for directions. Everyone knew of the bypass, but opinions varied about the exact distance. Some claimed it was 18 km away, others 35. I was ecstatic. I imagined reaching House of Kapaali by eight.

Suhani was expecting me the next morning for breakfast. I was going to show up for dinner unannounced and surprise her. Food for five uninvited visitors I didn't bother about. The

Mahajans would be having a splendid meal anyway; if that was finished there were always cooks who could be called upon to raise a quick meal; and if they were too sleepy or on holiday, we would rustle up a quiche banquet from the delicious leftovers that always crowded the massive fridge.

I haven't seen a family that entertained as wholeheartedly and as profusely as the Mahajans. There would be a party on, of that I was sure; and if there wasn't, what of it? We would start our own. I wanted to toast myself and the impending arrival. I left the moment the sun had set and caught a terrible stretch of road. 'No matter,' I thought, 'I would get to Greater Noida on adrenaline.' After my first 100-km cycle ride, I had foolishly told Shikaari, 'If I reach Madhya Pradesh Sir, I'll get to Delhi on adrenaline alone.' He had given me a wan smile, 'Don't think like that. Adrenaline works only for a short time.' It was time to pull adrenaline out.

The elusive bypass appeared. Only one section of it had been opened for use. Huts rubbed shoulders as slums ballooned. The mosquitoes came out to feast; I turned the pedals quicker to avoid getting bitten. The traffic belched fumes and farted horns. It was a poor suburb of the NCR crowded with the noise of people, the magic of lanterns, the criss-crossing sabres of traffic's light and shadow, and no electricity with only fireflies lighting the dust motes occasionally. As the huts and the squalid tenements disappeared, the people got sparse. The bypass disintegrated into a gravel track. The adrenaline evaporated. The further away we got, the less people seemed to know about the bypass. We began to doubt the existence of the road.

People counselled us to travel to Noida and then Greater Noida. Around 20 km came and went. We stopped again. Two options remained—cycle onwards to Noida, or head straight into Delhi. The crew were all for winding up the journey. It would be a fantastic end to the documentary—Agra to Delhi in a day! I was adamant. Three years in Delhi, I'd promised Suhani (and myself too) that I'd jump on my cycle and pedal the 50 km to her home. I had never done it. Now I wanted to surprise her, show up sweaty, rapping at her door, reminding her of the promise and finishing with a flourish, 'Now I've cycled 2250 km to see you.'

Naveen egged me on to Delhi, appealing to my reason. I got irritated. We took the road to Noida. A bumpy bridge sans electricity stretched across the Yamuna Barrage. The Innova disappeared ahead. I was peeved, it had sped away leaving me to flail in the darkness. Nautanki bounced and rocked against the undulations. I wondered if I was punishing her too much. When we reached the Mahamaya Flyover, it was goodbye to Prashanth. His brother had come to pick him up and take him back home to the children he doted over. Again the question was posed—Greater Noida or Delhi; the crew was beginning to get irascible too.

All of a sudden, I didn't care where I spent the night. I didn't mind sleeping on the road. We hit the Greater Noida Expresssway. I knew I was 25 km away. The Expressway was flat as far as I could remember. But it was different on a cycle. The cars whooshed in a fury of sound. I cycled slowly looking at the barricades that had been erected at the side of the road. This was the venue for the Cycling Road Race at the Commonwealth Games. I pretended I was a cyclist training for the race and tested out the course, but I was a tired and spent cyclist. I ploughed through the revolutions. I was bushed. I didn't want any party now. I wanted to have a bath and sleep. The bath was negotiable too. Nautanki passed under a sign that read 'Pari Chowk: 10 km away—another 13 km for us.

Nautanki slowed. I couldn't understand why she was

behaving stubbornly—she was making it tougher for me to pedal. I checked the rear tyre, it was depressed but it wasn't punctured. The effort of cycling became an onerous duty. I felt like a beast of burden, like a manual labourer working without enjoyment to make sure I completed my work for the day. It was stone-faced, leaden-footed, dull-hearted cycling. And then I began to feel the rhythmic shiver of the tyre and hear the repetitive click of the nozzle as it grated against the rim each time it flattened against the earth. I got off, and felt the tyre; it still didn't feel like a puncture, but I was low on blow. I shed the weight of the bag to lessen the load on the rear wheel. I got on again, begging Nautanki to hold out. I tried everything to ease the pressure on the back tyre; I stood on the pedals, I leaned over the horizontal till my nose touched the handlebar, I structured my entire body at right angles to everything. It didn't get any easier. Nautanki limped along. I gave up, I sat around and smoked a cigarette kicking Nautanki's rear wheel gently in frustration.

I was bugged. Of all the people in the world, Nautanki had given up on me when I needed her the most. I was being too harsh. I remembered flying along the Delhi-Agra highway, the ghostly ghastly bypass at Ballabhgarh, the minefield of a bridge across the Yamuna Barrage. All day I had been brutal while Nautanki had been brave. I forgave her, I even asked her forgiveness. I stroked her handlebar and whispered in her ear, I tickled her wheels and slapped her rump telling her she was the best girl I'd ever had, content to go about her ways unmindful of my moods. I began to laugh thinking that maybe it was poetic justice after all. After behaving impeccably for 21 days it was only right that she had chosen the penultimate day of the trip to throw a tantrum. Wasn't her name Nautanki after all?

The bright thing to do would have been to call it a night,

pack Nautanki into the Innova and drive to the House of Kapaali. But, no! The purity of the trip had to be maintained. It had been Nautanki and me against the weather and the roads till then and that was the way I wanted it to end. Thinking this and at the same time remembering the times I had grabbed fruit and restocked water on the go, sat in the car while the rain let up and cycled at night with the help of the headlights, it dawned on me that it was stupid and naïve to think it had been me and Nautanki all the way. This was how the purity of the trip had been maintained. This is the deception that exists in all man's truths.

Despite the daftness of the idea, I carried on. I knew there was a petrol pump at the end of the road. I led Nautanki to it. I jogged, I walked, I skip-walked, I tried cycling some more. We reached the petrol pump, but they didn't have the converter pin to get the pressure nozzle to fit Nautanki's tyre. There was nothing left to do but lug Nautanki the last 5 km. We sat around a lamplit cart and ate boiled eggs, famished from the day's work. I knew there would be a stellar meal waiting for us. The Mahajans had been forewarned.

We made space at the back of the crew car for me to sit down and and hang onto Nautanki's front wheel. We threw open the back door of the Innova and thus I carted Nautanki to House of Kapaali. The household was quiet, everyone had gone to sleep. It was Thursday and the Mahajans were stocking up on sleep for the weekend.

Suhani cracked up listening to Naveen, 'You don't know the places they made me sleep at,' he complained, 'places I've never slept in my life. Anywhere at all is okay for them; at the side of the road, they'll stop and sleep. They'd wake me up at four every morning after sleeping at 12 in the night and ask me to drive on the highway at 20 km an hour. I cursed them a lot in my head.' She asked why he agreed to the trip in the first place. Naveen said with a small smile, 'They told me they were going to do something great for the country.' As the laughter pealed, I blessed Arjuna.

When we sat down to dinner, I told Suhani that Naveen always ate with us on the trip. All along, there had been no distinction between crew members. Suhani said it was fine, but she had a business to run and drivers' egos to take care of, and there was no way she was letting Naveen eat at the table with us and bear the mutters and frowns and dark silences from the other drivers for the next few days. It was wise thinking. Now that we were back in the city, it was back to the familiar divisions of class.

After dinner, we went to the terrace for a celebratory beer. Suhani refused to be filmed. I told Achyu that all my friends were as camera-shy as I was. I thought about the day, setting out at 7:30 and not stopping until 15 hours later, except for a half-hour lunch and disciplined chai-and-smoke breaks in between. In the intervening period I had coasted, drafted, cycled, sped, flew, hung on, laboured, walked and finally hauled Nautanki a grand distance of 226 km. Achyu was telling Suhani about the trip. She was in splits. 'I'm so glad I quit my job,' Achyu was saying, 'Naveen drove, Arjun did camera, Prashanth did audio, Dominic cycled...and I slept.'

'Then what was your work on the entire trip?' she asked. 'I paid the bills,' Achyu retorted as we drank beer and the laugher drifted heavenwards. It was only when Achyu told Suhani he was flat broke, joking that he might even have to sell his blood to pay next month's rent, did I realize what a severe punt Achyu had taken on me.

3 October 2010

Opening Ceremony

I was slouched in a chair, looking anxiously at my phone willing it to ring. I was trying to stop myself from getting worked up into a cold sweat. Mitesh (DJ's contact) still hadn't called about my pass. Achyu told me to calm down, the call would come. He wished he'd bought a ticket earlier. There wasn't a ticket available, even the 5000-rupee ones were sold out. There were no passes to be had either. He hadn't known the Games would be so big, he said. He had only been away a month, and Delhi had been transformed. Now everyone had the bug, even if they didn't care about sports: and Achyu didn't care—not even about cricket.

With every passing minute Mitesh stayed unreachable, my franticness grew. At around three, the call came. I was to meet him at 4:30 p.m. outside the metro station of the Jawaharlal Nehru Stadium. We hadn't decided how the documentary would end. I was unwilling to cycle to India Gate and other stock monuments that had no relevance to me. We had abandoned the idea of shooting outside the stadium, convinced the camera equipment wouldn't be allowed through security. I thought of a banner. I asked Achyu if he had a sheet of white cloth. He dove into a drawer and came up with a light green sheet. He handed me a permanent black marker. In large block letters, I scrawled on the sheet:

MAW, POPS
I REACHED SAFELY!
DELHI CWG 2010 KM

Achyu looked at my handiwork and said the lettering wouldn't show. He came back with another marker; we started colouring in the letters. We gave up all pretensions to neatness; soon we gave up because it was taking too long. Achyu thought paint would be faster. First, he filled in the blanks with his fingers, time slipped; he scooped paint out and spread it across the letters. The paint would never dry, even if I held it flapping outside the train all the way to the stadium. It was running too. I looked at the ruined banner Achyu was kneeling on; he was blowing on it to dry the paint.

I bunched the banner into a roll and hit the roads skip-walking. I didn't trust my legs to run, they quivered tremulously when I used steps. I found an auto in the unpeopled streets. Without negotiating the price, I jumped in and sat forward to take in the sights. The roads were empty; the Delhi government had mandated that all business establishments down shutters for the opening and closing ceremonies.

Shops, bars, theatres, restaurants, malls, small businesses, ice cream parlours, medical stores, libraries—everything was closed. We sped through the barren roads, me gazing at the colourful signage dotting the city. I had never dreamt Delhi would look so pretty and empty. I hadn't imagined how big the Commonwealth Games would be. Throngs of cops were everywhere, most of them in camouflage outfits, lounging behind sand and cement bunkers toting guns. It looked like a city under curfew, like a ghost town in the midst of war. It didn't seem like a city hosting an international athletic extravaganza…until I came to the Green Park Metro Station.

Young volunteers darted into the underground entrance, access badges dangling from their necks. They all wore red tracks and the official Games T-shirts with Shera emblazoned on it. Delhi being Delhi, many of the girls looked like they had been cast-mould in those T-shirts. I wished I was a college kid in Delhi in 2010. I would have volunteered to see all the sports stars in action, and meet a sweet girl or two. I raced through the corridors of the station past the human horde. Kids were going wild and needed to be restrained, grandparents were shepherded carefully, husbands and wives added to the bustle, couples raced, gangs of friends joked as they walked at pace—it seemed like everyone was going to the Commonwealth Games.

The lines to board the train waited expectantly. As the train rumbled in, all semblance of queues and decency vanished. It was back to Charles Darwin and survival of the fittest. No one cared, no one complained; you pushed whoever was in front and dragged whoever was behind. We were packed in, body pressed against body, until they could pack us in no longer. We stopped at stations where the doors wouldn't open; there was no more space left to fill. People waiting in queues outside, jostled to peer into the tinted windows with cupped hands. We waved to them, they waved back. The train stopped in the middle of stations. I could see the cemented walls of the underground tunnel we were in. No one betrayed the slightest hint of paranoia, claustrophobia or irritation. Families spoke, people sang, groups laughed. Kindness and bonhomie filled up the spaces between peoples' ears.

It seemed like everyone on the train was being ferried to a mass picnic. Everybody was dressed up, gleeful and unburdened—many clutched their Opening Ceremony tickets in their hands. The train stopped again. Still no restiveness, no complaining about the teeming masses, only a few suggestions that more trains should have been pressed into service that day. This was followed by a stinging rebuke from a lady to her husband accusing him of taking more time than her to get ready. No one could see the lady, her voice seemed to pipe up from a hole at everyone's feet; more laughter was uncorked. It was difficult to not feel intensely comradely.

The train stopped and disgorged itself of passengers, vomiting them out in a projectile rush. Almost everyone got off the train; the few people who stayed on looked sad. The train had become a ghost train. The tunnelled corridors were peopled again, everyone raced to the sunlight. I turned and saw (for one last time) the earth spewing forth people. I looked for Mitesh, he was with four friends. He told me he had my pass, but I wanted the assurance of touching it; my heart soared as I caressed it.

We raced to the stadium. There were around 15 gates that ringed the entire stadium, and no one had directions. The metro station wasn't particularly close to the stadium either. Every clump of policemen we came across, we asked for help. They had grown tired of telling people they had no clue about the stadium either. The volunteers stood around looking helpless. There wasn't an exasperated soul around; everyone laughed, everyone joked. I was immensely proud of my countrymen—we were all imbued with a tremendous comic fortitude that day. A few volunteers raced around trying to paste arrows handwritten in crayon on loose sheets torn from notebooks; no one trusted the makeshift directions. At a turn, we glimpsed a view of the Jawaharlal Nehru Stadium rising skywards in a multitude of curves, diagonals and straight lines. This was the newly constructed showpiece for the 2010 Commonwealth Games and we would be the test of its tensile strength.

Most stopped to stare, to ponder, to take photographs. We tramped across the pontoon bridge the army had been called in to build. What the contracted company had failed to accomplish in six months, the army had pulled off in six days. A few people (me included) jumped on the bridge. When we got closer to the stadium, we were told our gate lay in a different direction. It was back to the pontoon bridge.

Finally, we found Gate Number 15. A seven-tier ring of security had been put in place, we were about to face the first one. My banner was taken away and dumped with the other confiscated items. There went our ending to the film. I was hustled along by the crowd. I slowed my walk remembering how I had helplessly watched Saina Nehwal walk away. I resolved to not allow vanity come in the way again. I sped up to Mitesh and told them to carry on; I would meet them at the next security check.

I explained to a policewoman that I needed to retrieve my banner. She said it wouldn't be allowed inside. I pleaded. She relented saying I would have to explain the banner past the three men guarding metal-detector arches with automatic guns. I walked up to them purposefully, they noticed my approach. One of them calmly, without saying a word, pivoted his torso so that the perforated muzzle of his gun pointed to my chest. I didn't break stride (smiling in my head) thinking it wasn't the first time I'd had a gun pointed at me in suspicion before.

I explained the banner to them, dwelling marginally on the statistics. I read out the banner and in faltering Hindi translated it too. They gave me a patient hearing, probably glad for the novelty. I thought I was convincing them. My parents were old and I wanted to ease their mounting concern, I told the soldiers. One of the soldiers asked why I didn't call my parents if I was so concerned. I had no phone, I said. He offered me his phone. While the other two policemen sniggered, he took the banner from my hand and threw it behind him. He told me to carry on.

Something about the arrogance with which he threw my banner away piqued me. I walked behind him and heard him ask what I was doing. As I folded the banner I deadpanned a monologue. 'I have cycled 2226 km from Bengaluru to Delhi.

2226. Think about that number; then think about cycling that distance. Have you ever done something that wasn't expected of you, that wasn't demanded of you, that wasn't your responsibility? What have you ever done for yourself that you weren't supposed to do, either as a son, or as a policeman, or as a father, or as a husband? What have you ever done for yourself for no other reason except to see what it would feel like?' I continued, all in broken Hindi. I stuffed the banner into his surprised hands saying, 'You won't get time now but before you go to sleep tonight, read that banner and think about the number. After that, worry about my parents. Till then I'll take care of them.'

Without waiting for a rejoinder, I left banner-less and irritated at rising to the bait of the clown in the group. Apart from being unafraid of policemen, I had learnt nothing on the trip. It was many more cycle yatras before I would learn to mend my ways.

Finally, we were in, it was close to six. The rehearsals were still going on. A massive pneumatic balloon that covered the entire stadium lay suspended many feet above the dancers' heads. When it began to rise slowly, the crowd roared in anticipation. The stadium was almost full. Every dignitary that made their way to their special enclosures was greeted with applause when they came up on the big screen. When they began to announce the big shots, Suresh Kalmadi was roundly booed. I imagined him shrinking in his new suit bought specially for the occasion—the mortification of being publicly reviled by thousands of people. Thank God we had grown past the age of mob justice. The dignitary that drew the most applause was A.P.J. Abdul Kalam—all he did in response was wave and smile like a child. I thought of Shikaari.

I called him, I called my parents, I called everybody that

wasn't in the stadium so they could hear what they were missing. The opening ceremony started promptly at seven—without a fumble, without a hitch, without a goof-up, just like Gopichand had said it would. The pneumatic balloon rose above the rafters and beams of the stadium. Whatever took place on the ground was projected onto the balloon against a background of bewitching designs. It was a surreal balloon—a kaleidoscope without colour but peopled with humans instead. We could see more on the balloon of what was happening on the ground because we were so far away. Cameras flashed incessantly, there must have been a hundred going off every second. I imagined every camera flash was for me. When the crowd swelled their voices as one, I'd stop cheering as the shouting and clapping reached crescendo to hear how loud it actually was. We sang the national anthem, thousands held their phones to the skies.

The athletes' parade started. I nodded off, waking occasionally when the crowd got loud, or when the spectator behind bumped into my chair. Each time I woke up, I instinctively raised my hand, yelled until my throat got scratchy and nodded off again. Countries I'd never heard of were announced; they sent a handful of athletes. Of all the countries that filed past, Pakistan was cheered the most. And then, finally, the Indian contingent emerged to a cacophony of war cries. The girls were dressed in saris and the boys wore sherwanis. There wasn't a person sitting down, everyone jumped and craned to see. We were too far away to spot anyone with a degree of certainty. We had a massive contingent; they took their time walking past. We goaded them into going slower by shouting more. I thought about the athletes and how they might feel during something so big for the first time in their lives, especially the young ones. For years, they would have sweated through the age-groups in an empty substandard stadium, watched over by teammates, coaches and family. As they strolled around the stadium, I wondered how they felt soaking up the adulation, the thousands of flashbulbs erupting like stars in a rural night accompanied by a manic bellow of pride that sounded so much like the baying for blood.

As they rounded the first corner, I sat down. This was what it had all boiled down to. I was convinced that apart from the athletes, there was no one in the stadium who felt more self-satisfied and content than I did. My father put it best when he said, 'Only 60,000 people have the privilege of watching the Opening Ceremony live, son, and you're one of them.'

When the athletes left, the entertainment started. I slipped into the cocoon of a deep sleep; I had seen the dress-rehearsal already. When the ceremony finished, Mitesh shook me awake and said he had wasted a pass on me. I stood up groggily. It was time to move on. There was nothing left to do but write all those books I had been promising myself over the years—about the women I had known and the men I had loved.

Epilogue

Arjuna was in Delhi, I stayed the night at his hotel. The next morning when I returned to the Whitebalance office that I used as my living quarters at night, I climbed a few stairs beset by the vague notion that something was amiss. I retraced my footsteps to figure out what it was. I discovered that in the space where Nautanki usually lay in stately repose, there was nothing but blank air. Even the chain that tethered her to the iron grill fence was gone.

It took me a few minutes to realize Nautanki had been stolen. I asked at the eight-seater restaurant (where they boiled chai and made rotis on the pavement) if they had seen her. The cook sympathized with me, *'Roz hota rahta hain, juye ke liye paise chahiye unko'* (This happens every day, they need money for gambling). It was Diwali week and four cycles had been filched in the previous few days.

I told the chole parathawallah boy to spread the word that a hefty reward was on offer if Nautanki was returned. He didn't place too much stock in my ambitions. He claimed that there were a lot of people in Hauz Khas village who were addicted to smack. *'Nasha ke liye paise chahiye,'* he philosophied. He even claimed whoever stole Nautanki would probably sell her for 150 or 200 rupees.

I cringed. When I had first bought Nautanki and was feeling her out on the roads of Bengaluru, she had been the pride of several security guards and petrol bunk attendants. They had all winced when I told them she cost 3400 rupees. Now Nautanki was going to be sold as cheap as scrap iron—for smack no less. I cringed some more.

I went back to the eight-seater restaurant to smoke a cigarette and drink some chai. I looked at where Nautanki usually lay. Slowly, the feeling grew that Nautanki hadn't been stolen. Maybe she had adopted a few random strains from me, like some pets do with their owners, like intimate friends and lovers do with each other. In three short months, she had racked up over 3000 km, listening to the sounds of the road and the stories of people I'd never imagined before. For the last three weeks, she had lain there as if in shock, unmoving and helpless. It was no way to treat a hard-travelling cycle. For three weeks, I'd taken her nowhere except for two short rides—one to get her shipshape, and the other to customize a thickly cushioned cycle seat. While I had been recovering, Nautanki had always been ready.

I went to the fence that had once supported her weight; I took a look around. Surely Nautanki must have gotten bored looking at the same old *istriwalah*, the same old *moosambi-juicewallah*; the same little eight-seater restaurant with its stock clientele of construction workers and labourers; the same old teenager lugging aluminium kettles whose spouts were crowned with columns of plastic cups, to the hundreds who work in the many offices that crowd the immense, narrow, studio-lined lanes of Hauz Khas village, needing chai like a drug to get through the tedium of another repetitive working day. Maybe she had gotten mortally bored chained up all the time.

And so gentlemen and gentlewomen, on our twenty-second day in Delhi, the same time it took for us to reach the capital, in the swaying sibilant shadows of the night, Nautanki busted her bonds and cut loose to go on a trip of her own making, this time with a new travel companion, hopefully another lover. I hope God keeps her wits about her.

Now only she can tell her stories.

Acknowledgements

There are many people I am indebted to for completing this piece of work. Thanks are due to—my parents, for being the most uncomplaining nutritionists not just during training but since my birth; Sibi, whose company on the long training rides freed my mind from unending doubt; Ponappa, for helping me train intelligently; Shree, for being so generous with good counsel; Sibi again, for giving me his laptop to write when I lost mine; Arjuna, for giving me his laptop when I lost Sibi's; Sibi, Arjuna, Apeksha, Kristen, Sammy and Suhani, for lending me their homes to write in; Achyu, for thinking this journey interesting enough to document; Joy, Robbie, Rishab and Ruth, for dream opportunities when I was callow; Kanishka, for believing when I was convinced of nothing; Dharini, for setting things in motion; Ishita, for taking things forward, and Aparna, for the patience to see things through.

And last, my deepest debt is to Shikaari, for mentoring my interest in physical activity and cultivating values that a sport teaches. I thank you for your instant forgiveness when I told you I lost your 'Nautanki Diaries'—the memoir describing your own journey from (then) Bangalore to Delhi—but most of all, for your smile, humility, fairness and for always being there.

Glossary

Aam janta	common people
Aloo bondas	deep fried spicy potato dumplings
Angootha chaap	illiterate
Ay thu	act of spitting
Bhutta	corncob
Bucch aata	hopscotch
Charitra	character
Chitranna	rice-based dish
Ek sau chawalis	Section 144
Ghungroos	musical anklet made of bells
Huchchaa	madman
Istriwaalah	a man who irons clothes
Jadi butiyaas	medicinal herbs
Kaaka kade	a small multipurpose grocery shop
Kachcha	crude and temporary
Keechad	mud
Keeda	itch
Mardangi takat	masculine strength
Marm	Tamil for brother-in-law; can also be used as a slang (meaning rascal)
Mazdoor	labourer
Mazdoori	labour
Moosambi-juicewallah	a person who makes sweet lemon juice
Murti	idol
Naitik shiksha	moral education

Nasha	drugs
Nati koli	country chicken
Pakka	permanent
Pakodas	deep fried snacks
Petha	translucent soft candy from North India
Poha	preparation of flattened rice, spices and vegetables
Puliyogare	tamarind rice
Rudraksh	seed used as prayer beads in Hinduism
Saagoo	mixed veg curry
Samvedana	compassion
Sanstha	organization
Sarson	mustard
Taka-tak	prim and proper
Taraste	to yearn
Tehsildar	tax officer
Theka	a local liquor shop
Thekedaar	contractor
Trishul	trident
Upasthith	to be present